A Rich
Young Man

A Rich
Young Man

*A Novel Based on the
Life of Saint Anthony of Padua*

JOHN E. BEAHN

TAN Books
Charlotte, North Carolina

Cover design by Caroline Kiser.

Cover image: *St. Anthony of Padua* from *Military and Religious Life in the Middle Ages* (French School, 19th century, litho, published London c. 1880) by Paul Lacroix. Private Collection, Ken Welsh. The Bridgeman Art Library.

ISBN: 978-1-61890-202-3

Cataloging-in-Publication data on file with the Library of Congress.

Printed and bound in the United States of America.

TAN Books
Charlotte, North Carolina
www.TANBooks.com
2013

And behold one came and said to him: Good Master, what good shall I do that I may have life everlasting?

Who said to him: Why askest thou me concerning good? One is good, God. But if thou wilt enter into life, keep the commandments . . .

The young man saith to him: All these have I kept from my youth, what is yet wanting to me?

Jesus saith to him: If thou wilt be perfect, go sell what thou hast, and give to the poor, and thou shalt have treasure in heaven; and come follow me.

Matthew 19:16–17, 20–21

A Rich
Young Man

PART I

1

LISBON knew nothing of the family De Bulhom before 1147. In that year, Don Raoul de Bulhom came from the north with the armies of Afonso Henriques to reclaim the city from the Saracens and to remain there with his wife and son. Lisbon speculated, but none could learn De Bulhom's origin, either as to family or country. Similarity of the name De Bulhom to De Bouillon inspired a conjecture that Don Raoul bore in his veins the blood of the great Duke Godfrey; but Don Raoul neither affirmed nor denied the speculation, and thus confirmed it by default.

Don Raoul's son, Roberto, almost permitted the De Bulhom line to expire. He had a knight's powerful body, but his placid, cheerful disposition turned him toward a peaceful life. When he was twenty, he began construction of Castle de Bulhom and became so engrossed in that activity that he did not marry until he was thirty.

Don Roberto built the great castle on a shelf, a little above the level of the city on the slope of St. George's Hill. Above it was the Cathedral, and on the summit above both was the Fortress of St. George. His project drew townsmen and innkeepers to build along the road from the city to the castle, and they built, one next to the other, to the very edge of the slope.

The outer walls of the castle displayed neither the cheerfulness nor peaceful intent of their builder. The building dominated Lisbon as a gloomy mass of stone without windows. Narrow slots, from which bowmen could drive off attackers, pierced the walls at regular intervals. The one entrance was the sally port, an arched tunnel cut through the west wing to connect the road from the city with the interior courtyard.

The sally port tunnel was sufficiently wide to accommodate a team of oxen drawing a cart and sufficiently high that a tall man on horse could ride through it upright in his saddle. Entrance through this could be blocked by closing the heavy wood and iron gates at the outer end or by closing the grilled iron gates at the inner end. The sally port was so designed that a small group of raiders could be trapped between the outer and inner gates, then slaughtered by bowmen from slots in the side walls or by fire and hot oil poured down from openings in the ceiling.

The tunnel opened into a courtyard, a large rectangle formed by the four wings of the castle. It was open to the sky and paved with cobblestones. The four walls around it, unlike the grim outer walls, were cheerful with doorways and three levels of windows.

In the east wing, directly across the courtyard from the inner opening of the sally port, was the principal entrance—twin doors of oak that opened into the Great Hall, with its dozen windows. The first doorway beyond the two windows on the right was the entrance to the living quarters of the family, which occupied the remainder of the wing.

Through the hours of light, except at midday, carts rumbled heavily on the cobblestones of the courtyard, anvils in the forge and armory rang almost continually, grooms and horses fought loudly but without rancor. The lighter chorus of human voices swelled and diminished with the labor of the day. In the first hours of the morning, knights and squires grouped noisily before the stables while they waited for grooms to bring the horses. Only at midday and at night did the clamor cease.

Don Roberto had completed the castle two years after his marriage but his wife lived only three years to enjoy it. When she died, after the birth of their son, Martinho, Lisbon knew that a man who had married for the first time so late in life would not enter readily into a second marriage, and the De Bulhom line again depended on the one son.

Young Martinho went far to the north country as squire in the service of the King's brother. Lisbon did not see him from his thirteenth year until he returned in 1194 with his sword of knighthood and his royal bride from the Taveiras of Asturias. They saw then a broad-faced, heavy-jawed youth, confident in the strength of his powerful body and proud in his heritage. They saw, too, a young and pretty Dona Tereza, whose low, happy laugh contrasted with the intensity of her husband.

Soon after, Lisbon's sharp tongues wagged the news of Dona Tereza's dowry—the whole rather than a part of her family's lands along the River Tagus. Her dowry, joined to Don Martinho's lands in the valley north of the city, made the family De Bulhom the wealthiest of Lisbon.

Lisbon's tongues wagged again in 1195 when Don Martinho's son, Fernando, was born. Dona Tereza had not recovered as she should and remained some months in bed. When she did arise, she was delicate and could walk no farther from the castle than to the Cathedral or ride, in the chaise, no farther than the city walls. Fate again held continuation of the De Bulhom name to one son.

Thereafter, Lisbon's interest in the family De Bulhom changed steadily and imperceptibly. The city became accustomed to Don Martinho, with a group of his knights or with only his knight commander, riding slowly through the narrow, crowded streets; accustomed to the food and fuel and clothing that flowed from the castle above to the needy below; accustomed to Master Fernando serving Mass each morning in the Cathedral and to the parents who waited afterward in the emptied church until he joined them.

2

FERNANDO walked calmly and quietly at his mother's left in small imitation of his father at her right. He could maintain his calmness and gravity until they descended the steps of the Cathedral and had taken a step forward on the road to the castle. There, where his father's requirement of silence and gravity ended, Fernando's tongue and body reclaimed their freedom. With gay abandonment he related the events of the night, of the morning, and of the sacristy; then ran before his parents to explore anew the familiar road, to shout each new discovery, to point each new interest. August heat held no greater power than January cold to suppress him.

"Fernando!"

He dropped the stone he had lifted in his search for lizards and looked back at his parents. His father's expression was ominous; he looked quickly to his mother. For the moment, he felt misgivings as her black eyes looked at him steadily and seriously; then his heart lifted again as she smiled and her white teeth gleamed from the surrounding darkness of her face. He smiled quickly in return and ran toward them.

"Can we not train the boy to hold his tongue, Trese?"

Safely at his mother's side Fernando carefully avoided looking at her even when he knew she had turned to glance at him. If he turned his head his eyes might meet his father's.

"Fernando is noisy, Martinho," she scolded with soft indirectness.

"He talks without end, Trese," his father persisted.

When his mother spoke again, her voice had softened more as it always did when she was troubled. "Does he talk more than before, Martinho, or are you more aware of his talking?"

"Trese, you are not fair," Don Martinho protested sharply.

The road lowered gently before them to the towering bulk of Castle de Bulhom, where it seemed to end abruptly against the great stones of the east wall. On either side of the road, olive trees formed straight lines into the depths of their orchards. Dull green leaves, unruffled in the morning stillness, foretold the heat of the day. The hill and the Fortress of St. George behind shielded them from the morning sun, but the sky was cloudless, and the month was August.

Don Martinho pointed toward the heavy stones of the castle and let his arm sweep away to include the olive trees and the country beyond. "Which will be master, Trese— Fernando de Bulhom or Castle de Bulhom?"

Fernando's mind grappled with the strange question. His father's voice was angry, but it held also a tone of foreboding, as though this castle that was their home could suddenly become a monster and devour them. His eyes ranged along the great stones of the wall, laced with mortar and the bowmen's slots. His mother seemed to understand the question.

"Please, Martinho, I was unfair," Dona Tereza admitted softly. "But you are too tense—so anxious . . ."

Fernando waited for the scolding that must follow withdrawal of his mother's protection. But when his father spoke again, all traces of temper had disappeared. "Trese, I am more sensitive now to his faults. If the King appoints me, I may become even more sensitive. But if I am not the king's magistrate, Fernando's faults remain, and we must still correct them. Someday, all this will be his. He will have the power of this wealth. He will be responsible for all these people."

Slowly at first, then more quickly as his parents discussed other matters, Fernando's spirits regained their accustomed level. With difficulty he remained silent through the remainder of their walk. He was relieved when, at last, he followed his mother through the doorway into their quarters.

In the trencher room, a waiter prepared the table for breakfast. The room was small and plain, its stone walls bare with an incongruously large window open to the noise and confusion of the courtyard, and a table with four benches placed around it. Don Martinho's accustomed place was at the end of the table nearest a door leading into the kitchen. Dona Tereza sat at the right of her husband, between him and Fernando, whose bench was nearest the window. Three knives and three goblets were on the table.

"Sir Thomas?" Don Martinho asked.

The waiter straightened from his work. "Sir Thomas went early into Lisbon, Don Martinho. He left no message."

Fernando waited until his mother and father were seated, then pulled his own bench beneath him and recited grace. He fixed his mind firmly on the necessity for continued silence.

"You had a birthday last week, Son?"

Fernando nodded quickly at his father. "On the feast of the Virgin," he said and smiled.

"And you were eleven?"

Fernando hesitated, warned by the question. His eyes darted toward his mother, but Dona Tereza studied the table before her. His smile faded. "Yes, Father," he said.

Don Martinho leaned his big body forward over the table to emphasize the intensity of his words. "Fernando, you are only eleven, but you talk more than most men." His voice was sad rather than stern. "You begin to talk as soon as your foot touches the ground before the Cathedral, and you will not stop until you sleep at night."

The waiter brought the bread and meat of breakfast. The noises of the courtyard magnified in the silence of the room. Don Martinho paused. He examined the meat before him, lifted a piece of bread, and turned it critically. His manner was elaborately patient and oppressive until the waiter finished his work and fled through the door into the kitchen.

"Fernando, all your energy is in your tongue. Your mother must awaken you each morning, must brush your hair, must care for your clothes and your shoes. You talk at home, and Canon Joseph complains that you talk at school. In a few years, you will want to enter service in some other house as squire. Your master will not endure your talking as we have. Any master will demand improvement or will send you home as unworthy of knighthood. Or, if he keeps you, you know what he will call you." Don Martinho's voice had been low and even, but now it rose suddenly with contempt. "Sir Triple Tongue!"

Fernando held his gaze steadfastly on the food before him. Belatedly, the offending tongue endeavored to disown its guilt. He looked up only once—a startled look when his knife slipped from his hand and rattled loudly on the wood of the table. The noises from the courtyard dominated the room.

"This afternoon," Dona Tereza said, "I shall need an escort into the city."

Fernando glanced up hopefully but turned his eyes downward again immediately. "Perhaps you will need both of us, Trese," he heard his father say, and raised his head quickly again.

The return of Sir Thomas interrupted them. Chain mail and great sword rattled in the outer passage while the knight commander stripped the camail from his head. When he appeared, he had not delayed to towel his wet hair and face, though there was no urgency in his manner. He smiled as he paused casually at the doorway.

"God's Morning!" he said—"Dona Tereza!—Don Martinho!—Master Fernando!" as he looked at each in turn.

The knight commander was a big man, an inch or two taller than Don Martinho, with wide shoulders and slender body. He was not handsome—a nose broken at least once and a blunt, heavy chin denied the possibility—but his alert smile and deep-set eyes imparted a singular impression of loyalty and devotion. When he walked to the vacant bench at the side of the table opposite Dona Tereza, he carried the weight of the chain with distinctive grace.

"There was trouble in the city this morning, and I took a group of the men down. That trouble was already settled, but we stumbled on three men—archers from Anglia—beating one of King Sancho's knight couriers. The courier was that braggart, Roberto, who talks so much. He was hurt, but he was still anxious to talk. He said he had been here for two days, but when he left Coimbra, the King had already selected a magistrate for Lisbon and was sending another courier to announce it."

Don Martinho shook his head doubtfully. "King Sancho would not send a courier to announce a magistrate. He would come himself."

"His Majesty has been placed under interdict again, Don Martinho. Roberto claims he will not leave Coimbra because the churches are closed wherever he goes, and the people become angry."

"What caused this interdict?"

"He interfered with a legacy to the Cathedral in Oporto. The Bishop protested, and King Sancho ordered his magistrate in Oporto to expel the Bishop and occupy the residence."

Dona Tereza looked up suddenly at the tall knight commander. "Even a king's magistrate need not obey that order, Thomas," she exclaimed.

Sir Thomas hesitated for a moment. "It is difficult for a king's magistrate not to obey, Dona Tereza."

Dona Tereza turned quickly toward her husband as though to appeal to him, but Don Martinho raised his hand that he understood. "There is no danger of that in Lisbon, Trese. King Sancho has no interest in lands so near the country of the Saracens."

Fernando sat quietly at his place, turning his eyes as the others spoke but restraining his own impulses. His dark face flushed when Sir Thomas described the "braggart, Roberto, who talks so much," but the others did not notice. He rose readily from his bench, when Dona Tereza stood, and followed her from the room.

In the room which was his parent's bedroom by night and his mother's sitting room by day, Fernando remembered briefly his father's admonition about silence. He sat in the end of the window seat, his back to the stones that framed the window. From that post, he had only to turn slightly to the left to see the noisy activity of the courtyard or to the right to watch the quiet movements of his mother. When. Dona Tereza sat at the other end of the window seat with her breviary or needlework, he could divide his interest between her and the courtyard merely by shifting his eyes.

Fernando's interest languished quickly both in Dona Tereza's monotonous examination and counting of linens and in the slow movements of the hot courtyard. "If Father becomes magistrate, could King Sancho tell him to put the Bishop out of the Cathedral?" It was an idle question—he watched a team of oxen plodding in their ungainly manner from the sally port.

"Fernando!"

Disappointment and fear mingled together strangely in his mother's voice. He turned quickly toward her. "I didn't mean to hurt you, Mother," he whispered. The pain in her eyes frightened him. He walked slowly toward her as though not yet comprehending the nature of his offense. When he stood before her bench, she put both hands on his shoulders so that he would look at her.

"Fernando, you do not think your father would do that?"

His startled eyes looked up to her. "Father would never harm the Bishop," he protested.

"Oh, Fernando! Learn to control your tongue. Ask the Holy Virgin to give you her silence."

He lowered his head with shame, but his mother lifted it again and smiled faintly. "Forget what has happened, Son . . . I want you to ride away from the castle to the other side of St. George's Hill—stay away until the Angelus bell. Think about silence."

The slow ride and morning heat, the view from the summit of St. George's Hill and the coolness of the trees on the farther slope, swept away the troubles of the morning. When he dismounted in the midday stillness of the courtyard, Fernando had forgotten the morning.

He stepped into the room of his parents as the Cathedral bell struck the first note of the Angelus. Dona Tereza sat on a bench she had drawn near the window. She did not look up from the breviary in her lap. Fernando went silently across the room to his own.

The command "Honor!" sounded loudly from the quiet courtyard. Fernando turned quickly to the window—the word announced either his father or a noble. A rattle of chain mail and strike of iron on cobblestones told the progress of men and horses in the sally port. The knights at the inner gate stood stiffly facing each other. Men—Fernando saw they were strangers—rode in pairs from the darkness of the sally port into the sun-filled courtyard but turned toward the stables. Twelve men appeared, then a tall, slender noble. Following were twelve more men. Fernando leaned forward eagerly to watch the group dismount, talking and laughing noisily before the stables.

Don Martinho appeared suddenly to run across the courtyard. Fernando saw the noble run from the group to meet his father. The two men met, embracing and laughing as friends long parted. Household knights and squires came from the building, grooms ran to take the horses, other men brought buckets of water and towels for the visitors.

Fernando backed from the window, plunged a towel into a pitcher, mopped his head and face, and ran into his parents' room. Dona Tereza stood by the window seat, smiling at the group in the courtyard. Fernando glimpsed his father and the stranger walking toward the doors of the Great Hall.

"That's Prince Pedro, Son." Dona Tereza glanced toward Fernando, and she laughed. "Son, brush your hair!" Fernando rushed again to his own room then back to rejoin his mother. A page stood in the doorway of the outer passage. "Don Martinho asks that you come to the Great Hall, Dona Tereza."

The Great Hall was a turmoil of men and sound when Fernando entered with his mother. The vaulted ceiling echoed and multiplied the voices. Fernando had an impression of big figures, clad in mail, laughing and talking. As his mother entered, voices repeated, "Quiet! Dona Tereza!" and all the knights stood silent.

Prince Pedro's low voice sounded clearly in the room, "Dona Tereza! Beautiful Dona Tereza!"

Fernando heard his mother say, "Castle de Bulhom is honored again after many years, Your Highness"; then the turmoil of the room resumed even louder than before.

Prince Pedro saw Fernando and smiled delightedly. "Fernando?"

Fernando smiled. He liked this vibrant man of extravagant tongue and extravagant manner.

Prince Pedro stooped to embrace him as he had embraced Don Martinho in the courtyard. "You are a picture of your mother, boy. Your mother will sit at my right; you will sit at my left."

Fernando's father was standing beside the Prince smiling happily. His father put his hand on his son's shoulder and turned him toward a knight whose left shoulder bore the gold insignia of a knight commander. "My Son, Fernando,

Sir Richard." Behind Sir Richard, Fernando saw the alert smile of Sir Thomas.

Benches scraped on the floor of the hall, and the men stopped talking until they were seated at the long tables. Fernando followed his father and Prince Pedro to the smaller table at the head of the hall and sat happily facing his mother. Sir Thomas was beside him, across from Sir Richard. Don Martinho sat on the bench at the far end of the table, and Prince Pedro went to the end between Fernando and Dona Tereza. The hall quieted again when Prince Pedro did not sit immediately but stood in his place at the end of the table to speak.

"It is customary and proper," he said so that all could hear, "that my father, the King, should come himself to Lisbon to announce appointment of his magistrate. Unfortunately, he may be prevented from visiting Lisbon for some indefinite time in the future."

A murmur arose, as though some of those present had begun to laugh.

Prince Pedro flushed angrily, and his eyes swept over the room. In that instant, his pleasant smile disappeared. He raised his head higher and his expression hardened. The room of men was quiet—tense and without movement. "His Majesty, the King," he said, "considered that he should send my brother, the heir, to represent him and to speak in his name. But he determined that friendship would overshadow statecraft. He selected me to be his representative and his courier.

"No assignment has ever given me such great happiness as this—to bear the scroll from the hand of my father appointing as king's magistrate of Lisbon my own loved friend, Don Martinho de Bulhom."

A great cheer burst from the men at the long tables. They pushed back their benches and stood, shouting and whistling shrilly, pounding the tables with the heavy drinking mugs. Sir Thomas and Sir Richard rose and cheered. Fernando saw the slight motion of his mother's eyes and jumped up to add his own cheers. At the end of the table, Don Martinho's smile did not vary.

The room quieted somewhat after the benches scraped into place and the men started eating. The business of eating interfered with conversation and, as they finished, they went in groups through the doors into the courtyard.

Prince Pedro talked and laughed, but his gaiety had dimmed, and he seemed to retain some of the anger from the time the men had laughed. He ate and drank quickly, as he did everything, and his wine goblet was always empty. His anger seemed to disappear completely once when he asked Fernando his age.

"Eleven, Your Highness."

Prince Pedro reached forward to feel Fernando's shoulder and arm. "You need more food, Fernando," he decided with mock seriousness. "You should enter the service of a good master as your father did. See his big body?"

Fernando glanced at his father, but his father did not look at him. His father's expression was serious again.

"Your father and I were in the service of the King's brother, Fernando. How would you like being in the service of the King's brother?"

Fernando puzzled at the question before he realized that Prince Pedro was speaking of himself as though his brother were already king. The Prince did not wait for an answer but looked at Don Martinho. "Remember that, Martinho! When it is time for the boy, send him to me."

After that, Prince Pedro's anger returned. He talked more, and his face became more serious while the others said little. A waiter refilled his wine goblet regularly. When the room was almost emptied, he nodded toward the few men remaining at the long tables. "Some of your men seem to find amusement in the King's troubles, Martinho."

Fernando turned expectantly toward his father, but Don Martinho shook his head slowly, unhappily, without speaking. It was such a strange manner of answering that Fernando turned quickly to Prince Pedro. His father's action was final proof that Prince Pedro was drunk! Fernando felt the sharpness of disappointment.

The Prince's voice became louder, and the last of the men left the long tables. "My father will show the landowners they cannot ignore the Crown. He will show them that lands cannot be handed over to the Church and removed from his control. The Church and the bishops will learn they cannot swallow the whole of the country.

"What happened to the Bishop of Oporto is a lesson to the rest. Let them impose interdicts! Let them tell the whole country! Everyone in Portugal knows my father is under an interdict." He looked around the silent table until he saw Fernando. "Even you know it, don't you, boy?"

Fernando was unable to answer—unable even to turn away from the Prince. He looked at him with a fascination as of horror.

"Answer me, boy!"

The savage demand shocked Fernando from his silence, though his eyes continued to hold to the face of Prince Pedro. "Everyone in Portugal," the words flowed evenly and swiftly, "knows that King Sancho is greedy for land." His voice was clear and distinct in the silent room. "Everyone

knows that King Sancho ordered the Magistrate of Oporto
to commit a sin—"

"Fernando!" His father's shout broke the spell that had
fastened on him.

Fernando's whole body leaped in response to his
name. His eyes widened with the sudden realization of the
words he had spoken and the disgrace he had brought upon
himself.

"Go to your room, Fernando!"

He fled from the anger he had never before heard in his
father's voice.

3

FERNANDO remembered the day his father was appointed Magistrate of Lisbon as a day of sorrow succeeded by other days and weeks and months of sorrow. He remembered the sounds of his mother's movements, in the room next to his own, as she prepared for her ride into the city; remembered the sound of her footsteps to the outer passage; remembered watching her from his window and watching the chaise disappear into the sally port with his father and Sir Thomas riding beside it.

Slowly and painfully, he learned the fullness of his father's displeasure. He was required, rather than permitted, to ride into the city as escort to Dona Tereza. He was required to ride with Don Martinho for the periodic visits to their lands along the Tagus and those north of the city.

As the habit of silence developed and the necessity for vigilance diminished, pleasure revived; the sights and sounds of city or country were not less enjoyable because he could not speak of them. His eyes and mind began to penetrate below surface appearances. He understood little of the life he saw among the people of Lisbon and strangers from overseas, but much that he understood repelled him.

Accompanying his father, he learned gradually of rents and yields, which of the serfs worked industriously, the seeds and supplies needed by each of the serfs' villages.

He came to know the leaders appointed by his father from among the serfs of each village. He began to understand the management of their estates.

The resentment of nature subsided within him. What at first he did reluctantly, he learned through the months to do with quick pleasure. Penalties and reproofs diminished, but he saw greater proof of his progress in the quickening smile of his mother and closer union with his father.

He awoke one morning in July of 1207 and lay for a time looking at the heavy gray of the sky brightening with dawn. The bell of the Cathedral had not rung; Dona Tereza had not shaken him. He knew he could shut his eyes and sleep again. But a feeling more insistent than bell or voice clamored a summons. He knew why it was there and what it meant.

When the Cathedral bell rang, he had already washed and dressed. He waited quietly at the door of his parents' room until he heard Dona Tereza's footsteps. When they were very near, he swung the door wide suddenly to surprise her. "God's Morning, Dona Tereza," he said and bowed stiffly from the waist in the manner she had told him the pages bowed at the royal court in Coimbra.

"Fernando!"

He stood confidently but unsmiling for her inspection. His hair was brushed straight; light caught and reflected from the silk of his shirt that fell loosely from his shoulders. The felt of his shoes was clean.

"Fernando, you are handsome this morning."

He smiled then, matching her smile and her pleasure. Then he saw her eyes glisten suddenly, and a new fear touched him that again, in some unknown way, he had hurt her. The lightness of his heart became an emptiness.

He looked beyond her at Don Martinho, but his father seemed unaware both of him and his mother's tears.

When they came from the Cathedral and descended the steps, his father was the first to speak. "You made your mother happy this morning, Fernando."

Fernando looked up at his mother walking between them. She was smiling now—smiling as though she had not cried when his father did not see her. He turned toward his father. "Why did she cry?" he challenged.

Don Martinho's glance shifted quickly from his son to his wife and back to his son. Amusement touched his face. He formed his lips tentatively, then shook his head slowly as though he had confronted a great wonder. "I think that is one of God's own mysteries, Son."

Dona Tereza drew the two of them close to her and laughed softly.

After that day, he sensed he was not restricted as before. He could speak if he wished, and he did speak—with the fluent ease of his mother and the deliberate manner of his father—but he spoke infrequently and reluctantly, aware that his boy's voice rendered ludicrous his adult manner. Only when he spoke of knights and knighthood did he forget the incongruity between voice and manner. The rides with his father and Sir Thomas and the knights had opened his mind and heart to the future.

One day in September he was standing in a group of knights and squires before the stables when a page summoned him to his father, who was in the accounts room.

Don Martinho was at his table pushed against the window, through which he could see all the varied activity of the courtyard merely by raising his head from the work before him. When Fernando entered he pulled a bench beside his own so that both of them faced the window and the courtyard. Fernando slid onto the bench, trying to feel within himself some of the power that was so much a part of his father's big body when he watched the men of Castle de Bulhom from this window.

"Did you ever notice, Son, that different men hold to different sections of the courtyard?"

The group of knights and squires dwindled as men mounted and went into the tunnel of the sally port. Grooms turned back leisurely to the stables. At the far end of the courtyard, serfs unloaded carts.

"Your grandfather built Castle de Bulhom, Fernando, so that this section of the courtyard in front of us would be reserved for us and for our guests. Other sections are reserved for knights and serfs. None may enter our section except when they are ordered or required by their duties." His father turned to look at him. "That rule applies to us also, Fernando."

Fernando frowned slightly with disappointment as he realized his father's meaning. "I am not to be with the men?"

His father did not answer directly. "You are becoming anxious—thinking of knighthood, aren't you, Son?"

Fernando nodded eagerly.

His father looked out at the activity of the courtyard. "That is not necessary for you, Fernando. You will be Don Fernando with as many knights as you wish in your employ." As though he realized the disappointment his words would cause, he added quickly, "But this is not the time to talk of that."

"I'm twelve now," Fernando objected.

Don Martinho nodded. "Instead of sending you away

to learn the business of knighthood, Fernando, I must send you on the business of a noble. Which do you prefer?"

Fernando hesitated. Suspicion born of past experience warned him against pursuing his own desire when his father permitted him a choice.

"Do you think you have learned why we must go each month to our lands outside the city and what must be done on those trips?"

Fernando nodded cautiously. He was aware of an indication of secret amusement in his father's manner.

"Then one last question, Son. Would you like to ride on those trips yourself and do that work we did together?"

Fernando straightened very suddenly on the bench. He smiled quickly even as he examined his father's face doubtfully for signs that his father was not serious. "I will be in charge?" he whispered.

Don Martinho nodded. "You will be in charge," he assured. "You will be in charge of the knights with you, you will talk with the leaders of each village, you will inspect their equipment, and you will inspect the lands to see that they care for them properly."

Fernando's smile faded with loss of confidence. "I cannot do all that, Father."

Don Martinho waved aside his objection. "You will learn, Fernando. And, sometimes, maybe you'll take your father with you just to be sure you are doing your work properly." He paused. "Your mother does not yet know of your appointment, Son."

Fernando leaped happily from his bench toward the door. Behind him, he heard his father's laugh.

The joy of his new position did not long endure. The mere absence of his father and Sir Thomas gave him a feeling of isolation, despite the presence of the knights who rode before and behind him. Long hours of silence and the monotony of the country soon made him realize that he rode no longer for pleasure. He learned to ride as the knights—unconscious of time or place, withdrawn into himself.

Late in December, the sight of some Saracen raiders enlivened a ride to the lands along the Tagus, but the raiders turned while they were still far off and fled across the river to their own country. When the men assembled for the next trip, early in 1208, Fernando saw that four more knights with their squires were added to the column. "I feel like a baron with big bags of gold," he grumbled to his father. His voice was no longer the voice of a boy, nor was it yet the voice of a man; grumbling concealed its variations.

When they started through the sally port, the courtyard was dark except for lanterns and torches. The column turned at the outer gate, and the horses stumbled along the uneven road that descended to the King's Highway. In the darkness along the slope, Fernando could do no more than distinguish the forms of the men and horses immediately in front of him. The rattle of chain mail and weapons and the sharp beat of the horses on the hard earth emphasized both the cold and darkness.

They had entered the highway at the bottom of the slope when a knight's challenge sounded from the darkness ahead. "Canon Joseph," a voice replied casually. Fernando strained into the darkness to see the priest; the form of a rider moved from the darkness beside the road and joined him.

"God's Morning, Fernando."

"God's Morning, Canon Joseph."

"May I ride as far as Santa Lucia in your protection?"

Fernando laughed at the priest's request but stopped abruptly and embarrassed. He was conscious that his changing voice made his laugh sound raucous, but he was more aware that Canon Joseph had stated his request seriously as he might have to Don Martinho. "I didn't laugh at you, Canon Joseph," he mumbled awkwardly.

The small hand of the priest reached out from the darkness and pressed his arm lightly. "I understand, Fernando. I asked only as a matter of form." The casual voice excused his awkwardness.

Darkness of the night lessened when St. George's Hill turned away to the right; the valley outside the walls of the city was a cold plain that disappeared uncertainly into the grayness of dawn. The youthful form of the priest emerged from the darkness and became a person, a slight person with a calm smile and direct eyes that absorbed everything they saw and revealed nothing. Fernando rode uncomfortably beside him, guarding carefully against another blunder.

Canon Joseph seemed unconscious of embarrassment or restraint between them. When the day advanced so that he could see the number of men in the column before them, he turned to look at those behind, and his smile widened. "We are better protected than I thought."

"Saracens," Fernando replied. He frowned. "All these men are not necessary. If my father went, he would take no more than four knights and Sir Thomas with him."

"Your father and Sir Thomas are powerful knights themselves."

Fernando was conscious of his own slightness. "I could be a knight," he said. "I am older than some of these squires, but Father won't let me enter service yet."

Canon Joseph began to talk of other things then—of the

fields, of the King's Highway, of the birds, of the mountains that now became clear in the distance along the edges of the valley. Ordinary sights acquired new color and new interest as they acquired the light of a new day, and the priest's words transformed them from the ordinary and commonplace.

After Canon Joseph turned from the column at the serfs' village of Santa Lucia, Fernando felt again the monotony of his work. He tried to see ordinary sights with the extraordinary view of the priest, but he could see nothing more than fields and serfs and villages as they were before, and he abandoned the effort.

On the return ride, he looked eagerly ahead when they drew near Santa Lucia. Only when they had advanced sufficiently that he could see into the open side of the village square did he see the priest in the act of mounting. Canon Joseph seemed to pause for a moment after he mounted and raise his hand as though in blessing before he turned and galloped toward the highway. For the first time, Fernando wondered idly what business would bring a Canon Regular of St. Augustine from the Cathedral to this serfs' village, cause him to remain all day among these people, and leave as happily as Canon Joseph's smile indicated.

The priest's happiness seemed even to increase as he drew rein beside Fernando. "God is good today, Fernando." He spoke as though in thanksgiving. "He offered me protection with you this morning, He has blessed my work today, He offers me protection with you again into Lisbon."

Before Fernando could think of some answer, Canon Joseph turned in the saddle toward the village of Santa Lucia and raised his arm above his head in farewell. Fernando saw two figures—they seemed to be a man and a youth—raise their arms hesitantly in reply then draw them down quickly. The men must be serfs; others would not respond so fearfully.

"Are you so astonished, Fernando?"

Canon Joseph's casual question awakened him, and he realized he had continued staring back at the two figures. He turned his head forward quickly. "Are they serfs, Canon Joseph?"

"Serfs, Fernando. The younger man wishes to be a priest; the older one is his father."

Fernando studied the priest doubtfully. "Can serfs become priests?"

"Where else would Holy Mother Church obtain priests, Fernando?" Canon Joseph's voice was casual as before. "His Excellency, the Bishop, has assigned me to enlist candidates for the priesthood. Where will I find them? Knights have their wars and their tournaments; merchants have their affairs of business and their affairs of money. So Our Lord directs me to look among the serfs as He looked among the fishermen."

Fernando felt a compulsion to defend his own people against the implied criticism of Canon Joseph. "Some become priests, even bishops," he grumbled, uncertain of his freedom to disagree. "All those studying at San Vicente are nobles or knights or merchants."

Canon Joseph nodded agreeably. "But most of them are brothers, Fernando. Few become priests."

"But the nobles cannot all throw aside their responsibilities, Canon Joseph." He remembered his father saying something about that. "They must care for the lands and be responsible for all the people."

The priest turned his head to Fernando, and his eyes

lighted as though the adult words were more amusing than convincing. "Would you like to know of a great noble who disagreed with that, Fernando?"

Fernando felt his certainty of noble obligations waver before the casual voice of the priest. "Not Our Lord?" he asked cautiously.

Canon Joseph shook his head. "Our Lord was a King, but we do not think of Him as a noble. No, Fernando; the noble I mean was like any other—as a matter of fact, he was much like you. His family was wealthy and powerful, they owned a tremendous amount of land, he was born to command men and ride about the affairs of their estate just as you. He did have brothers and a sister—that was one difference between you and him. And he lived only a little more than fifty years ago, so he is even of your time."

Fernando thought differently about a man who had lived more than fifty years ago being of his own time, but he remained quiet.

"He grew up, as you did, in a castle. He went to school about as much as you did. He even wanted to be a knight."

Fernando was disappointed. "Didn't he become a knight?"

"Something more than that, Fernando. Knights are the work of kings. A king lays a sword on a man's shoulder and dubs him Sir Knight. No king ever laid a sword on this man's shoulder, and no one ever dubbed him Sir Knight, because God reached down from heaven and laid a cross on his shoulder and dubbed him St. Bernard."

"Saint!" Fernando had not expected the story to end in that manner. "Then, he was not like other nobles."

Canon Joseph did not press his views but found other matters to discuss. The column climbed the slope of

St. George's Hill. Horses and men quickened with expectation. They approached the corner of Castle de Bulhom,
where a road branched along the north wall toward the
Cathedral.

"Will you ride in our protection again, Canon Joseph?"
Fernando attempted awkwardly to offset his blunder of the
morning.

"If I may, Fernando, I should like to ride with you
whenever you go to the villages in either direction."

The rides thereafter were not monotonous; the priest's
knowledge and casual voice raised each ride to the level of
adventure. Gradually and unconsciously, Fernando opened
his mind and his heart as to a friend.

Life became more vibrant also at Castle de Bulhom.
Settlement of the dispute between King Sancho and the
Bishop of Oporto was reflected in the increased numbers
of royal couriers riding in and out of the courtyard, in the
increased number of Lisbon nobles visiting the king's magistrate for business or pleasure, in increased entertainment
of guests in the Great Hall. When entertainment at the castle
palled, Fernando rode, aimlessly and with a knight trailing
him, to the Fortress of St. George, to the Monastery of San
Vicente, or wherever his fancy directed. Occasionally Don
Martinho rode with him, and they hunted with falcons or
with arrows. When he was with his father, no knight trailed
them, and Fernando relaxed in his freedom and in the lux-
ury of the blue of the sky and the brown and green of earth
and mountains.

Spring ended completely Fernando's interest in the
entertainment of the Great Hall. Warm sun and the wonders of nature overshadowed all lesser entertainment. He
was seized by a tremendous restlessness that was not stilled

by rides into the city beside Dona Tereza's chaise, and became overpowering when his father summoned him to the accounts room to learn the business transactions of Castle de Bulhom. The bickering and vile language in Lisbon repelled him; the business of the castle revolted him.

In May a noble, the giant Don Ruggiero, arrived from the north country with his son. Fernando had never seen a man as big as Don Ruggiero—thick and powerful as his father, but as tall as Sir Thomas. And the boy with him was nearly as tall as Don Martinho. Fernando stood fascinated, looking at them until Dona Tereza pushed him gently on the shoulder, and he remembered his responsibility. He walked to the other boy, and they shook hands shyly without speaking.

Don Ruggiero made supper a gay feast. He told stories in a big, rumbling voice that made even Don Martinho laugh. Fernando and young Ruggiero sat next to each other without speaking, smiling and laughing because their fathers and Dona Tereza and Sir Thomas laughed. Fernando remembered how Prince Pedro had talked and laughed; but he saw that Don Ruggiero touched his wine goblet as infrequently as his father.

Several days passed before Fernando realized that his father and Don Ruggiero were watching them and listening to them recount the adventures they found each day. A hope formed in Fernando—a hope that was realized shortly after when Ruggiero, smiling and frowning alternately, told him he was to stay at Castle de Bulhom. "I'm squired to your father." Fernando smiled at first then also frowned as he remembered that he was not permitted to mingle with the squires. But at supper, his father also announced that Ruggiero would remain and added, "He will have his bed in your room, Fernando. Don Ruggiero's son will not live apart from us."

For a time, the presence of Ruggiero countered the attractions of the world beyond the sally port. When the tall squire finished his duties in the armory and Fernando was released from the accounts room, they would go to the room above that of Fernando's parents. With Don Martinho's weapons, Ruggiero would demonstrate the arts of knighthood, and Fernando would try valiantly to imitate him.

"You haven't enough strength," Ruggiero commented during one of these demonstrations.

Fernando closed his eyes firmly against his failure. "I could learn if a knight taught me," he retorted.

They tired of the game, the one because of boredom, the other with discouragement, and turned to riding. Fernando discovered an unsuspected superiority in the graceful agility that enabled him to stand in the saddle while his horse galloped slowly and to invent other unorthodox attitudes which the awkward Ruggiero could not duplicate. But this game also lost its fascination, and by the time of his thirteenth birthday in August, Fernando reverted to his melancholy view of the future.

"I will never become a knight as long as you make me work here," he complained to his father in the accounts room. His voice had steadied then, and he could complain impressively as a man. "I'm thirteen but am not yet even a squire. I am not permitted with the knights and squires here, but Ruggiero may be with them. He can learn from them, but I am not permitted to learn anything more than these accounts."

Don Martinho bowed his head as a man whose patience is tested. "Fernando, Ruggiero is an unusually strong and powerful boy. He has the physical strength to be a knight among knights. But you have other gifts. You can be a man among men if you will value the gifts God has given you, and if you will realize that your gifts are not in physical strength. Why don't you teach Ruggiero to read and write instead of trying to imitate him?"

Fernando looked at his father with astonishment. "Ruggiero can read and write," he protested unbelievingly.

Don Martinho shook his head. "Ruggiero never went to school, Fernando. Their home is not near a church of the Canons of St. Augustine."

The new game between them proved more successful than the others. Through the last months of 1208, Ruggiero copied laboriously and painfully the characters Fernando taught him. During the early months of 1209, Ruggiero persisted with the reading of Dona Tereza's breviary, but rather because of Fernando's insistence than his own desire. "You're fitted to these things, Fernando," he said in excuse.

"A man who cannot read or write is ignorant and lazy," Fernando retorted mercilessly. He matched his energy against Ruggiero's unwillingness and ineptness until the big squire could read slowly and haltingly from the breviary. The duties of the accounts room, visits to the villages with Canon Joseph and Ruggiero, and the contest against the forces of ignorance slowly consumed the months of rain and cold. Yet when the long, disagreeable winter ended and the warmth of spring flooded over Portugal, Fernando went out into the courtyard more restless than before.

In April a change in the manner of his father and the expression of his mother alerted him to some impending development. His father went each afternoon to the accounts room as well as each morning. His mother was unusually interested in the condition of his clothing, his father's, and Ruggiero's. The mystery of activity was revealed unexpectedly at supper on the last Sunday of that month.

"How long have you been at Castle de Bulhom, Ruggiero?" Don Martinho asked casually.

"Eleven months, Sir."

Fernando looked up curiously at his father.

"Do you ever think of home and your father, Ruggiero?" Don Martinho pursued.

Fernando looked at Ruggiero beside him. The big squire was just lowering his knife slowly to the trencher before him, and his eyes were fixed downward. "Often, Sir."

Don Martinho smiled happily. "We will start for your home tomorrow morning, Ruggiero," he said.

*   *   *   *   *

Their arrival at Don Ruggiero's home was a disordered, noisy, milling confusion of men, voices, and horses. Fernando saw that Don Ruggiero's home was much like those of the nobles near Lisbon. But the square, formed within the three wings of this home, was festooned with bunting, flags, and knightly pennants, and the walls were bright with shields fixed beneath each window. Everything reflected the gaiety and good humor of its owner.

Ruggiero's mother, Dona Maria, did not wait for them to enter the building as Dona Tereza would. She stood in a doorway as the column approached until Ruggiero galloped forward. Then she stepped into the courtyard that she might greet him as he jumped down from the horse.

Dona Maria was a big woman who seemed small when she stood beside her son. Fernando was surprised that she was quiet like Ruggiero and not noisy like Don Ruggiero. Fernando followed his father through the doorway into a large room that might have been called a great hall but which was small in comparison to the Great Hall at Castle de Bulhom. Don Ruggiero hurried in front of them to present the four brothers and three sisters of Ruggiero.

Fernando was aware only of Anna and, being aware of her, he was suddenly shy and silent. She was pretty; and she smiled with the friendliness of her father in her black eyes and the friendliness of her mother in the gentleness of her mouth. She was small, too, and not big like some of her brothers and sisters. Because Anna was there, Fernando was glad he was there; but he felt at once miserable in her presence.

The week at Don Ruggiero's was a week of hawking and hunting and listening to a minstrel who had wandered to this house at the head of the valley and had never gone away, even though the good-humored noise and confusion inseparable from Don Ruggiero often overwhelmed the thin, sweet evenness of the minstrel's songs. It was a week, too, of admiration of Fernando by Don Ruggiero and Dona Maria and Anna and the rest of the family. Ruggiero, with unrestrained enthusiasm, extolled Fernando's ability to read and write and ride as though he had suddenly acquired his father's own extravagance.

Supper, rather than dinner, was the great occasion of each day. When they rode in from the hunt, the courtyard between the wings would be filled with long tables. It was there, instead of inside an enclosed great hall, that nobles and knights gathered for the evening meal and to listen to Don Ruggiero or, less often, to the minstrel. Near the end of the week, Don Ruggiero proudly silenced the entire company and made his son stand and read for them from a breviary. As soon as he finished, the courtyard broke into noisy cheers for this accomplishment of the boy. Ruggiero stood uncomfortably for a moment, then cried out, "Fernando is the one you should hear. He taught me." The cheering grew louder both in tribute to Ruggiero's compliment and to Fernando.

Fernando laughed uneasily and uncomfortably. He felt Anna turn and look at him admiringly. "You are the only boy Ruggiero ever admired," she told him. Fernando was happily miserable because she spoke as though he were the only boy she, too, had ever admired. After that, he enjoyed less the sport of the others; he was dreamy and quiet. He saw his father looking at him as though seeking signs of illness. Don Ruggiero whispered to Don Martinho and laughed, but his father's expression was one of displeasure. Fernando tried to become interested in the activities of the others and forget Anna; but he lapsed soon again into his silence.

The ride to Don Ruggiero's had been monotonous, but the return to Lisbon was a melancholy, somber succession of trees and mountains, or warm sunshine and cool shadows. Fernando saw as little of it as he could. Ruggiero was equally quiet, but his was the quiet of satisfaction, and his responses were quick and eager when Don Martinho spoke.

In the afternoon of the first day, Don Martinho sent Ruggiero forward to ride with the advance group of knights. As soon as the big squire had started from them, Don Martinho spoke very low, that others could not hear. "You are an infant, Fernando—an infant who speaks like a man."

The intensity of his father's voice shocked Fernando.

"You are no longer a child or a boy," the accusing voice

continued. "But you have not yet indicated you are a man. I do not mean only this past week. Your conduct at home has been as childish as ever."

Fernando flushed slowly as though from sullen anger rather than embarrassment. "I am treated as a child," he retorted quickly.

"You will be treated as a child until you show awareness of your manhood." Anger tinged Don Martinho's voice.

Fernando did not answer. He sat straight in the saddle, looking at the squire in front of him. Trees muffled the rattle of mail and weapons along the column; soft earth counted the dull beat of the horses. His father's horse slowed and, automatically, Fernando drew rein, and the column in front moved slowly away from them. He saw his father signal the men behind to fall back. He was uncomfortably aware that his father was preparing space before and behind them that he might talk freely.

"Son, you are completing one of life's great changes. That change is in your body. But it is so tremendous that it also affects your mind. You will think differently of much that you see. You will lose interest in some things; you will find interest in others that never seemed interesting before."

Fernando looked cautiously at his father. He had expected a continuation of Don Martinho's displeasure, but all trace of anger had disappeared from his father's voice. Don Martinho was intense as before, but it was an intense seriousness that had supplanted passion.

"There is a new power in you, Fernando—a power that God put in you. It has been growing gradually—that's why you have been restless and dissatisfied." Don Martinho's voice lowered almost apologetically. "That's why you acted as you did this week, Son. That's also why you must learn to be master of yourself, to control your body and control your mind.

"It's a tremendous power, Son—almost like the power God Himself used when He made Adam. It's so strong that it begins to boil inside you even though you are hardly aware that it is there. In some men, that power boils over like water on the fire. Those men make no effort to reduce the fire to control the power. Good men ask God to let them use this power the way He wants them to use it. They pray, Fernando, and God helps them."

He did not understand all that his father said. He felt rather than understood that he was to be either master or victim of some tremendous force—that he must be master or he would be victim. Fear and determination came alive and churned about: fear that he might fail to be master, determination that he must be. His restlessness was not now the friendly haven it had been when his father had excused him before Dona Tereza; that restlessness, with the dissatisfaction, the craving for excitement, the yearning for new scenes and new adventures, was an indication that he did not know the force within him and had done nothing to subdue it. He had not prayed to be master—he did not know he should, or needed to, pray.

4

THROUGH the summer of 1209, Fernando grew more aware of his restlessness as he grew more aware of his inability to subdue it. Repeatedly he grappled with an enemy he did not understand; repeatedly he resigned himself to his restlessness and rode with Ruggiero to find new distractions, new adventures. For a time, he found peace in the churches they discovered; but Ruggiero's curiosity discouraged that.

"Why do you always want to visit these churches?"

Fernando edged carefully from the subject. He could not reveal to Ruggiero the fear in his heart; he could not revive the subject with his father and could talk with him only when Don Martinho asked softly, "Progress, Fernando?"

"When I pray," he admitted once. "But Ruggiero wants to know why I always want to visit churches when we are riding," he complained.

Don Martinho paused thoughtfully. "Can't you tell him you are praying for something and want him to pray also? A friend won't ask more questions if you will say that."

Fernando repeated the words to Ruggiero, and the big squire shrugged his shoulders to disclaim curiosity. "I'll pray with you if it's that important."

"It is important," Fernando insisted. He was not sure himself what he was praying for; but the intensity of his father had impressed him with the importance of it. He prayed for something and against something without understanding either.

In September, a disagreement between Don Martinho and Dona Tereza intensified his conflict. That evening the rattle of armor and sound of a horse approaching the doorway from the courtyard interrupted supper. Guards at the gate had not "honored" the rider and had permitted him to ride far enough across the courtyard to identify the unknown as a royal courier. Sir Thomas rose from his place at the table and went through the outer passage to meet the messenger. A murmur of voices ended quickly, and Sir Thomas returned with a paper for Don Martinho. Fernando looked disinterestedly at the paper and his father's slow efforts to open it.

"People are rioting in Coimbra," Don Martinho announced without turning his head from the paper. "King Sancho orders that the city garrison be sent to Coimbra and also knights from the Lisbon district to suppress the rioters." Don Martinho refolded the paper and pressed it down on the table. "Thomas, after supper, send word to the commander that the garrison must start tomorrow morning to Coimbra; then, notify all nobles that they and their knights will assemble the next morning on the King's Highway at the city gate prepared to go to Coimbra."

Sir Thomas nodded, and Dona Tereza asked immediately, "Has King Sancho been placed under interdict again?"

Don Martinho cut a piece of meat and answered absently: "By the Bishop of Coimbra."

Dona Tereza placed her knife slowly on the table in front of her. The room was quiet. Noises drifted from the courtyard through the open window, but they were the slight noises that marked the end of the day, the noises of children at play. "Martinho, nobles are not permitted to send knights when the King engages in dispute with the Church."

Don Martinho glanced at his wife as though he had already forgotten the message laying beside his hand. "They are not required to engage in the dispute, Trese. The men are required only to suppress rioters." He turned his attention to the food before him.

"That is an evasion, Martinho."

Fernando looked quickly at his mother. He had never before heard her speak so insistently to his father. Her voice was soft, but Fernando saw that her tone had surprised and irritated him.

Don Martinho picked the message from the table and put it before his wife. "Read the message, Trese, and see that the men are required because of the rioters."

Dona Tereza did not look at the paper. "Martinho, the people are rioting because the churches are closed. The churches are closed because of the interdict, and the interdict has been imposed because King Sancho is engaged in another dispute with the Church."

"Dona Tereza," said his father, "we are not enemies of the Church because we must suppress rioters and maintain order."

Fernando forgot about his food. He looked from one to another as his mother and his father and Sir Thomas spoke. He realized that this was not another of his mother's minor protests which his father would pretend to hear reluctantly before he agreed and did as she asked. His father's manner and Sir Thomas' defense emphasized their determination to do what she firmly opposed.

Dona Tereza raised her voice when she spoke and looked at her husband, at Sir Thomas, at Fernando, and last at Ruggiero. "I expect that the men of this house will be courageous not only against enemies of the body but also against enemies of the spirit."

"Courage is not foolhardiness, Trese," Don Martinho retorted angrily. "Should I resign as king's magistrate rather than interfere with rioters?"

Fernando looked at his mother. Her lips still curved gently, but he could see that she was not smiling. He wanted to speak for her, to ward off his father's anger, but he understood only part of the disagreement between them. None spoke, and Fernando began again to eat, uncomfortable in the stillness of the room. Beside him, Ruggiero had almost finished his supper.

In the morning as they walked from the Cathedral, he knew that the disagreement remained between his mother and father though they talked together and to him and Ruggiero. His mother's smile had lost its gaiety, and his father's manner was guarded as though he expected her to say more about the message from the King.

Breakfast was calm and placid, but Fernando felt uncomfortably that a stranger had entered among them. He was relieved that he and Ruggiero must ride that day to the lands along the Tagus. When Canon Joseph joined the column at the corner of the castle, he could do no more than return the priest's "God's Morning!" and lapse again into his silence.

From the wall of the city, the road was straight and level, holding close to the river on the right. On the left, the ground rose steadily higher until it bulked upward and formed the mountains. Orchards dominated the land from the road to the mountains; the buildings that were the serfs' villages were visible only occasionally in the distance at the base of the mountain. On the right, beyond the Tagus, little more than the shoreline was visible, for that country was flat.

They had passed the bend that marked half the distance of their ride when the column halted suddenly. Fernando stood in the stirrups and stretched to see over the heads of the men before him but could see nothing more than the foremost knight leaning down from his horse and talking to a serf in the road. The serf gestured wildly and pointed farther along the road and across the river. Fernando settled again into the saddle until the sound of a horse galloping toward the column drew him up again in the stirrups.

The knight who had talked to the serf charged past the forward section of the column, drawing in the reins so abruptly beside Fernando that his horse slid on the loose earth of the road. "Master Fernando! The Saracens have raided and burned San Bruno! They killed the serfs and burned the building."

Fernando's heart jumped suddenly in his chest, then began to beat rapidly. He felt the eyes of the men in the column look to him for decision and order. Even Canon Joseph turned as he might have to Don Martinho. "When did this happen?" he demanded. His voice was shaking, but he controlled it against its own tendency to rise higher.

"In the last hours of darkness. This man hid in the fields until the Saracens went away at dawn."

"How many were there?" Fernando felt his voice steady and he felt more confident.

"The serf doesn't know, Master. He thinks there were forty or fifty."

Fernando looked quickly at the men in the column. He had ten knights here and their squires. He saw in the faces of the men their eagerness to go forward; but they would need help if the enemy was double their number. "Ruggiero! Take the last knight and his squire from the column. Ride back and tell Don Martinho what has happened."

The big squire did not move. His eyes widened with astonishment. "You cannot go forward, Fernando. You are not armed," he protested.

"Now!" Fernando ordered.

Ruggiero swung his horse from the column and turned without offering more objection.

Fernando waved his arm forward over his head. The column began to move. "Take your place, Sir; the column will follow your pace." The knight galloped along the side of the column, then into the clear space of the road until he joined his squire waiting with the serf. The knight gestured the serf from the road and settled his horse into a hard run. Fernando saw the men in front of him straightening with interest for an encounter. He was conscious of passing the serf, an exhausted figure crumpled and sobbing beside the road. Then he realized that Canon Joseph had turned from the column. He looked back to see the priest dropping from his horse at the place where the serf lay on the ground.

Thin white smoke from burned-out fire formed a pillar over the site of San Bruno, far back from the road at the base of a mountain. Orchards hid the building until they came to the narrow road that led between the trees to the square of San Bruno. The leading knight changed the pace to a gallop, and the column pounded after him to the very edge of the square.

His first impression was of a space of brown, trampled earth, enclosed by the three sections of the burned building, and of figures, still and helpless, against the brown earth. Before him, not more than eight paces, the body of a man lay face downward, his clothing bearing the imprints of the horses that had trodden on him. A little farther was the body of a woman, stripped of all clothing; a dull red against the darkness of her throat showed the manner of her death. Death claimed and silenced the square of San Bruno.

Fernando dropped from his horse and felt the weakness of his knees. The horse pulled back from the smell of carnage, and he had to take hold of the bridle; the effort revived his strength. The men grouped to either side struggled with the horses or looked dazedly at the square before them. Someone retched loudly. His own stomach contracted, and he did not trust himself to speak. He thrust the reins of his horse into the hands of a squire and moved forward past the body of the man and past the body of the woman. "Let the squires care for the horses." His voice echoed against the wings of the building along the sides of the square. "See if any of these are living."

He moved beside the body of a girl—she was not older than Anna—and knelt to touch her cold face before he saw the depression in her head where a mace had crushed out her life. After that, he was not aware that he moved from one crumpled figure to another, not aware that only some of the knights had moved forward on either side of the square, not aware of orders he spoke, not aware of time. A powerful arm circled his shoulders gently, and he looked up at his father beside him. For a moment he fought against weakness, but tears overpowered and blinded him. His father's arm tightened and pressed him against the hard mail. "Bigger men than you have cried at scenes like this, Fernando."

Canon Joseph and another priest, apparently from one of the other villages, moved from body to body with the Oil of Anointment. As they straightened, serfs picked up the bodies and carried them from the square around the wings of the building.

Sir Thomas came to his father in the early afternoon. "The bodies will be in an open grave until this priest can celebrate Mass tomorrow morning. We should leave a guard—animals . . ."

That, even in death, these bodies might not lie undisturbed, lighted a fire of rage in Fernando. In that instant, and with a shock greater than when he had first looked on this courtyard of death, Fernando saw his own restlessness— the fierce power that boiled within—as the beginning of lawlessness, and the crumpled bodies in the courtyard as the end of lawlessness in the men who had done this.

The sun had progressed far across the sky when they mounted. Fernando sat erect and alert. He measured the long line of men and horses ahead and behind—his father had brought most of the men from Castle de Bulhom— a striking force that would be his to use someday. None spoke. His father and Sir Thomas rode in front of him. Canon Joseph was beside him and Ruggiero beyond. Even the priest was silent and recollected as though he too had been overwhelmed by the carnage of San Bruno. Fernando held his tongue; he would have opportunity later to demand action and vengeance of his father.

When they had passed the bend of the road, half of the distance, Don Martinho turned to Sir Thomas. "Send a messenger tonight to recall the city garrison. Send a message to the nobles not to assemble tomorrow morning. Tell them to assemble on the second morning with knights only at the Santarem gate for an expedition against the Saracens."

"The King?" Sir Thomas asked.

"We have greater need of the men than King Sancho, Thomas. Let him make peace with the Church, and the people will stop the rioting."

Rage flamed higher in Fernando. He must be a part of this expedition. He must be granted an opportunity to turn his fury against those who had spent themselves at San Bruno. His father must let him witness the retribution against the Saracens. He asked at supper that night, but Don Martinho merely shook his head.

"I can take part. I proved that today," Fernando persisted.

"Fernando," Dona Tereza interrupted, "you did not prove your strength in combat today. You proved your courage, but not your strength."

"I would have strength against the men that raided San Bruno," he replied recklessly.

His father ended his hopes. "Fernando, even the squires are ordered to remain here. You will stay with them."

Fernando quieted, but he determined stubbornly to find other methods to present his request again. When the supper ended, he followed Sir Thomas through the outer passage and into the courtyard. "Speak to my father for me, Sir Thomas. After today, he should take me with him."

In the darkness, he could not see the knight commander's expression, but the voice rebuked him. "Don Martinho gave you an order, Fernando." He felt Sir Thomas turn away and heard his footsteps diminishing on the cobblestones of the courtyard.

He would not yield. He had been leader of the men at San Bruno. He must have part with the avengers. After breakfast, the following morning, he followed Dona Tereza to her room to beg her assistance.

Dona Tereza shook her head firmly. "If the squires cannot go, Fernando, certainly you cannot. Ruggiero is bigger than most of the men who are going, but your father will not take him."

A final, desperate appeal to his father at supper was discouraged by the presence of Sir Thomas. Fernando could not risk the knight commander's contempt. He had no other opportunity, for Don Martinho left the Cathedral immediately after Mass the next day, and the column was prepared to leave the courtyard when he returned with his mother and Ruggiero.

"You are in charge of Castle de Bulhom, Son."

"May the Holy Virgin go with you," Fernando said clearly.

Breakfast was an ordeal. As soon as he could, he went to the accounts room, where neither Dona Tereza nor any other could see him.

After a long time, he moved from the corner of the room to his bench at the table. Through the window he watched the men and carts. There was little activity; the actions of the men were slow and hesitant, as though all of Castle de Bulhom already began to wait news of the expedition. He saw Ruggiero come from the doorway of the armory and walk across the courtyard. The big squire hesitated at the doorway into their own section, then looked at the window of the accounts room. Fernando lifted his arm without enthusiasm, and Ruggiero turned and came toward him.

Fernando did not turn when Ruggiero entered. He

supported his head with his arms braced on the table, watching the courtyard without interest. Ruggiero pulled up a bench.

"I had to leave the armory," he grumbled almost as though apologizing. "Those other squires are talking about organizing their own expedition to follow after the knights, and they won't stop asking me to go with them."

"They were ordered to remain here," Fernando said.

"I told them that. I told them Don Martinho would discipline everyone who violated his orders. Then they started talking of asking you to go with them, so I left."

Fernando drew back slowly from the table and lowered his arms. For a moment he continued staring at the courtyard with his eyes fixed on the doorway of the armory, then he turned to Ruggiero. "They want me to go with them?" he questioned softly.

Ruggiero regarded him curiously, puzzled by Fernando's sudden interest. "That's why I left—" he began, then stopped abruptly. He scowled with disgust. "They don't want you, Fernando. They want your protection."

"I would be their commander," Fernando retorted.

The big squire refused to retreat. "If they won't obey Don Martinho's orders, they wouldn't obey yours."

Fernando turned back then to the view of the courtyard and braced his arms again on the table. They sat silent for a long time. Ruggiero stirred restlessly and finally stood up and started slowly to the door. "Why don't you go down there and order them not to leave the castle?"

Fernando did not turn from the window. He held his face fixed to the view he did not see. "If they won't obey Don Martinho's orders . . ." he repeated. The door behind him closed violently.

He tried to talk at dinner, but Dona Tereza answered without enthusiasm, and Ruggiero would not speak except to answer questions. Fernando stayed all afternoon in the accounts room. Supper was eaten in almost complete silence. In the morning, after Mass, Dona Tereza had regained her cheerfulness and talked with them as they walked from the Cathedral and through breakfast, but Ruggiero refused to join them.

After breakfast Fernando followed Ruggiero through the passage into the courtyard as he had followed Sir Thomas. "Why don't you try to talk? Mother is worrying about my father, and you should help her."

The big squire looked down at him. "Your father said you were in charge here. Why didn't you speak to the squires?" Ruggiero walked away toward the armory.

Fernando frowned. He had to run to join Ruggiero. "I'll give them that order if you think it is that important," he offered sullenly.

Ruggiero stopped abruptly and turned around. "You should have done that yesterday," he said angrily. "The squires rode away while we were at Mass."

A sense of failure and of loss dominated that morning. In one day he had neglected his father's trust and had lost Ruggiero's admiration by refusal to speak to the squires. He remembered, too, his own interest when Ruggiero had told him the squires wanted him to go with them. He was quiet at dinner, but Ruggiero talked to Dona Tereza, and they did not seem to notice his silence.

"I'm going to see Canon Joseph," he explained to Ruggiero after dinner, then turned away quickly because Ruggiero looked curious and he did not want to explain. He was not sure he could explain.

A lay brother admitted him and led him to the visitors' room. Fernando wandered from one window to the other, looking down the slope at the castle until Canon Joseph entered. The priest joined him at the window so they could stand and look down on the olive trees. Far off to the left, they could see a small fragment of the river. Standing in this way, it was easier to tell Canon Joseph of the squires and of his failure to stop them, though the effort to speak of failure brought excuses to minimize his responsibility. "They did not obey my father's orders," he repeated Ruggiero's challenge as an excuse for himself.

Canon Joseph added another excuse for him. "It is possible too, Fernando, that you did not speak to the squires because you don't want to command men."

Fernando considered whether the priest's comment was favorable or unfavorable. Lack of desire to command men seemed a reproach in itself. "I have no choice," he answered. "Someday I must command them."

The answer did not satisfy Canon Joseph. "That is not sufficient. One man may be a bad man but a good commander because he wants to command others; another may be a good man but a bad commander because he does not want to command men. A very good man may become a very bad man by trying to do what he has no talent to do." The priest turned from the window and leaned with his shoulder against the sill. "Do you ever think of life, Fernando—what your life will be, or what you will do with your life?"

The question startled him. He was looking at the castle and lands he would own, he could picture the men he would command, he could imagine that he might also be Magistrate of Lisbon, he would be a good master to the serfs in the villages as his father was. Canon Joseph need not be told this. Fernando thought of the knighthood that had claimed his dreams and all his hopes; but the dreams had evaporated, and his hopes had dried before the reality of his slight body. He glanced at the priest but could see no indication of humor or amusement. Canon Joseph was neither more serious nor more casual than at any other time. "I don't know what you mean," Fernando admitted.

Canon Joseph did not explain his question; he appeared content with the admission as if that were sufficient answer. "We have wandered from the subject, Fernando. You came here because you were troubled that you might not have done your duty by ordering the squires to remain in the castle. You should forget that. Your order would not impress them more than Don Martinho's. In fact, if you had given that order, they might have been angry at Ruggiero for telling you their plans."

Fernando's cheerfulness and confidence revived while they talked. The sense of loss and failure that had oppressed him vanished before the priest's approval. When he returned to the courtyard, thought neither of the squires nor of Ruggiero disturbed him. He found a new hope that the squires would return before his father and the knights; if they did, his father would modify his discipline. At supper Ruggiero looked curiously at him but did not ask questions. They talked and laughed together to cheer Dona Tereza. A new determination possessed Fernando to sustain his mother and to discharge his duties in the accounts room.

A man of the city garrison, hurt when his horse fell beneath him, brought information that the expedition had learned the identity of the group that had ravished San

Bruno and was riding through Saracen country seeking them. The man had returned slowly to Lisbon because of his injuries, however, and the expedition might already have encountered the group they pursued.

Three days later Fernando was at the table in the accounts room when the command "Honor!" sounded from the guard at the inner gate. He half rose from his bench and watched the sally port eagerly. He saw his father enter the courtyard alone, and noted that he was not stopping at the stables but was forcing his horse to canter across the treacherous cobblestones. Fernando turned to the doorway and hurried through the passage to the courtyard.

"Father!"

Don Martinho had jumped from the horse at the very entrance to the family section and had started toward the doorway. He turned as Fernando ran toward him. "Fernando! Thank God! Thank God!" He caught Fernando in his arms and held him tightly against the hard mail. "Thank God! You are here, Son." His strained voice changed suddenly to a laugh of relief, and he took his arms from around Fernando. But the strain returned immediately and he said: "Ruggiero! Where is Ruggiero, Son?"

"In the armory, Father." He saw the figure of the big squire running toward them. "He is coming now."

His father turned quickly as if words were not sufficient and he must have the assurance of his own eyes. The laugh of relief returned to his voice. "Ruggiero is here with you, Fernando!" He stepped forward as though to take Ruggiero's hand then impetuously embraced him.

Fernando noticed for the first time the strangeness of his father's actions, his tenseness and his relief, the dirt-streaked face, the dirt on his clothes and armor. He saw the horse, head lowered with exhaustion, walking wearily and unattended toward the stables.

His father put one arm around his shoulders and held Ruggiero with the other. He turned both of them to the doorway. "Come in with me!" Fernando heard again the relieved laugh.

Dona Tereza waited in her room. Fernando wondered idly if his father would grasp her impulsively as he had himself and Ruggiero; but his father was smiling, and there was none of the rough impulsiveness in his greeting to her. He kissed her cheek lightly as he always did, and Fernando heard him saying, "I was worried about them, but they were here." His mother smiled but seemed puzzled as though she did not understand his words.

Don Martinho saw his wife's bewilderment, and his expression sobered again but without the tenseness he had displayed in the courtyard. He turned to look at Fernando and Ruggiero waiting in the doorway. He seemed to waver uncertainly for a moment before saying to them, "Leave me with your mother for a time."

Fernando and Ruggiero returned to the courtyard. The big squire stopped, but Fernando turned without hesitation toward the entrance to the accounts room, and Ruggiero moved beside him.

"Don Martinho was worried that we were with the squires, Fernando."

Fernando looked up at Ruggiero. "Are you guessing or did you hear him?"

Ruggiero shook his head. "I wouldn't repeat it if I heard him say anything. But I'm not guessing."

They waited in the accounts room without speaking. Fernando sat at the window, where he could see when a page stepped from the doorway of the family section. Ruggiero went to a table at the end of the room and lay full length on his back staring at the ceiling. The bell of the Cathedral rang the Angelus, and they looked questioningly at each other, but neither spoke. Fernando turned back to his vigil at the window until a page appeared at last and looked toward the accounts room. Fernando raised his arm and jumped to his feet. Ruggiero rolled from the table and they went together to the courtyard to meet the page.

"Don Martinho sent for you, Master Fernando."

Don Martinho and Dona Tereza were already in the trencher room. Don Martinho had bathed and had discarded the chain mail, but Fernando saw that his father's eyes were red and he was tired. His face was serious again, though he smiled when they entered. Dona Tereza was smiling, but it was a subdued smile, as though she was troubled about something Don Martinho had told her.

"You will want to know all that happened," his father began when they had recited the grace. "I will tell you now only that we found the group that raided San Bruno. I'll give you the details after dinner."

"But what happened when you found them?" The question rose spontaneously.

"I can tell you that Sir Thomas was hurt," his father continued. "A Saracen tried to ride me down, and he would have done it except that Thomas intercepted him. That Saracen was riding at a full charge when Thomas rode in front of him. Both of them went down and, when Thomas got up, he could not remount. I think all of his ribs are broken on the right side. He is coming home in a cart."

"Will he recover, Don Martinho?" Ruggiero asked anxiously.

"In six weeks, Ruggiero."

Fernando looked again at his mother, but she was interested in the story about Sir Thomas. Her smile and her eyes retained their sadness, but he knew that Sir Thomas' injury was not the cause. He thought of the disagreement between his mother and father, but the recall of the city garrison and the expedition of the knights had ended that. She was little interested in the food before her, and soon laid her knife down and sat waiting until the others had finished. She rose from her place then and left the room. Fernando and Ruggiero looked expectantly at Don Martinho, who now turned a serious face toward them.

"We learned from people in the Saracen country where the group came from that raided San Bruno. Then we learned who they were. There were thirty-two of them. We went to their town, but they were not there, so we divided our force into five units to hunt for them. Our unit found them. They ran from us until they saw that our unit was no larger than theirs, so they turned around and fought. Six of them were killed in that fight. We hanged the others."

Fernando felt the elation of justice but with it a surge of revulsion. He saw that his father's face hardened as he spoke as though he also disliked the story.

"During that same time," Don Martinho continued, "another unit of the knights came upon a Saracen village where the buildings were burned and the people slaughtered just like San Bruno. That unit pursued the raiders, thinking it was the same group that had attacked San Bruno. When they caught them, they discovered they were the squires from Castle de Bulhom."

Fernando did not move nor speak. He continued watching his father while his father's words slowly formed into images and pictures in his mind. Then his father's face disappeared, and he saw again the pillar of smoke and blackened window openings of San Bruno, the width of brown earth that was the square of the village, the body of the man, and the other crumpled bodies. He heard the sound of the man who had retched somewhere to the right. And now his own stomach contracted, and he fled blindly from the room and through the outer passage to the courtyard.

He became aware of the courtyard noises after a time, became aware that he was leaning with his arms outstretched against the wall beside the doorway and that men and women in the courtyard saw his sickness and strange behavior. He pushed himself from the wall and started walking toward the stables.

Ruggiero came from behind him. "Your father told me to come out with you," he said simply.

Fernando shook his head. "Tell him I went to Canon Joseph."

He did not see the groom who brought the horse nor the guards at the gates nor the tunnel of the sally port nor the country and river. Yet he saw many things plainly that had been mere feelings or formless masses before. More clearly than all else, he saw his own blindness, saw the fury that had claimed him at San Bruno, saw the determination for vengeance that had so nearly joined him to the squires. He tried to tell all his thoughts to the priest, but he told them badly and confusedly, though Canon Joseph insisted he understood them.

"With God, nothing is impossible, Fernando. Almighty God draws good from evil. He drew good from the evil at San Bruno, and He drew good from the evil of your pride. Your father recalled the men he had sent to help King

Sancho against the Church. And your pride prevented you from going with the squires when you knew they wanted you only to protect themselves. God only permits evil that He may draw good from it. He permitted one evil to protect you from a greater evil. Have you thought how you will thank Him?"

Fernando shook his head slowly, trying to understand what the priest meant.

"Two weeks ago I asked you if you ever thought about life and what you would do with your life. Have you thought of that?"

Fernando shook his head again. "There is nothing for me to think about," he said slowly. "My life is settled."

"Do you want your life to be what you think it will be?"

Fernando could not answer. None had ever suggested that his life could be other than his father's or his grandfather's. There was the castle and the lands and the people who would look to him. There were the countless details he must learn, countless responsibilities he must accept, countless orders he must give. No one before had asked if this were a life he wanted. This was a life that was given to him.

5

THROUGH the last months of 1209, Fernando sparred
fitfully with Canon Joseph's question. He felt no compulsion to answer the priest, made no effort to consider
the question even that he might answer to himself; yet the
question persisted before him, nourished by the very life
that had been given him and which it challenged.

Riding to the lands beside the priest and Ruggiero,
his eyes contemplated the figures of the men in the column before him. Sometimes he swung about that he might
see the equal column that followed. The knights balanced
their bodies in slow and rhythmic cadence to the movements of the horses, without effort, without consciousness; they were silent and withdrawn—animal bodies from
which reason and will had fled into a timeless numbness
as though eager for that final timelessness that was their
proper environment.

When he sat beside his father in the accounts room,
his eyes lifted repeatedly to the life of the courtyard. He
watched the endless procession of serfs and carts bringing wealth from the lands to increase the wealth of the
family De Bulhom. To what purpose did his father gather
and increase this wealth—for what indefinite purpose
did any man continue the pursuit of wealth long after he
had acquired sufficient for his life and the lives of those

61

dependent on him? He sensed that all this was necessary, that someone must continue to direct and order this activity of the courtyard to its appointed end, but the purpose was concealed from him.

"What will you do with your life?"—the question clamored more stridently when he rode beside his mother's chaise into the city and saw what other men did with theirs. Their words, their anger, their coarseness repelled him; their actions revolted him; their pleasures frightened him.

The question clamored with greatest intensity when he rode alone to San Vicente to dispute with himself, to try to arouse within himself what was necessary to live the life that had been given him. He watched the monks who entered the sanctuary to kneel on the altar steps or sit in the stalls of the choir for a time. They were nobles and knights and merchants, he knew. They were men who had known wealth and had sought wealth, men who had seen the lust of Lisbon—perhaps the lust of men in other places also. They knew the deceits of pride and of the world. These quiet, slow-paced men in the sanctuary had turned away from all that the world offered and all that the flesh craved. They had come to San Vicente to give their minds and their hearts to God. Fernando watched them kneel and plead that God would accept them.

He did not know the precise moment when the answer to Canon Joseph had formed in its fullness; he was not sure of the week nor even of the month. He thought that it might have been in December that he himself knew the answer fully. Yet no answer is fully formed until it is spoken.

In January of 1210, Don Martinho announced the release of the squires who had raided the Saracen village. "They are paroled to their fathers—those who have fathers.

The others are paroled to their nearest male relatives." Don Martinho announced the release while they were eating dinner; but he put his knife on the trencher while he talked, as though the subject were too important to be diminished by food or movement. Fernando saw that his father's eyes turned alternately between himself and Ruggiero beside him.

"You two must never forget those squires. Not all of them were guilty of that terrible crime, but they were guilty of disobedience, and their disobedience involved them in the crime of the others. Their youth saved them from being hanged, but now their reputations are ruined. They can never be knights; they can never raise their heads and their eyes among honorable people. For the remainder of their lives, they are marked as men who failed their trust and failed their God.

"Both of you will encounter a multitude of temptations during life. If you are faithful to God, He will protect you and support you when those temptations are thrust before you."

Fernando watched his father's expression and marked the intensity of his voice, as though there was more he should like to say but had not words to frame his thoughts. He saw his father's face relax gradually and his eyes turn to the trencher and the food before him. He saw his hand move toward the knife.

"I am going to enter the service of the Church," Fernando said quietly, as though his own purpose was directly connected with his father's words.

His father raised his eyes slowly and casually, but he lowered them again immediately, more interested in the food before him than in Fernando's announcement. Dona

Tereza looked toward him also but with no greater interest than his father had shown. Sir Thomas did not interrupt the steady movements of his knife and his hands.

"I am going to enter the service of the Church," Fernando repeated.

Don Martinho nodded his head without looking toward him. "Every boy decides, at some time in his life, that he is going to enter the service of the Church, Son."

Fernando flushed as he realized that his father had virtually accused him again of childishness. He looked uncertainly at his mother, then at Sir Thomas, but neither of them seemed interested in his statement or his father's comment. He felt Ruggiero turn and look toward him briefly. "I have thought about this for months," he answered. "I'm going to enter the service of the Church," he insisted.

Dona Tereza touched her napkin to her lips and smiled at him. "Fernando, entering the service is not something you decide. That is something God decides. He calls men to service in the Church; He doesn't ask them to decide."

Fernando retreated momentarily from this unexpected assault. He felt his inability to answer his mother directly. He strained for an answer that would be adequate. "Canon Joseph would not say that."

Dona Tereza smiled with pretended surprise and interest. "What would Canon Joseph say, Fernando?"

"He has already asked me twice what I intended to do with my life. So, if I told him I wanted to enter the service of the Church, he would not say I could not decide that." Fernando felt the comfortable security of defense in the words of the priest.

Don Martinho raised his head alertly at Fernando's answer. "What did Canon Joseph say to you?"

Fernando shook his head quickly. "He didn't say anything to me. He asked me a question. He asked me what I wanted to do with my life. He didn't say I should do anything. He only asked me." Don Martinho regarded him for a moment uncertainly then returned his attention to his dinner without comment.

Fernando looked from his father to his mother and let his eyes wander back and forth, waiting for either of them to speak, but neither seemed interested in the subject. "I'm going to tell him now what I want to do with my life," he persisted. "I can tell him now that I want to enter the service of the Church." He emphasized the finality of his decision by taking up his own knife and cutting at the meat on his trencher.

At supper that same night, he resumed the attack. "I told Canon Joseph the answer to his question this afternoon. I told him I wanted to enter the service of the Church," he announced. "Ruggiero went with me so he can tell you that Canon Joseph did not say that it was something I could not decide." He looked around at the others triumphantly. "Canon Joseph only said that I must have your permission to enter San Vicente."

Don Martinho seemed as though he had not heard. "King Sancho is ill," he announced. "A courier brought the news late this afternoon."

Fernando waited and listened while Don Martinho, Dona Tereza, and Sir Thomas discussed the illness of the King. Ruggiero also put down his knife and listened, interested in all that pertained to the kingdom of which one day he might be a knight. The conversation deteriorated quickly; Don Martinho knew no more than he had already announced; the others could add nothing but conjecture about possible changes in official positions should the King's illness be fatal.

When it was evident that their conversation was exhausted, Fernando began once more to prosecute his own interest. "Father!" he waited until Don Martinho glanced up. "Canon Joseph said I need only your permission to enter San Vicente."

Don Martinho nodded his head slowly and patiently without looking at his son.

Fernando watched his father curiously, uncertain whether the shaking of the head was an indication of deliberate patience or mere acknowledgment.

Dona Tereza answered him. "Fernando, you cannot decide impulsively that you are going to enter the service of the Church and immediately receive permission to enter."

Fernando prepared to deny that he had decided impulsively, but his father anticipated him. "He cannot decide such a thing as this, Trese, whether impulsively or deliberately." Don Martinho turned from his wife to his son. "You are doing nothing more than distracting your mind from your duties and your responsibilities, Fernando. For a time you thought of nothing but becoming a knight. Now you want to enter the service of the Church. Your responsibilities are here at Castle de Bulhom. This is your life. Give that your attention, and stop your imagination from wandering."

Fernando sat helplessly silent, resentful that his father revived the past as though that were significant of the present or of his future; more resentful that his father had revived the very facts he could not deny; most resentful that he himself had provided the very facts his father now turned against him. Stubbornly he determined that they would understand the necessity of what he desired and would not revive the past to accuse him of vacillating and of impulsiveness. He would let his father see his disinterest in the affairs of the accounts room, he would let him see his disinterest in their lands, he would let his mother see his repugnance for the sights and life of the city.

When he told his intentions to Canon Joseph, the priest disagreed. "What would you prove, Fernando? You would prove that you do not like the work of the accounts room, that you do not care to inspect the lands, and that you do not like the manner of the people in the city. Would you prove that you should enter the service of the Church?"

Fernando shook his head grudgingly.

"The heart of the matter is that your father and mother are entirely correct. In just one day you told them your intention and insisted that they give you permission."

"I told them I had thought of this for months," Fernando protested.

Canon Joseph nodded agreement. "It may seem strange to you, Fernando, and you may not understand it, but your father and mother are doing the will of God by opposing you."

Fernando searched the priest's face carefully.

"If your parents did not object but gave you permission immediately to enter San Vicente, then Prior Gonzalez would refuse you entrance. Come into the library and I'll explain."

They went from the visitors' room some distance along a gloomy passageway that was lighted only where doors opened into various rooms. The library was a large, square room with two large windows facing to the south. Books rested on shelves against every wall and filled more shelves built in the center of the room.

The priest took a small volume from a shelf and motioned toward the windows. Fernando looked at the book in the priest's hands but could not recognize it. It was not a breviary. It was small, and the monk or cleric who had copied it had made small letters.

"Did you ever hear of the rule of St. Benedict, Fernando?"

Fernando shook his head. "I've heard of St. Benedict," he added hastily.

Canon Joseph found a page then closed the book, holding his finger between the pages. "St. Benedict was a very great abbot, Fernando. He founded many monasteries; and he wrote this book to guide the abbots of those monasteries and the monks in them." Canon Joseph opened the book. "This is the section, Fernando, where St. Benedict told his abbots how to test vocations. A great many people come to monasteries and ask to be admitted; many of them are not fitted for that life. St. Benedict wanted to keep those men from wasting their time and endangering the vocations of others, so he provided a test. Listen to this! 'When anyone is newly come for the reformation of his life, let him not be granted an easy entrance; but as the Apostle says, "Test the spirits to see whether they are from God." If the newcomer perseveres in his knocking, and if it is seen, after four or five days, that he bears patiently the harsh treatment offered him and the difficulty of admission and persists in his petition, then let entrance be granted him, and let him stay in the guest house for a few days.'" Canon Joseph snapped the book closed. "Do you understand now why I said your parents are doing the will of God?"

Fernando hesitated doubtfully. "They will not give their permission," he answered hesitantly.

"They are trying the spirits, Fernando; they want to see if the spirits are from God. They want to see if you will bear patiently the harsh treatment offered and the difficulty of admission and want to see if you will persist in your petition."

Fernando could not pretend to understand completely the meaning of St. Benedict. He knew only that an obstacle impeded the realization of his desire and the obstacle was his father and mother. "What can I do?"

"Have you asked Prior Gonzalez for permission to enter San Vicente?" Canon Joseph knew he had not asked.

Fernando shook his head.

"He must agree to accept you, Fernando."

*　*　*　*　*

The church and monastery of San Vicente—memorial to those who had fallen when Afonso Henriques had retaken Lisbon from the Saracens—was a gray stone rectangle. The brother who admitted Fernando ushered him first into the visitors' room but returned immediately to lead him to a smaller room, where Prior Gonzalez received him. Fernando had entered this room once before when he had accompanied his father and understood that it was in this room that Prior Gonzalez conducted the business matters of the monastery he directed. There was but one window, and Prior Gonzalez sat against the wall in the corner so that he could see all who entered or left the double doors of the church vestibule; but it was also an arrangement that permitted visitors to face the Prior across his table without being compelled to face the light from the window. The short, round prior was standing and smiling his welcome when Fernando stepped through the doorway.

"God's peace, Master Fernando!" A note of concern in the Prior's voice contrasted with his smile. "You were riding hard to San Vicente . . ."

Fernando realized that the Prior had observed his rush to the monastery and would attribute it to something alarming rather than to his own enthusiasm. "I am sorry, Reverend Prior. I had no reason for rushing as I did." He saw the face of the Prior relax almost imperceptibly. It was a smooth, fair, smiling face, with wrinkles framing the eyes so that the Prior seemed already laughing when he smiled only slightly. "I came to ask permission to enter San Vicente." The words burst from him, driven by the same force that had caused him to rush to the monastery.

Prior Gonzalez' eyes widened with surprise, amusement, and with pleasure. He gestured to the bench across the table and sat down on his own. "In that case, Master Fernando, I think you should sit there and tell me why you want to enter San Vicente and why you galloped to San Vicente as though you were afraid that you would forget what you intended to say when you arrived."

Fernando smiled, and his dark face became darker with the flush of embarrassment. He sat uneasily facing the Prior, trying to think what he should say first—then the words rose easily, and he told the whole story from the question of Canon Joseph to the refusal of Don Martinho and Dona Tereza.

Prior Gonzalez' smile diminished while he listened. When the story ended, he shook his head doubtfully. "A monastery may not be the proper place for a boy raised at Castle de Bulhom, Master Fernando. Fine foods and soft garments are poor preparation for that life."

Fernando wished the Prior would not address him as "Master"; the title intensified the distance between them and between what he was and what he wished to be. He looked down at the sleeve of his silk shirt protruding from the woolen cloak. It was soft and shining. He was ashamed to look at Prior Gonzalez' habit. He knew already the harsh roughness of that wool. "I do not ask to come because of food or clothing," he answered. "I ask—" He stopped as a new thought entered his mind. "O Reverend Prior, I know you want to test the spirit to know that it is from God, but my father and mother are already testing it by refusing to give me permission."

Prior Gonzalez' eyes opened wide with delight. "Excellent! Excellent, Fernando! You already know that the spirit must be tested."

Fernando lowered his eyes as though he had revealed something that should have been concealed. "Canon Joseph read that to me this morning from the Rule of St. Benedict, Prior Gonzalez," he admitted.

The Prior turned his head toward the window and looked to the road Fernando had traveled. The direction of his gaze revealed something of his thoughts, for he looked toward Castle de Bulhom, hidden by St. George's Hill, and his expression became serious again. "You are the only son of a great noble and landowner, Fernando." He turned away from the window to face Fernando. "Ever since you were born, your father has anticipated that you would assume control of Castle de Bulhom and all the estates. It is a tremendous sacrifice that is asked of him now, Fernando. And your mother is asked to make a tremendous sacrifice also because you are her only child."

"My mother would not refuse permission, Reverend Prior," Fernando objected. "She would be willing if my father were."

Prior Gonzalez spoke slowly and softly and confidently. "I know your father; I know Don Martinho will also agree—he will agree as readily as Dona Tereza. But he will not agree until he is certain that you know what you want. He will not give you permission merely because you ask it. You must prove to him that this is your life."

Fernando grew desperate. "How can I prove, Reverend Prior, what is of the future?"

Prior Gonzalez' smile returned in all of its fullness. "That, Fernando, is God's business." He leaned forward and rested his arms on the table between them. "There is not such urgency as your ride here indicated. God may not always act today or tomorrow as we would wish Him. And I think it is according to the will of God to tell you that, even with your parents' permission, you should not enter San Vicente before your fifteenth birthday."

Fernando could not conceal his disappointment. "But that will not be until August, Reverend Prior, and this is January."

Prior Gonzalez rose from his bench, smiling and kindly, but indicating firmly that their interview had ended. "Between now and August, Fernando, you will pray constantly that your parents will grant their permission. Between now and August, you will also come to me every second week to tell me that your determination has not lessened. If you do not come, I will understand that God wants you for other purposes."

Fernando had never thought of life as a matter of problems and obstacles. His inexperienced mind grappled with the problem of this present desire, turning it about, examining it, exploring whatever method promised a solution. He prayed, he implored God's help, he insisted upon the help of the Holy Virgin and all the saints. He returned at the end of two weeks to Prior Gonzalez and again after another interval of two weeks. Impatience overwhelmed his piety at last, and he resumed direct methods of assault on his parents. But God, the Holy Virgin, and all the saints seemed to ignore his pleading. His parents refused him.

In March, news that King Sancho's health was failing put a new and insurmountable obstacle before Fernando's objective.

The courier reported that the royal family and the court at Coimbra had abandoned hope of the King's recovery. All plans were being recast with the view that Prince Alphonso would soon ascend the throne. As king's magistrate of Lisbon, Don Martinho would be expected to present himself to court officials without delay.

Fernando heard announcement of his father's plans as fresh discouragement. He had no alternative but to set aside his own purpose and hope that the trip itself would afford opportunities to plead his case again to his father.

The journey to Coimbra was an ordeal of seven tedious, almost silent days; and the death of King Sancho, on the very day of their arrival, closed the shops and markets and stilled the life of the capital. Respect for the dead monarch required all to remain indoors unless their work related to the funeral; so that the reception of the king's magistrate from Lisbon was a subdued greeting by the king's marshal at the city gates, from which he was escorted by his ten knights to the estate house assigned for use of Don Martinho and his men.

The unnatural stillness of the city ended with the morning. From daybreak, the estate house quickened as the company of Don Martinho and the servants of the house prepared for the royal funeral. The city, too, returned to life, for those not participating in the funeral came early from their homes to line the road between the royal castle and the Cathedral.

Outwardly, Fernando maintained a severe gravity, but neither the dull ride to the capital nor the quiet induced by the death of the King stilled his eager interest in his new surroundings. He looked covertly at the houses, the streets, and the people of the capital while he and Ruggiero rode behind Don Martinho and Sir Thomas to the royal castle. He was attentive to the movements of the knights and bowmen moving into position for the funeral procession, and to the court officials moving through the main doors of the castle, whispering instructions to lesser officials and messengers. Soon the king's marshal appeared and raised his baton to signal the beginning of the funeral.

Knights of the royal household issued first from the castle. Immediately behind them, eight men supported the casket on their shoulders. Then followed a woman clothed entirely in black, accompanied by a short but very fat man.

"The new King, Alphonso," Don Martinho said softly, "and Queen Urraca."

Fernando strained to see the new king, but Ruggiero distracted him by whispering disgustedly, "Alphonso, the Fat." Don Martinho heard also and frowned at Ruggiero. Others had heard, too, and some of those nearby covered their faces. They whispered to others, and the name rippled the length of the procession and even to the freemen and serfs waiting along the edges of the road leading to the Cathedral.

Fernando watched expectantly for the tall, slender

figure of Prince Pedro, but two girls, wearing the white of the unmarried, followed the new King and Queen.

"Princess Sancha and Princess Mafalda," his father whispered, half-turning as he did to warn against comment. Fernando was suddenly entranced. He forgot to watch for the appearance of Prince Pedro. His eyes remained unwaveringly on the nearer of the King's two daughters. Unmindful of her rank, he saw only a girl his own age, beautiful as Dona Tereza, delicate, graceful. He realized that his father was watching him, and the boy glanced at him with the expectation of disapproval. Don Martinho turned away from him, without comment—Fernando puzzled at the unusual look of satisfaction on his father's face.

During the course of the funeral procession, he saw the figure of Prince Pedro, and throughout Mass and the ceremony of burial, his eyes wandered repeatedly to the white veil of Princess Sancha; but he forced them to turn away as quickly as he became conscious of his action.

On the following day, Don Martinho and Sir Thomas left early without explanation, but without instructions that he and Ruggiero should remain within the grounds of the estate house.

"We can ride through the city," Fernando decided.

Ruggiero shrugged his shoulders. "We might get lost or wander into a bad part of the city," he cautioned.

Fernando laughed. "Canon Joseph told me where we should go while we are here and what places to avoid."

To conceal his real purpose, Fernando led the way first to the places of minor interest but barely paused at each of them. Before mid-morning, he had led the way to the edge of the city; Ruggiero's doubts increased in proportion as the number of houses diminished.

"We can't leave the city, Fernando."

Fernando pointed along the road before them where the wall of the city was clearly visible. "There is the wall, Ruggiero. We are inside the city." He swung his arm slightly to the right to a building of extraordinary size, surrounded by open fields, and separated from all else by a high stone wall. "There's our destination. Holy Cross."

"What is it?"

"Mother house of all the Canons Regular of St. Augustine in Portugal," Fernando responded with the lightness of superior knowledge. "The prior of Holy Cross is head of all the canons. He is even superior to Prior Gonzalez."

The big squire looked casually at the building then turned back to Fernando. "I thought from the way you looked at Princess Sancha yesterday that you had forgotten there were Canons Regular of St. Augustine." He repeated the full name of the religious order vengefully, savoring the opportunity to counter Fernando's show of knowledge.

Fernando flushed with angry resentment. "My father didn't scold or criticize me," he retorted.

Ruggiero's sarcasm penetrated more deeply than he intended or Fernando expected. For the remainder of the day, Fernando could not rid himself of the guilty feeling that he had acted little better than during the visit to Ruggiero's home when he had seen Anna. His distress increased that night when Don Martinho told him that King Alphonso and Queen Urraca had invited father and son for dinner on the following day.

Fernando endured the amused expression on Ruggiero's face when he told the big squire about the invitation. He built up within himself a renewed determination that he would prove to all of them the firmness of his intention.

He would abandon this life. He would not be dissuaded by the attractions of life in the world—not even by the loveliness of a royal princess.

His determination made him alert in the presence of the King and the Queen and Princess Sancha, who was even prettier than she had seemed before. He noticed that the King and Queen and his father were watching him and the Princess, and he wondered what had attracted their interest—why all three of them appeared secretly pleased.

Princess Sancha seemed also to become aware of the attention of the adults and lapsed gradually into silence. Fernando began to wish that dinner would end and that he could escape before some word or action might ruin the day. The interest of the others pressed so heavily that he, too, lapsed into silence to guard against some blunder. When the dinner did end and he rode with Don Martinho to the estate house, something cautioned him to answer with a noncommittal grunt when his father asked if he thought Princess Sancha was pretty.

Ruggiero grinned at him knowingly when he dismounted but waited until Don Martinho disappeared before he spoke. "Did you like her?" he demanded.

Fernando flushed and turned away and followed quickly after his father. He was inside before Ruggiero was able to hurry beside him. The big squire caught his arm and held him against his struggle to escape.

"I didn't mean anything wrong, Fernando," the other pleaded.

Fernando saw the sincerity of Ruggiero and stopped struggling. "Why do you continue talking about the Princess, then?" he demanded.

Ruggiero looked down at him uncertainly. "I only

wanted to know if King Alphonso and Don Martinho agreed, and they would not agree unless you liked Princess Sancha." Fernando's eyes opened wide with astonishment. The whole meaning of the dinner, of his father's satisfaction, of the interest of King Alphonso and of Queen Urraca burst suddenly on him. Stupid! He was stupid as a child. "What do you know?" he demanded. Ruggiero regarded him fearfully as though he had already said more than he should. "What did you hear?" Fernando pursued savagely.

The big squire had no escape. "One of the knights told me," he admitted.

"What did he tell you?"

Ruggiero resigned himself to inevitable confession, but the words struggled from him reluctantly. "He said the King wanted to arrange a marriage with the De Bulhom family because your father is the most powerful man and the wealthiest in the southern part of the country. Besides, there are only two other families greater than yours in the country, and their sons are too old."

Fernando raged inwardly, partly at his own stupidity, partly that his father would subject him to such humiliation before Ruggiero, before Sir Thomas, before all the knights of the household. He went directly to his father's room, but his intention was defeated by the presence of others, and he had to retire without speaking.

Through the remainder of that day he had no opportunity to speak to his father. Preparations for the return ride, messages, business with other officials of the King, claimed all of Don Martinho's time and barred Fernando's efforts to express himself. At supper, Fernando and Ruggiero sat at the end of the table that others might be near his father to discuss their business, and again he was denied an opportunity to speak. After supper, he had no alternative but to go with Ruggiero to their room and prepare for bed.

"I don't know what you intend to do," Ruggiero offered hesitantly in the room, "but you ought to keep in mind that Don Martinho is very happy."

Fernando did not answer. He did not know himself what he intended doing. He had concentrated his efforts on finding opportunity to speak to his father but had not planned what he would say when he found that opportunity. Ruggiero's sober comment drove his mind in a new direction, and he planned his thoughts and the words to express them. Anger gave way to preciseness of detail. He remembered that they had climbed gradually as they had approached the capital. He fixed the bottom of that slope as the place where he would demand his father's attention. His mind continued planning until, at last, he slept.

His determination wavered uncertainly in the morning. Then memory recalled the day of the King's funeral, the dinner with the royal family, the apparent pleasure of the new King and Queen; his resolution returned with greater intensity than before. As soon as the last man of the column descended the slope below the gate of Coimbra, he began the attack.

"Father!"

Don Martinho turned in the saddle. He smiled slightly.

"May I speak to you?"

Don Martinho drew in the reins of his horse until Fernando and Ruggiero came on either side of him. Don Martinho motioned to the place beside Sir Thomas, and Ruggiero moved his horse forward obediently. "Is this confidential, Son?"

Fernando nodded. They drew back from Sir Thomas

and Ruggiero, while those behind obeyed Don Martinho's signal and fell back an equal distance. Fernando remembered the space his father had arranged the day he had scolded him for his interest in Anna. The memory helped support his resolution.

Fernando drew a deep breath. Deliberately he abandoned the discipline that had checked his tongue for three years. Words flowed from him as though by their very number they would crush all opposition. He did not look at his father; he was afraid that, whatever his father's expression, it might discourage him from continuing. "I know what I want to do with my life," he concluded, "and I am the one who has the right to decide what I will do," he spoke quietly but almost defiantly. He turned only then to look at his father. "I want to enter the service of the Church."

Don Martinho's face was impassive. All expression had disappeared. His happiness had vanished, but there was no indication of disappointment. Fernando saw that he had accomplished nothing more than to set his will against his father's.

"Is that all you wished to say?"

Fernando looked helplessly at his father. Desperately he wanted to add more, to justify all that he had said, to explain the necessity of what he proposed. He could say nothing. His father had drawn away from him, had closed his mind against all that he might say. There came into his mind again the picture of men kneeling in the sanctuary of San Vicente, of men offering their prayers for him, of Prior Gonzalez' assurance that those prayers would win the objective if only he persisted in his determination; but he felt defeat now rather than the encouragement the picture should have inspired.

Fernando said nothing to his mother, either of Princess

Sancha or of his words to his father; he did not know whether Don Martinho related the incident to her. She could know that some disagreement had occurred between them merely by the constraint that marked their relationship during the ensuing weeks. Neither did he confide to Ruggiero, though sometimes he saw the big squire looking unhappily from him to his father. He avoided entirely any private conversation with Sir Thomas; the knight commander made no effort to conceal his contempt for Fernando.

It was May before he realized that his mother was striving to end the dispute between her husband and her son. There was no intimation in her efforts that she wished to sympathize with either; she seemed interested only in reestablishing confidence between them.

That same month, Prince Pedro came again to Castle de Bulhom. Fernando had gone to continue his scheduled reports to Prior Gonzalez—dispirited reports they had become—and returned to a courtyard that was overburdened with men, horses, carts, and supplies. He recognized the gold and scarlet gonfalon held stiffly upright at the entrance of the accounts room. He began to walk hurriedly from the stables across the courtyard to escape from the crowd of knights he did not know, but who seemed to know him, because they nodded and smiled as though they thought well of him.

He had put his hand against the door to the family quarters when a strange voice called his name—a low voice that yet carried strangely over the sounds of the courtyard. Fernando turned to the open window of the accounts room and saw Prince Pedro beckoning to him. He ran forward past the standard-bearer and through the door that led to the accounts room.

Prince Pedro was standing, but Don Martinho sat on a bench. Fernando saw that his father was unhappy, almost morosely unhappy, while Prince Pedro's welcome to him was extravagantly artificial. "Come in, boy, come in. Let there be one member of the De Bulhom family here who agrees with me against a grasping king."

Fernando stopped and looked automatically toward his father. He had wanted to avoid another encounter with this prince; now the Prince seemed to have trapped him into some position opposed to Don Martinho. He could do no more than let his eyes tell his father that he was guiltless in this, that he had no sympathy for whatever this prince pretended of him or presumed of him, that he was loyal to his father. His father shook his head slowly that he should not speak.

"Master Fernando, it is known that you prefer to enter the service of the Church rather than allow your father to arrange a marriage agreement with the daughter of the King."

Fernando opened his mouth to deny the terrible misrepresentation of the Prince, but he saw his father shake his head again and he held his silence.

"Your father has abandoned everything in his new alliance with the King, Master Fernando. He abandons not only his friends but even his son."

Don Martinho jumped up from his bench. Fernando had never seen his father so prepared to strike as at that moment. Prince Pedro did not move from his place; he bent forward slightly as though expecting Don Martinho to attack. Fernando wanted to turn and run out through the door at his back, but he moved forward impulsively with three quick steps to stand with his father. The movement distracted Don Martinho, and he did not move from his place. His arm raised and encircled Fernando's shoulders. "You will leave Castle de Bulhom immediately, Your Highness," he rumbled calmly. Prince Pedro's expression did not change, nor did he acknowledge Don Martinho's order. As though he alone had decided his action, he went immediately through the doorway. Fernando heard his footsteps sounding in the passageway, heard the outer door open, then knew from the sudden silence of the courtyard that the Prince was outside the building.

Don Martinho turned toward the window, holding his arm on Fernando's shoulders. Together they watched the Prince's men form their column and mount. The courtyard quieted as they disappeared into the sally port. His father released him, and Fernando stood for a moment wondering what was expected of him. The great bell of the Cathedral rang the Angelus. "Go in with your mother, Fernando. It is almost time for dinner." His voice was heavy and spiritless.

During the succeeding days, Fernando and Ruggiero discussed and conjectured the reason for Prince Pedro's visit and his sudden departure. Fernando could not reveal the words he had heard—words that were a lie but that could be turned against his father by anyone who wished to injure him.

Nine days after the event, Fernando escorted his mother to the city. When they returned, he sat on the window seat looking out silently at the courtyard. Dona Tereza, at the opposite end of the window seat, was absorbed in needlework. Fernando could look at her without moving his head. He had said nothing to her about the encounter between his father and Prince Pedro. His mind alternated between a sense of guilt that he was concealing from his mother something that she should know and a sense of frustration that his own objective was no nearer to realization.

"Your father is most unhappy, Fernando."

He turned his head completely from the courtyard. He felt again an emptiness that always attacked when he thought of the conflict between himself and his father. "I know," he acknowledged.

Dona Tereza laid the cloth in her lap and looked at her son. "Are you going to ask him again for permission to enter San Vicente?"

Fernando turned his eyes away. He did not see the courtyard, though he had turned toward it. He saw only the indication that his mother was joining his opponents.

"Do you still want to enter the service of the Church, Fernando?" she persisted.

Fernando nodded unhappily. "But I wasn't going to ask father again for permission as long as he is unhappy," he said.

"You will make him happy if you will ask him now, Son."

Fernando looked incredulously at his mother. He could not doubt the sureness of her voice; he could not doubt the softness of her eyes nor the certainty of her smile. He could only doubt that she knew all that had happened. "You don't know, Mother," he whispered.

Dona Tereza's smile increased, and her confidence was even more evident. "I do know, Son. I know what happened at Coimbra and what happened on the road from Coimbra. I know also what happened in the accounts room when Prince Pedro was here. Mother knows some things, Fernando."

Fernando smiled apologetically. "I didn't mean that, Mother."

"Do you know why Prince Pedro visited your father?"

Fernando shook his head slowly.

"King Sancho's will directed that certain of his lands should belong to Prince Pedro, and the rest should belong to the new king. But King Alphonso claimed that their father had not the right to divide the lands—that all were attached to the crown. So he claimed the share that belonged to Prince Pedro. Prince Pedro came here to ask your father's help in taking the lands by force of arms. Your father refused. That would cause civil war. He asked Prince Pedro to submit the controversy to the Church. Then Prince Pedro became angry and refused to submit to anyone. That was when he called you to the accounts room.

"He spoke lies about Father," Fernando grumbled.

Dona Tereza's voice softened. "Your father thinks there may have been some truth in what he said, Fernando. He thinks that when he refused you permission to enter San Vicente and discussed a marriage arrangement with the King that he may have been sacrificing you to his ambition."

"He wouldn't do that!" Fernando disagreed emphatically.

"He will not be sure, Son, until he gives you permission to enter San Vicente, and now he is afraid that what he did changed your intention of entering. He is waiting for you to ask him again."

6

ANOTHER youth had preceded Fernando to San Vicente. On the morning that Fernando entered, Prior Gonzalez brought the two novices together in the chapter room, a long, narrow room with a platform at one end on which was a single bench. The platform continued around the room with a great number of benches on it.

Introductions were reduced to a simple recitation of their names: "Stephen, Fernando." Prior Gonzalez did not tell Stephen that Fernando was of the family De Bulhom nor tell Fernando the origin of Stephen, but Fernando saw that the short, stout Stephen was so like Prior Gonzalez—even to the same round, smooth face—that the two were related.

From the chapter room, Prior Gonzalez led them through the entire monastery. Fernando examined everything curiously and eagerly. The Prior led them to the dormitory, then to the room where, as novices, they would study, hear lectures, and enjoy their recreation apart from the others of the community, and to the refectory with its long tables and benches and few utensils. Throughout that day, Fernando grappled with a seemingly endless variety of duties, counsels, advice, strange terms, passageways, and rooms. "Can you remember all this?" he whispered once to Stephen. The other frowned at him disapprovingly to remind him that he had violated the rule of silence.

What seemed so complex and confusing on the first day became simple and habitual in the days and weeks that followed. Achievement of his goal, contentment, concentration on study, performance of the few duties given him as a novice, and the regular periods of prayer transformed Fernando's life into a period of enchanted happiness. Infrequently, his thoughts turned to his parents, to Ruggiero, and to the comforts of Castle de Bulhom; but the thoughts fled from him when he deliberately recalled also the torments that had filled him. Each day, each month seemed to have no purpose other than to increase his happiness.

Through the winter, community activities were restricted to the monastery building; but with the warmth of spring, Prior Gonzalez announced resumption of processions and chanting in the cloister garden. On the first occasion, Fernando looked around the garden, uncertain of his place in the procession. He saw the lay brothers gathered near one end of the garden and Stephen near them. He had started walking in that direction when another figure among the lay brothers attracted his eyes.

It was not possible! He had stopped when he saw the big figure in the lay brother's garb. Others moved in front of him and obscured his vision. He moved forward again, slowly now, looking eagerly but almost fearfully to the group at the end of the procession. Then he saw him again. It was Ruggiero!

He had almost cried out to him, had almost run to him. The first notes of the chant sounded. He had reached, unknowingly, his place beside Stephen. The voices of the community recalled him, and he responded automatically to his duty.

They moved in slow procession along the cloister walk.

Fernando looked at the book in his hands, but his eyes could see nothing there. When he had forced his eyes to see the words, his mind could not comprehend them. Ruggiero here! Ruggiero in this line! Ruggiero following no more than six places in back of him! Endlessly, the community continued the procession.

They began the last psalm. He would go immediately to Prior Gonzalez. He could turn, as soon as the office ended, and wave to Ruggiero—that would not violate the rule. His mind alternated between the book before him and the tall youth in back of him. The voices of the community raised and lowered. Verse followed verse. As the community continued the procession, the Prior, as though by accident, was beside him. The last note sounded, and Fernando turned eagerly to his superior.

Prior Gonzalez anticipated him; his finger was pressed tightly against his lips to demand silence. He was smiling at his own huge joke. Before Fernando could look for Ruggiero, Prior Gonzalez gripped his arm and held him turned steadily away from the brothers. Still holding him, he guided him from the garden and into the building. Only when he had hurried him along the corridor and into the room that was the office did he release him. "Now you may speak, Fernando."

Someone had followed them as they moved through the corridor, and Fernando knew it was Ruggiero, but the Prior had held his arm so that he could not look behind. He swung around now, and his glad cry of recognition joined Ruggiero's. They embraced and laughed and pounded each other on the back; Prior Gonzalez hastily closed the door to the corridor. "Less noise! Less noise!" he demanded, but he was laughing noisily himself.

"You're really a brother in the community, really a brother?" Fernando persisted as though he couldn't believe Ruggiero's repeated assurances. "You're really a brother!" "Don Martinho said I would do better as squire for you than for him, Fernando."

Prior Gonzalez quieted them at last. They could only laugh happily together. Fernando could ask no more questions. He could think of nothing other than the wonderful fact that Ruggiero had come to San Vicente with him. That thought crowded all else from his mind. He could not ask about others. He could do nothing more than laugh happily.

Prior Gonzalez took Fernando by the arm again and moved him to the door. "You can talk together at recreation time tonight, Fernando."

After supper, Ruggiero followed silently after Fernando to the recreation room. Stephen greeted the new brother, but his expression revealed his misgivings.

"Prior Gonzalez gave special permission, Stephen," Fernando assured him. "He said that Ruggiero could join with us each evening this week and on Sunday. After that we must follow the Rule again."

Ruggiero seemed unhappy when Fernando mentioned the Rule. "Does that mean we are not allowed to speak to each other, Fernando?"

Fernando and Stephen laughed. "You learned some of the Rule today, didn't you, Ruggiero?"

"But Reverend Prior didn't say anything about not speaking here." Ruggiero's tone seemed aggrieved as though he wondered whether the Prior had concealed some disagreeable fact from him.

Stephen defended his uncle quickly. "That part of the Rule applies to the novices, Ruggiero. We are allowed to speak during recreation after supper and on feast days."

Ruggiero shook his head doubtfully. "Everybody speaks of the Rule around here as if there is just one rule for the whole place and everyone in it. But the Prior told me ten or twenty rules for myself."

Fernando and Stephen both laughed at his apparent mournfulness. So lately themselves accustomed to the complexities of the Rule, they saw in Ruggiero their own confusion of a few months earlier.

"Never mind the Rule, Ruggiero. Tell me about the people I know."

"Your father and mother?"

Fernando shook his head. "I know about father and mother. Prior Gonzalez tells me about them whenever he sees them. I'll see them myself in another month. Tell me about Canon Joseph."

"He's no different. I saw him last Sunday to say good-by to him. Did Prior Gonzalez tell you that King Alphonso appointed Don Martinho as governor?"

Fernando and Stephen were both interested in that news. "What is a governor?" Fernando asked.

The question seemed to confound Ruggiero momentarily. "A governor is like a general or commander. He rules—that's what he does. Your father rules the Lisbon district. He can make laws or send troops or change commanders without asking the King. He tells the King about it after he does it. Didn't you know about that?"

Ruggiero's voice became low and confidential. "Your father is one of the most important men in Portugal. It's just as though he is the king as far as Leiria and Santarem. He is the most important man in Portugal outside Coimbra."

Fernando's mind returned to the events that had

happened immediately before he won Don Martinho's permission—to the angry words in the accounts room between his father and Prince Pedro, to his own tirade to his father on the road from Coimbra where the road leveled after sloping down from the capital, to the dinner when King Alphonso and Queen Urraca had openly admired and approved him.

"I was afraid King Alphonso might have been angry with father," he commented slowly.

Ruggiero did not understand his comment for a moment, then his expression lightened as he also remembered. He started to speak but looked quickly at Stephen and stopped. "He was more thankful for your father's loyalty against Prince Pedro than angry because of that other matter," he mumbled.

During their discussion after supper on succeeding nights and on Sunday, as Prior Gonzalez had permitted, Fernando gradually acquired more complete understanding of his father's new position and his prestige with King Alphonso. The time was approaching when he would be able to see his parents; he wondered about them now that his father had become so important. He was a little afraid they would not be as they had been before.

When they came, it was as though they had never parted. All three cried out their greetings to each other as soon as Fernando rushed into the reception room where they were waiting for him. He embraced his mother with a wild extravagance and his father in a manner little more restrained. All three tried to talk at the same time until Don Martinho and Fernando laughed and Dona Tereza touched her handkerchief to the corners of her eyes.

She looked just as he had expected and, without knowing why, he was glad. He loved her because she was his mother and because she was good; but he could love her, too, because she was pretty. He had only begun to realize she was pretty when they had returned from the funeral of King Sancho. She was slender, and her face was smooth and dark. He had thought his father would look differently. Fernando pictured a governor as a pompous, portly person whose importance would be apparent. His father was neither pompous nor portly; he had always seemed a person of importance. Don Martinho was the same grave, strong, courtly father he had always been, and Fernando was as glad of that as he was that his mother was pretty.

They made him tell them about his daily life. Don Martinho wanted to know his entire schedule from the moment of rising in the morning, but Dona Tereza seemed interested only in the other members of the community. Fernando told them first of the duty that would be most amusing to them. That was the task of wielding the rush broom in the novitiate room, the passageways, and the church. Dona Tereza smiled while he told them of his proficiency, but Fernando saw the doubt in his father's expression. "Shouldn't the Governor's son do such things, Father?" he laughed.

Don Martinho smiled at that. "Do you like to sweep the floors, Son, or wouldn't there be more benefit if you applied that time to your studies?"

"Oh, Prior Gonzalez didn't ask me what I wanted to do. That's one of the tasks assigned to me."

"But didn't you ask Prior Gonzalez to assign you to tasks more fitted to you?"

Fernando grinned. "There are no rents to be collected for San Vicente, Father. Everybody here must do something like that; some tasks are more disagreeable than sweeping."

If Don Martinho was disturbed by the duties assigned

him, Dona Tereza was apprehensive when he told them of Stephen. "What kind of boy is he?"

"You needn't ask me, Mother. You'll meet him this afternoon because he and Ruggiero will be with us all afternoon." He wanted them to like Stephen; he wanted them to like the duties required of him. He was proud, he realized, that here in San Vicente there were no rights for some that were not given to all; there were no barriers between men because some were nobles, some were knights, others were merchants.

They liked Stephen. He knew they would. That countered his inability to convince them that the life of San Vicente should be the model of life elsewhere. He made Stephen tell them of the daily life at San Vicente because he knew that Stephen's description would be more elaborate and enthusiastic than the one he had given. Deliberately, he referred other questions to Stephen until Don Martinho and Dona Tereza automatically directed questions to the other novice as well as to himself and Ruggiero.

On the next day, Fernando went, for the first time, for instruction with older members of the community. Prior Gonzalez was standing at the entrance to the lecture room. He drew Fernando from the others. Fernando wondered why the Prior's expression seemed serious.

"Are you dissatisfied with the tasks given you, Fernando?" Fernando considered for a moment; the Prior's tone alarmed him. He remembered his father's interest when he had described his duties. He frowned. "My father must have spoken to you, Reverend Prior. He does not understand such things."

The answer satisfied the Prior. The subject was not mentioned again. For a time, Fernando was alert to comments when Don Martinho and Dona Tereza visited him; but his father said nothing more, and the Prior also seemed to forget the matter. Fernando thought of it again only when Dona Tereza noticed the deepening color of his face. Fernando did not explain that the community worked two hours each day in the fields. "We are outside more in the warm weather," he told her.

Through the summer months, life settled into a routine pleasantness. Fernando enjoyed the hours in the fields. In the beginning, he tired quickly, but his body became accustomed to the labor and, as the evidences of their work appeared and grew, the earlier pains were forgotten. He saw the approach of colder weather regretfully.

On the first Sunday of October, Sir Thomas came to San Vicente. The visit surprised Fernando. He had not expected the knight commander to come alone. Fernando was alarmed when one of the brothers summoned him and told him who had come. He went immediately to the reception room to greet the knight.

Sir Thomas had changed not at all in appearance. Fernando thought that the year since he had last seen him might have been no more than a day. Sir Thomas' manner was entirely different, however, and Fernando felt relief that the knight commander had put aside his manner of contempt and seemed now to have only the friendliest and kindest attitude toward him.

Fernando could not conceal his anxiety. Sir Thomas began to relate some trivial incident that had happened in the city, but Fernando interrupted him. "Something more important than that brought you here, Sir Thomas. My mother and father—are they well?"

The knight considered for a moment before he nodded,

but with the attitude of a person who doubts his own conclusions. "They would say they are well, Fernando."

The knight's words and manner frightened Fernando. "Are they sick?" he pleaded.

Sir Thomas breathed deeply as though he had determined that he must say something unpleasant and disagreeable. His smile softened to display sympathy before revealing the reason for his sympathy. "Fernando, you know that I am your friend." His words were both statement and question.

Again, Fernando recalled the knight commander's unconcealed contempt for him—the darkness of the courtyard when he had asked Sir Thomas to ask that he might go with them against the Saracens, and the knight's attitude when he had insisted that he would enter the service of the Church. Memory held other more favorable pictures of this same knight commander, and they rushed now to overwhelm the unfavorable. And anxiety could not tolerate disagreement with this man in the very moment of his greatest friendliness. Fernando nodded his head quickly in full agreement.

"I am a knight sworn to serve your father, Fernando. My oath is greater than that. Nothing is more important to me than his happiness and the happiness of Dona Tereza." Sir Thomas paused. "That happiness has been endangered, Fernando." The knight commander regarded him in such an unusual manner that Fernando thought guiltily that he was expected to know what had endangered the happiness of his parents. "I intend to do all that I can to protect their happiness as I would to protect their lives. They would say nothing to you, Fernando, but I have decided that you must know, because you are the only person who can determine whether they will be happy or unhappy."

Fernando felt his heart emptying of the happiness he had enjoyed ever since Ruggiero had joined him at San Vicente. Each word of the knight commander increased his fear.

"Your mother is not happy because of the people with whom you associate here." The knight gestured as if to include all of San Vicente.

Fernando started. Disappointment replaced the happiness he had known. He had thought that his mother liked Stephen as much as he did himself—not as she liked Ruggiero, because Stephen was the son of a merchant—but that she had accepted Stephen as a youth who would one day be a priest. "She said nothing of that, Sir Thomas. Mother was surprised when she first learned about Stephen and some of the others but was satisfied after she met Stephen." The knowledge that he was opposing himself to the statements of the knight commander deprived him of conviction. He wanted to believe each word he spoke, wanted to make Sir Thomas believe; but his words were lifeless and weak.

Sir Thomas ignored his protest. "Would you say, too, that your father is satisfied? Do you think yourself, Fernando, that the son of the Governor of Lisbon should be sweeping floors in a monastery?

"I know it has never occurred to you that your action was cruel and selfish. You would not have entered here if that had occurred to you. You are Don Martinho's and Dona Tereza's only son—the one person for whom both of them lived and enjoyed living. When you left—when you insisted that you receive your father's permission, you were thinking of yourself." The knight commander raised his hand impressively to prevent Fernando's indignant denial. "That is not my opinion, Fernando. Everyone in Lisbon—everyone in

Coimbra—all of them say that you thought only of your own wishes, that you think nothing of your parents, nothing of your responsibilities. You followed a boyish impulse and went away to the monastery." Sir Thomas paused dramatically. "Some people even say that you are not well." His eyes glanced significantly at Fernando's forehead.

Fernando had slumped down on his bench. The words stung as physical blows. Surely people—the people he had known—surely they were not as unjust as this.

"Your mother and father know all this. People are very sure to tell them what others say about you. What others say may not disturb you, Fernando. You are closed up safely here where you will not hear what they say. No! It is your mother and father who must suffer for you. Haven't they suffered enough, Fernando?"

Fernando looked steadily at the stones of the floor. He could not answer the knight's question. He had never thought that others might view his vocation differently from the way he viewed it. There had been no reason to wonder what others might think. He had cast from his mind the unjust words of Prince Pedro that he was entering San Vicente only to escape a marriage agreement.

He wished that Canon Joseph or Prior Gonzalez were present. They would answer! Immediately doubt followed the wish. Could they answer? Could one person answer the problems of another?

"The opinions of others do not disturb a Bulhom," he retorted defiantly. He remembered that his father had said that—how long ago had it been? How unconvincing it sounded now when he repeated the words!

For the moment, Sir Thomas faltered; but he, too, had heard Don Martinho. "Your father does not mean that a

Bulhom is stubborn in his mistakes. Even the Devil quotes Scripture to his purpose."

Both were silent. Fernando had never been more miserable. He was selfish. He was cruel. He could understand that now. His father and mother would not accuse him. They had let him enter San Vicente as they had tolerated so many of his actions. They had not complained. They would not complain despite the comments of others.

The knight commander left his own bench and walked slowly to the huddled figure of Fernando. He sat down beside him on the bench and put his arm over his shoulders. "I'm sorry this news has depressed you, Fernando. I would not have done it if it were not absolutely necessary. I put it off as long as I could. Do you know that an expedition is being prepared to be sent against the Saracens next year?"

Fernando shook his head slowly and straightened. "We hear nothing at all about such things."

Sir Thomas sat up indignantly. "The united armies of all the Christian kings of Hispania will move against the Saracens, and you are told nothing!

"Next year, Fernando, a great Christian army will conquer the Saracens forever. No longer will the enemy be allowed to move first against one kingdom then against another. This time all the forces of Christendom will strike together. We will crush them completely. You must be at home then to care for your mother and for the estates. Your mother must not be left alone; neither can the lands be left to the serfs."

"Is my father to go with the expedition?"

"Every noble, every knight, every freeman—all of them must join this Crusade, Fernando. Don Martinho will be one of the commanders. All those who cannot take part in the Crusade itself must take the places of those who will go. Your part will be to care for Dona Tereza and to supervise the estates and all the serfs. In that way, Fernando, you will also have a part in the Crusade."

When Sir Thomas had gone, he went to the church. "Thy will be done. Thy will be done." There were others there, others who sat quietly talking to God, others whom God wanted to be there. "Thy will be done." He had no other prayer.

There were compensations. God always did seem to offer compensations. Fernando felt a new contentment. He need no longer deny himself the dream of Christmas in the Great Hall: He would be a part of it again this Christmas. He would enjoy again the cushions he had tried so hard to forget. He could enjoy, too, the fine food and soft garments Prior Gonzalez said did not prepare a man for service in the Church but which were so fitting to the life he had known. Others would sweep and clean for him. Oh! he would be a model—he had learned virtue here at San Vicente, and he would not forget it. He would so live that other nobles would copy his example; he would so live that the knights and serfs and freemen would all honor and love their Don Fernando.

There was no need to hurry to Prior Gonzalez. Certainly he must not appear anxious to leave San Vicente. He must prepare what he would say; he must explain to the Prior that his vocation was to live in the world. He would not be of the world, as Our Lord had warned; but he would be in the world to live a good example for others.

A week passed and another Sunday. On Thursday of the second week, he was satisfied. He had memorized everything. He had arranged the items he must explain according to their importance. Strangely, he had not his usual confidence or courage. He searched for some item the Prior might think of that he had overlooked. Was there some aspect he had not considered? He dismissed his misgivings; he could wait no longer.

Prior Gonzalez was sitting in his accustomed place, a big book open on the table in front of him. Fernando waited quietly and the Prior raised his head. His air of recollection gave way slowly to recognition of his visitor.

Fernando had prepared well. He had no difficulty telling the Prior of his obligations. The Prior did not interrupt; but the wrinkles slowly disappeared from around his eyes.

"You do have a problem, Fernando."

Fernando felt the satisfaction of agreement by a superior.

"The solution is not pleasant," Prior Gonzalez continued slowly. "It may be very painful. It is the solution St. Benedict and St. Bernard prescribe for pride."

Fernando could not conceal his disbelief. Pride was a vice related to those vain people who thought themselves more handsome or more talented than others and were always preening themselves or seeking praise. "This is not a matter of pride, Reverend Prior. It is just that I cannot ignore my responsibilities and obligations."

"St. Benedict wrote that the first degree of humility is attained when a monk holds his eyes to the ground and does not allow them to search about restlessly. If a monk does that, he cares nothing—knows nothing—about the opinions others may form about him."

"But I am not proud, Reverend Prior."

"Will you submit your humility to a test, Fernando?"

Fernando contemplated the question gloomily. They

had wandered far from his purpose. But he could not refuse the challenge. "I will do whatever you require."

Prior Gonzalez relaxed and leaned back against the wall as though he had waited tensely for the answer. "You will scrub the floor of the kitchen after supper tomorrow, Fernando, and every evening until I relieve you."

Fernando heard the order unbelievingly. He stared at Prior Gonzalez, whose eyes did not wander, but fastened on his to emphasize that this was a challenge, a test to which he had submitted voluntarily.

Brother Cook received him coldly when he appeared in the kitchen. The brother pointed to the far corner of the room. "There is your bucket."

Slowly, resentfully, carelessly, he scrubbed the unwilling stones. Brother Cook dropped a scraper beside him, but Fernando did not use it. If spots of grease lay on the floor, let those responsible return to clean them. As he scrubbed, he moved backward slowly on his knees toward the door.

"Go to the far end and start again!"

Fernando straightened and looked at Brother Cook. The other looked down at him. "Scrub and scrape," the brother emphasized, "until the floor is clean."

He endured through November. Hands and muscles hardened. He forgot the Crusade, forgot Sir Thomas, forgot the opinion of the world in the fury of his effort to prove himself to Prior Gonzalez. He knew that the others of the community wondered at the punishment imposed on him, and he determined he would not explain, even to Ruggiero. "Let them watch and talk; let them see a De Bulhom scrub the kitchen floor. Let them see that a De Bulhom is humble."

On the last Saturday of the month, he went to confession. Few others were in the church. He knelt and recited slowly, piously, the prayers the priest had assigned for penance because he was a manual worker. His eyes wandered to the great crucifix and the figure of the dead Christ. Automatically, his mind responded, "May I offer these trials and sufferings in reparation."

It was an inadequate gift, a disproportionate gift to offer for what God had given him, for what God had suffered for him. These were the soiled fruits of Cain. Conscience rebuked him that he was trying to deceive God, that he was pretending to offer his trials in return for the sacrifice depicted before him, when he knew that he was endeavoring only to prove his love for himself and to prove himself to Prior Gonzalez.

"Love for self." The words echoed in his mind. "Love for self." But that was pride! "Pride is the inordinate love of self," he recited wonderingly. His mind searched about awkwardly and vainly. This discovery was too big, too enormous, too gigantic to comprehend. "Love for self," his mind repeated. "Love for self is pride."

"Thou shalt love thy God with thy whole heart," Our Lord had said. And Prior Gonzalez had said that when we love God wholeheartedly, "there is no room for love of anything else." But he had loved himself!

He was smiling when he went to the kitchen after supper. Brother Cook looked at him curiously. Momentarily, Fernando expected a scolding for some oversight or negligence. Brother Cook said nothing, but Fernando felt the brother watching and studying him. Carefully and thoroughly, yet more quickly than ever before, Fernando rubbed and scraped. He forgot Brother Cook. He realized only that he knelt here in the kitchen as he knelt in the church. Here he could bend over as his work required. He could bow down and, with each movement of his hands, he could pray, "Jesus, meek and humble of heart, make my heart like Thine!"

He stood at the end of the kitchen while Brother Cook inspected the floor. Brother Cook nodded his head with satisfaction, but he raised his eyes to Fernando as though his satisfaction pertained to Fernando instead of the floor. "You have learned something, haven't you, Fernando? You have learned something very great and valuable?"

Fernando smiled hesitantly.

"Your work is finished here, Fernando," Brother Cook said. "You have learned what Prior Gonzalez sent you here to learn. You are to go to him now and tell him I said you have finished here."

He waited until late the next morning to visit the Prior. He walked through the passageways quickly and lightly. His whole body had benefited from the work of these six weeks. More than that, he knew that his body was no longer burdened with a deadening weight. Joy filled his heart and displaced the sadness that had pressed down upon him. He turned into the Prior's office, rapping his knuckles against the doorway as he entered. Then he halted and backed away. The Prior was talking seriously and sternly to one of the community whose back was to the doorway. Prior Gonzalez glanced up then and motioned that Fernando should leave. Fernando saw that the one facing the Prior was Stephen.

It had never occurred to him that Stephen had troubles or problems to discuss with the Prior. Certainly it could not be that the Prior had discovered faults in Stephen that required correction. Stephen's whole being was submerged in the life of San Vicente and in precise fulfillment of his uncle's every regulation. Fernando backed out of the doorway.

When he saw Stephen again, the other's smile had disappeared; he was unhappy—Fernando thought of the word "sullen," but that word could never be applied to Stephen. "Prior Gonzalez is transferring me to Holy Cross at Coimbra," he told Fernando. "I am too loyal to him and to San Vicente," he added bitterly. Neither of them understood the explanation.

"You will learn more at Holy Cross, Stephen," he encouraged. "Canon Joseph told me about the monastery there. There are more students, and they have priests as masters who have studied in the school at Paris."

"I'm learning enough here."

Fernando would have said more, but Stephen would have disagreed with anything he could say. He thought then that perhaps he realized, faintly and obscurely, why Prior Gonzalez was transferring Stephen. "I'm learning enough here," Stephen had said immediately—automatically. No other monastery could be as San Vicente, no other prior as Prior Gonzalez, no other group of priests as those of the Canons of St. Augustine. There could be nothing good that might be said in Stephen's presence about Holy Cross or the instructors or of the school at Paris.

It was late afternoon when he reported to the Prior what Brother Cook had told him to say. Remembering the serious and stern expression of Prior Gonzalez when he was talking to Stephen, Fernando was relieved that the Prior smiled as soon as he heard the message.

"Have you learned humility, Fernando?"

Fernando hesitated. He smiled, then shook his head. "But I want to learn, Reverend Prior."

7

IN April, Dona Tereza mentioned for the first time the change that had occurred within him. "You are always smiling, Fernando. For a time, you seemed unhappy and troubled. Now you act as though you have no cares, as though San Vicente is a royal palace." Her voice was so joyful and her smile so happy that Fernando determined to become even more happy on each succeeding day.

In May, Prior Gonzalez announced to the community the impending Crusade on the peninsula. He summoned them to the chapter room, but not to tell them that there would be a Crusade. "I understand that news of the Crusade has penetrated even the walls of San Vicente."

His comment stirred a laughing murmur in the room. They should know of the outside world only as much as he chose to tell them; yet the events of the outside world were known as quickly in San Vicente as elsewhere.

Prior Gonzalez did have news San Vicente had not heard. "Our part," he explained, "must be restricted to prayer. That may seem to be a very small part when Christian knights are dying, but our prayer will be directed toward a resurgence of faith in all Christian kings and princes. Our cause has already suffered one reverse. The King of Leon has decided that participation by him or his forces would endanger his own country.

"In itself, his decision would have little effect on the success of our arms. But this decision must be considered in connection with another event. Our sovereign's brother, Prince Pedro, only recently attached himself with all of his followers to the Court of Leon. We know that it is Prince Pedro's purpose to enlist the aid of Leon in an effort to wrest certain lands from King Alphonso. The refusal of Leon to join the Crusade can only be received as warning that Prince Pedro has persuaded Leon to attack our country."

A heavy rumble of indignant disapproval interrupted the Prior. The men of San Vicente reacted as one to the news of treachery.

Fernando drew back slowly until he rested against the stone of the wall. He could not join the others in actual condemnation of Prince Pedro; he could not forget the friendly, extravagant man his father had welcomed to Castle de Bulhom, the prince whose happy laugh was so much like his mother's, the prince his father had loved when they served together as squires. He had hoped that someday Prince Pedro and his father would again be friends. But Prince Pedro had decided they must be enemies.

From their place of work in the fields, the men of San Vicente watched the army of the Crusade move from the city and pass beneath them on the road that bordered the river. Men, horses, and wagons filled the road from early morning until late afternoon. San Vicente knew that others were moving in the same direction on the road hidden by the mass of the hills. More were moving along the opposite side of the river. Those on the river road below San Vicente were but a part of the Christian army gathered at Lisbon, at Leiria, at Oporto, at Santarem, and in the cities of the Christian countries to the east. This once, the Christian kings were joined to destroy the last remnants of Saracen power. When they were gone, life slowed perceptibly in the city and surrounding country. Even San Vicente was aware of the change. All thought, all conversation, all prayer followed the single thread of victory for Christ.

Couriers, bringing messages to the commander of the city garrison, and drivers returning for supplies brought news of the progress of the army. Names of strange cities, names known to few, marked the movement of the Crusade army southward. Rumors, inevitable companion of ignorance, supplied whatever information messengers failed to bring.

Each day Prior Gonzalez walked to the city to hear the latest messages, the most recent news and rumors. News of importance, the progress of the army, or merely word of individual Crusaders he relayed to the community by summoning them to the chapter room immediately. When he returned but did not call them together immediately, they resumed whatever they had been doing.

Day followed day, news diminished, rumors multiplied. The news arrived late at night that Leon and Prince Pedro had struck. Near midnight, Prior Gonzalez summoned the community to the chapter room to announce that news. He led them to the church to pray for the protection of themselves and all of Portugal.

Leon and Prince Pedro had planned carefully. The main Portuguese forces were already beyond recall far to the south in Castile. Even were they to turn immediately, the invaders might hope to be so entrenched that dislodgement would be impossible, and they would enforce a settlement according to their own wishes. Fernando had clung to the hope that Prince Pedro would seek to settle the quarrel with his brother in some peaceful manner. Now there was no basis for hope nor could there be compromise; the invasion threatened all of Portugal, but especially his own mother and father.

The message to Prior Gonzalez had come from Dona Tereza. A courier had brought the news to her, and she had arisen immediately in the night to send the few knights and grooms of Castle de Bulhom to warn those nearby. Fernando prayed fervently that some force would rise to block the Prince and his ally.

During the day, the road bordering the river was deserted except for the couriers. Serfs held to their villages. Tradesmen and freemen of the city remained within the walls. The quiet of fear settled over the country. Couriers galloping past seemed symbols of desperate hopelessness.

The invaders advanced slowly, deliberately. They need not tire men and horses with rapid movement; they need hurry only if the main body of the Christian army turned back from the south. They moved steadily forward; each courier reported new advances. On the third night they camped beneath the walls of Santarem. The few men remaining within the town defended it against the attack on the fourth morning of the invasion; but the enemy brushed them aside and occupied the city.

Fernando hoped that his mother would go either into the city or to Fortress St. George on the summit. Prior Gonzalez told him he could not persuade her. "Castle de Bulhom is one of the defense bastions, Fernando. She is right about that. Don Martinho's men can delay the assault on the fortress, and Prince Pedro must seize the fortress before he can feel secure in the city.

None doubted that the enemy would march at once against Lisbon; those of San Vicente who had once been military men plotted the path an invader would follow. Hope died that the main army would return; couriers from the south told the progress of the Christian forces and of skirmishes with minor units of the pagan foe.

More messages arrived from the outposts facing Santarem. The invader had turned away from Lisbon! They were turning into the roads leading directly to Coimbra. Their major objective was the capital. In San Vicente and throughout the district of Lisbon there was both rejoicing that their own area was spared and hope that whatever forces had been left to guard the capital would be sufficient to defeat this invader. At San Vicente, military men heard the news doubtfully, then smiled faintly with hope.

Rumors revived with greater strength. An unknown force had attacked and routed the invader. A counter-rumor protested that an unknown force had indeed attacked the invader but the invader had crushed this force. A third rumor held there had been no engagement whatever, and the invader was continuing the slow march against Coimbra. In some mysterious manner, the rumors penetrated San Vicente and spread as quickly as they had through the city. Often Prior Gonzalez returned late in the afternoon and summoned the community to the chapter room only to inform them of rumors already known. They benefited only by his careful separation of fact and rumor.

In mid-July, Prior Gonzalez smiled happily as the community filed into the chapter room. As soon as they had taken their places, he told them Prince Pedro and Leon had been defeated.

There was a general stir in the room and a low hum of voices. This news was the same as one of the rumors, except that the Prior announced it not as a rumor but as a verified fact.

"God has honored San Vicente in a strange way," he announced when the noise subsided. "Portugal and Lisbon have been delivered from the treachery of these invaders by the fathers of two of our brothers here with us."

Fernando felt his heart give a great leap in his breast. His father! Don Martinho! As quickly, he thrust the thought from his mind. He was not humble, he accused himself, when he grasped every such opportunity and, without reason, applied it to his father.

"We thought of ourselves as defenseless," the Prior continued. "When we saw the armies leave Lisbon and heard of their progress against the Saracens, we feared that Prince Pedro and his ally would have no difficulty if they chose to attack. So also did our royal enemies.

"We know now that we were not completely defenseless as we thought; the enemy has learned this to his own great sorrow and utter defeat.

"Don Martinho de Bulhom foresaw the danger to which we and all of Portugal were exposed and provided against it. When the main armies left Santarem and turned southward, Don Martinho appointed one of his ablest lieutenants to take a force apart into the mountains above Santarem and to lie in wait there for the forces of the invaders. That lieutenant was Don Ruggiero."

A burst of sound that was part cheer, part relief, part prayer interrupted the Prior. Nobles, knights, and merchants of San Vicente responded gladly to the Prior's words. A hard lump formed in Fernando's throat, but the brother who sat immediately beside him hammered him on the back and cheered "Don Martinho!" loudly in his ear, and the lump subsided. Across from him, Ruggiero smiled proudly as though he were afraid to believe the Prior's words.

The brother who was doorkeeper for the day burst suddenly into the chapter room and ran to the Prior. He whispered excitedly to him. The room quieted. Prior Gonzalez seemed to question whatever message Brother Doorkeeper had given him. Apparently satisfied, he smiled and stood.

"We have even greater and happier news," he cried. "The armies of the Crusade have crushed the Saracens!"

A tremendous cheer greeted his words. Every man in the room jumped to his feet cheering and laughing. The sudden outburst startled the Prior. Then he held his arms high and joined their cheering. Discipline was suspended. Within the chapter room were men who had been knights of kings and nobles, men whose minds had followed the armies of the Christian kings as their bodies had once followed their own commanders. Others here had been men at arms whose hearts exulted in the victory of Christian arms. As knights in the service of the King of kings, they cheered His victory.

The rule of silence was suspended for that day and for the next also. Tomorrow would be a holiday; they would make it a great feast day of thanksgiving. As they learned more of these great victories, they could talk as they would.

Fernando went directly from the chapter room to the church. The church was deserted when he entered, but he had only genuflected when others followed him. In orderly procession, the entire community came to thank their king.

News arrived steadily that day and the next. A new name, an insignificant place in southern Hispania, became at once more noteworthy than the names of great cities or countries—Los Navos dos Tolosa—an imperishable name that would be forever the glory of Portugal and Castile and Aragon and Navarre. At Los Navos the armies had met, the great united force of the Christian kings against the confident and careless generals of the Emir. At Los Navos, Christian knights and Christian blood won freedom at last from the threat of the Saracen.

The news of the great victory of the Crusaders completely overshadowed the victory of Don Ruggiero. Fernando and Ruggiero discussed the defeat of Prince Pedro; the others were interested only momentarily when more news was received. Ruggiero and Fernando pieced together what news was received until they understood what had happened and the greatness of Don Ruggiero's victory.

Groups of armed men appeared on the road below San Vicente, riding toward the city. They were the first to return from Los Navos. The groups increased steadily in size, and Fernando began to anticipate news of his father.

Don Ruggiero arrived unexpectedly at San Vicente near the end of July to visit his son. Fernando wanted to see this great giant of a man again, but he forced himself to wait until late in the day that Ruggiero might enjoy the day with his father. When he did go to the visitors' room, their meeting was noisy and boisterous as when Don Ruggiero had received them at his home.

Don Ruggiero was even larger than Fernando remembered him. He seemed to fill the whole room. And his voice—Fernando heard him the length of the passageway from the room—his voice filled the room and overflowed it.

Don Ruggiero was sitting at the far side of the room when Fernando turned into the doorway. The knight leaped to his feet and crossed the room with one swift motion. Before Fernando could enter the room, Don Ruggiero had gathered him into his arms and embraced him. "Don Fernando! Don Fernando!" the big voice rumbled. This great man loved him, Fernando knew. Because Don Ruggiero loved Don Martinho, he must also love Don Martinho's son.

Don Ruggiero would say nothing of the battle with Prince Pedro. "I have told Ruggiero about it. Let him tell you. While you are here, we must talk of Don Martinho. He is the great one. He is a greater man than ever before—the greatest man in the kingdom of Portugal."

Fernando smiled happily. He was happy to hear this great knight speak of his father. He saw Ruggiero look at his father cautiously as though to warn him or to remind him of something. Don Ruggiero waved his hand to brush aside his son's objection.

"Your father, Don Fernando, is not only a very brilliant man, he is also a very brave man. It was your father who earned much of the victory at Los Navos. One of the reasons I came here today was to tell you that."

Fernando puzzled over Don Ruggiero's words. The knight's tone of voice changed as he spoke, and he became more serious.

"Another reason for coming today, Don Fernando, is that your father asked me to come."

Fernando knew then that Don Ruggiero had some unpleasant message for him. He was not alarmed. Don Ruggiero had said that his father had asked him to come.

"Your father wanted you to have exact information and not some distorted tale," Don Ruggiero continued. "That was part of his message. He asked me to tell you that he was hurt at Los Navos, to tell you that he will not be home as soon as many others because he must be brought in one of the wagons. But your father will be home, Don Fernando. He said to tell you that he will be living—the wound will not kill him."

Fernando struggled to receive this message as Don Martinho's son should receive such a message and in the manner Don Ruggiero was helping him to receive it. "How did you receive this message, Don Ruggiero. Have you seen my father?"

Don Ruggiero shook his head. "Don Martinho's clerk wrote the message. He sent it to me by courier. I came at once to see you."

"Does my mother know?"

"I shall tell her tonight."

Fernando tried to think how his mother would receive the message. The thought of leaving San Vicente and resuming his life at home returned to his mind. He had defeated that temptation; he had determined he would not. Yet he knew that this message from his father had weakened his determination.

In the weeks succeeding Don Ruggiero's visit, other nobles and some knights visited San Vicente to greet the son of Don Martinho de Bulhom. Fernando remembered a few, others he had heard mentioned, many more were strangers. He went eagerly to meet the first of these visitors, hopeful of a message from his father or news about him. The visitors brought neither. They wanted only to speak to him, Fernando, son of Don Martinho. They wanted to praise his father and did with such lack of restraint that Fernando realized that their principal purpose was to make themselves known to him. He realized also that they examined and appraised him, searching for weakness. On his seventeenth birthday, in 1212, a visitor less clever than the others forced him to remember all that Sir Thomas had told him: People thought him a fool or, if not a fool, a youth who had hurled himself into the monastery to escape his father's will.

Two days after his birthday, a knight rode to San Vicente to announce that Don Martinho would pass soon on the road beside the river. Fernando stood with the others in the field on the slope watching the road. The column appeared—a long line of men and a cart midway in the column. He tried to see movement—the appearance of his father's head or an upraised arm. He raised his own arm until, at last, a knight—a knight immediately in back of the cart—raised an arm in acknowledgment.

He should not be here in the field watching with the others. He should not be at San Vicente. He should be there on the road beside his father. He should be at home caring for his mother. He should be supervising the lands and serfs. He should accept the duties his father had borne so long. He looked along the column for the tall figure of the knight commander. Sir Thomas would return now to torment and persuade and convince him again. Sir Thomas would visit San Vicente now—Fernando was certain of that. Sir Thomas loved them more than his own life. He would come again to tell him he must leave San Vicente. Fernando drew his eyes from the column moving along the road. Stubbornly he turned them to the ground before him.

Prior Gonzalez visited Don Martinho and Dona Tereza that same afternoon. "They are very brave people, Fernando," he told him when he returned. "Your mother told me today that God had given both of them health, strength, and wealth, and they are grateful to Him that they were given these to enjoy. She said they may not complain if now He decides they should have them no longer."

Fernando felt tears rise to his eyes. He fought them back. He could not be less brave than his mother.

"Your father is almost joyful. He was always so serious and tense before; now he laughs easily. Your father told me he was more grateful for their troubles than he had ever been for their blessings. He said that what has happened has shown him at last the true value of things of earth."

"Is he badly hurt, Reverend Prior?" Fernando whispered the question. Something held his throat.

"Physically, yes. But physical hurts are not always important. His leg is broken above the knee. One of those savages struck him with a mace. It must be very difficult for a man as active as he was to become an invalid. Yet now he thanks God for his troubles."

Prior Gonzalez had spoken slowly and softly as though he was meditating instead of talking. He was not recounting a mere succession of events or telling news of another. He was describing a spiritual experience.

"They will have good care, Reverend Prior. Sir Thomas can manage the estates and serfs and business affairs." Fernando tried to speak in the same manner as the Prior. He fought desperately to rebuild his own courage.

The Prior looked directly into his eyes, then shook his head slowly. "Sir Thomas did not come back, Fernando. He died at Los Navos."

Fernando had a feeling that he was cowering down, that he was trying to fend off blows that fell on him unceasingly. He had tried to delude himself that his father's wound would heal, had tried to convince himself that Sir Thomas would relieve and shield his parents. One by one, the slender pillars he had used to support his courage failed. How could man love God more than his own parents?

"Am I still to remain at San Vicente, Reverend Prior?" He tried not to let his tone become bitter. He was grasping frantically for support. Let the Prior, let this leader of souls, decide for him!

Prior Gonzalez did not answer. "We have talked enough for today, Fernando. We had better talk for a time with God."

Next day the brother summoned him to meet another visitor in the reception room. "Prior Gonzalez has given permission," the brother told him.

Fernando had never seen the man before. He had never heard his name—he was sure of that. From the moment he met him, he disliked him. He disliked the smile that was intended to be ingratiating. He disliked being addressed as Don Fernando by this man he did not know. He disliked the man's manner and words. He was polite, but he escaped as quickly as he could. Impulsively he went to the Prior.

"These visitors are disturbing me, Reverend Prior. I do not know them. I never before saw that man who came here today. Please do not give permission for me to see any more of them."

The Prior motioned toward a bench. "This is not a closed monastery, Fernando. If people come to visit, they must be received."

"They are not here to see me, Reverend Prior. They come only because they think I will take my father's position and his title. Please bar them."

Prior Gonzalez hunched himself up on his elbows so that he leaned far across the table toward Fernando. He looked directly at him. Then his eyes turned away and darted about the room. He drew back slowly as though he had decided against speaking his thoughts. "Let me think about it, Fernando. Let me think what we may do."

Fernando rose slowly from his bench. He was not satisfied; yet the Prior had virtually agreed that some escape would be given him. Another thought occurred to him. Coimbra! He could go to Holy Cross where Prior Gonzalez had sent Stephen! His face brightened. "Transfer me, Reverend Prior! Send me to Holy Cross."

Prior Gonzales could not conceal his astonishment. He had relaxed when Fernando stood. Now an entirely new and strange proposal was added. "Let me think, Fernando," he temporized.

Fernando waited four days. He felt the tenseness increasing within himself and knew the turmoil of his mind. More visitors arrived and he endured them. Then a knight arrived who asserted he had been with Don Martinho at the very moment the Governor was wounded. From that visitor, Fernando went directly to the Prior. He abandoned all pretense of restraint. "Why must I see these people, Reverend Prior?" The question burst from him, part sob, part complaint.

"Sit down, Fernando," Prior Gonzalez said softly.

Fernando sank down on the bench. "For four days, I have done nothing but pray, Reverend Prior. All of Saturday and all of Sunday. I was sure this morning my prayer would be heard—there would be no more visitors. Prior Gonzalez, find some way to keep these people from me."

"God did not see fit to answer your prayer, Fernando?"

Fernando struggled against resentment. The Prior's comment was almost a rebuke.

"You told me you wanted to learn humility, Fernando. You learned a little. Have you abandoned that?" Fernando shook his head. "I still want to learn humility," he muttered.

"You will never learn it if you avoid the opportunities God puts before you."

The words stung Fernando. All the pain he had endured, all the thoughts he had suppressed swelled angrily together. "Does humility demand that I hear how my father was wounded at Los Navos?" he said fiercely. "Does it require, Prior Gonzalez, that an eyewitness tell me how the Saracen struck my father with a mace and crushed his leg?" He saw the sudden contraction of Prior Gonzalez' face. "Does that disturb you, Reverend Prior?" A cold anger possessed him—an anger that deepened and leveled his voice. "I have endured as much as I can, Reverend Prior." He spoke slowly and deliberately. "I cannot forget that my father lies disabled only a short distance from here. If I could forget, these visitors would remind me. That is why they come here—to remind me that I am cruel to my parents and foolish for myself. 'You cannot remain here,' their eyes and their smiles tell me. 'You cannot remain at San Vicente.'"

Fernando rose suddenly to his feet. "I know that, too, Reverend Prior. I cannot remain at San Vicente. I must leave here. I must either go to Holy Cross or I must go to my parents." He turned without waiting for the Prior to answer.

He went to the church. He could not pray. He could only kneel silently. St. Benedict's second rule of humility taunted him: "Speak few words and in a quiet voice." He had spoken many words and had almost shouted them.

And the ultimatum! He had not planned to say that. He had heard the words as though someone else had spoken them. Now that they were spoken, he could not turn back. Holy Cross or life in the world—it must be the one or the other.

It must not be the one or the other. There must be no choice, no decision. Prior Gonzalez must transfer him! "Holy Virgin, he must, he must!"

PART II

1

THE cloister garden of Holy Cross Monastery was a space or an open area or a rectangle, but it was not a garden. It was a portion of plain earth surrounded by the four galleries of the monastery. During the rainy season, it was a quagmire none dared to enter. In milder periods, it was the center of community life where students and priests gathered in large or small groups according to their interests. Small groups indicated lack of disagreement or of discussion material; large groups indicated lively discussions that (Prior Vincent had observed) generated so much heat that some members could not endure even the shaded portion of the garden and were forced to withdraw into the building.

On the fifteenth day of August, 1216, four groups had formed. Twenty or more were in the largest group clustered on benches in one corner. Fernando and Stephen stopped tentatively at the edge of the group, ignoring vacant places on the benches until they knew the subject of discussion. "The principal difficulty," one voice lectured, "is that he never wrote his thoughts completely. He wrote notes rather than complete treatises. Aristotle did not want to write so that all could understand; he wanted to draw students to his lectures." Fernando turned away disinterestedly.

The "Saracen" beckoned to him from another group.

He was not a Saracen; but he had come from the Saracens' capital, which, together with his dark skin, invited the name given him. Others looked up from their places to nod recognition as Fernando joined them. The Saracen moved along his bench that Fernando might sit beside him.

"We are having an outdoor Scripture class," the Saracen explained, but his amused smile belied his description.

Simon Rolandino was talking. He spoke slowly, haltingly, awkwardly, groping heavily from one word to the next. "St. Peter had just proved that he loved Our Lord," his heavy voice labored. "As soon as St. John told him, 'It is the Lord,' St. Peter threw himself into the water and swam ashore. He wanted to be at the side of Jesus again."

"Then you would say," another objected, "that Our Lord was asking an unnecessary question when He asked St. Peter if he loved Him."

Simon Rolandino shook his head slowly in disagreement with the proposition, but his manner indicated his uncertainty. His expression revealed his inability to clarify his thoughts. He looked hopefully around the group seeking an ally. "Fernando! You agree with me!"

Invariably Fernando did agree with Simon. Slow-speaking, slow-thinking Simon—Fernando wondered if this bulky figure did not portray that other Simon of the great heart and elaborate promises. This Simon Rolandino so loved the Holy Words that his heart penetrated where his mind seemed unable to follow. "I do agree," he smiled. "I agree, Simon, except for one small detail, and I think that one detail strengthens your opinion. I am not convinced that St. Peter swam ashore as you said."

"The boat was two hundred cubits from shore," someone observed.

"Fernando means that St. Peter did walk on the water this time," another added, and the group laughed.

Fernando laughed with them. "That is the clue," he countered. "It is St. Matthew who tells us of the time St. Peter started to walk on the water, then became frightened that he would drown. St. John is the one who wrote that St. Peter cast himself into the water. He did not describe the action as diving or jumping or plunging as he might if he wanted to intimate that St. Peter swam ashore. He used the word 'cast' as though to indicate complete abandonment."

"Fernando silences all opposition again," the Saracen intoned derisively. "When the new master arrives, we must appoint a committee to acquaint him with Fernando's erudition; then our master must either subdue Fernando or return to Paris."

The group laughed appreciatively.

"Is that the rumor for the day?" Fernando taunted.

"A new master?" The Saracen shook his head. "It was a rumor—was a rumor for a full ten minutes after dinner; then Prior Vincent came out and confirmed it. That ruined our rumor."

Fernando laughed. "We will have a new rumor tomorrow. Tell me more about the new master."

"Matthew. Master of theology. School of Paris," the Saracen recited. "Origin unknown. Manner unknown— probably stuffy," he added disrespectfully. "Date of arrival uncertain. He will also be spiritual director." The Saracen grinned suddenly at Fernando. "I am happy to know that you do have moments of ignorance and that the Saracen can acquaint you with the momentous developments, the more portentous developments, at Holy Cross."

Arrival of a new master, especially a new master from

the school at Paris, was a development both momentous and portentous. Students of slow and painful progress under their present master anticipated hopefully that the new master would prove their slowness to be the fault of the old master. Students of greater progress correspondingly resented the advent of someone unknown as presaging change in their progress. Fernando had learned that his own progress, at least in Sacred Scripture, seemed unaffected by changes of masters; and a master from the school at Paris should bring to Holy Cross greater clarity of expression and greater breadth of knowledge.

When Master Matthew did arrive, some days later, initial reaction to his physical appearance was generally one of disappointment. He seemed young—little older than the deacon students. He was thin and obviously not strong, despite the quickness of his movements and firm volume of his voice. Fairly tall, very thin, with bony shoulders turned forward in the unmistakable posture of a student, Master Matthew was protected from general dislike only by an intangible suggestion of age intermingled with his apparent youth. He had the thin, lined face of a man who had suffered great pain—"a holy face," someone described it.

Despite prejudice, despite his youth, despite his appearance, Master Matthew was immediately successful. "We will study the Word of God together," he announced at the beginning of his first lecture, "according to the directives of Holy Mother Church, but according to the manner of the school at Paris. If the manner of the Paris school seems strange, you will have opportunity for exercising your charity. I am inclined to think that, at times, the manner of the Paris school tends to be godly rather than godlike."

They laughed doubtfully. If this was his manner

of lecturing, there would be no bowed heads in Sacred Scripture classes. Priests, too, who had come to hear the new master laughed and nodded their approval. Hesitantly at first, then completely and fully, Holy Cross students accepted the new master.

None complained. Those who had progressed under former masters continued to progress; others moved into the group with them. Master Matthew was quick to compliment those who progressed, was patient with those who lacked ability but who endeavored to understand; but he was impatient toward those who endeavored to explain by reason what could be understood only by faith.

"There is no greater wisdom than the Word of God," he told them one day. "What will you accomplish if you can read and memorize the *Ethics*? Will you be the better priest? Or a more brilliant teacher? A small child or woman who knows and loves and lives the Beatitudes is more brilliant than those who are learned only in the science of the mind. Virtue is lived, not learned!" he cried out in a tone that belonged to their spiritual director rather than the Master of Sacred Scripture.

Fernando listened to Master Matthew's lectures with an attention bordering on fascination. Words vanished as this master talked. Centuries faded away. Christ, now gentle-voiced, now thundering, always purposeful, lived and breathed and walked and preached. Fernando had never thought, had never reason to think, of the smile of Christ. Master Matthew re-created the Christ who smiled, kindly, humorous, at the quick-witted faith of the Canaanite woman, the Christ who smiled as He startled Nathaniel by describing him beneath the fig tree.

Fernando had studied and labored over rhetoric and

dialectics and natural science. Sacred Scripture he had loved so that he had neither to labor nor study as he had those other subjects. The only obstacle to his love had been the fear of other masters that the bold expeditions he proposed into the Word of God might lead to error and destruction.

Master Matthew held no fears for him as had the others. "There is danger, Fernando, for those who read the Word of God because they love wisdom; but there is no danger for those who read the Word of God because they love God. Those who love God will read the Word of God in the spirit of God and according to the guidance of God's Holy Church."

Fernando frowned doubtfully. "How can I know whether I am reading for love of myself or love of God?"

Master Matthew raised his thin shoulders expressively. "You cannot know, Fernando. There is no answer to your question. There is only a safeguard, the same safeguard that applies to everything we do. That is to love God with the whole heart, the whole soul, the whole mind as Our Lord said we should love Him. When we do that, there is no reason to fear nor reason to doubt. When we do that, all that we do, all that we think, all that we say will be for love of Him."

Late in Advent, Queen Urraca's messenger brought to Holy Cross both greetings from Her Majesty and expression of her intention of visiting the community on the day following Christmas. However good her purpose, the message interrupted the orderly routine of the lay brothers and suspended the tranquillity of priests and students.

Lectures were suspended during the week preceding Christmas that every effort might be given to preparation for the royal visit. Priests, students, and brothers practiced daily the matter of arranging themselves into line, one behind the other according to size, approaching a throne erected in the community room, bowing, backing from the throne, then turning to their appointed places. As a smaller member of the students, Fernando was forward in the line immediately in back of the priests; as the largest of the brothers, Ruggiero was last in line.

Fernando wondered what the Queen would look like now—whether she had changed in the six years since he had last seen her. The thought that she might recognize him startled him, but reason dismissed that; she did not know he was present at Holy Cross—had forgotten him long before as the noble youth of Lisbon who had suffered some mental illness and had fled to San Vicente.

Queen Urraca resembled but slightly the woman he remembered. He remembered an attractive woman with soft, black eyes and smooth, round face who had smiled approvingly at his words and his conduct. He saw now a stately woman, small as before, stouter. Her bearing, her manner, her ease as she entered the building were the bearing, the manner, the ease of a queen.

Priests, students, and brothers lined both walls of the passageway when she entered the doorway. Her Majesty smiled quietly and impersonally as she went between the two lines with Prior Vincent following by a step. Two knights in full armor followed the Queen and the Prior. Fernando looked at them eagerly, but both were strangers. The community had been instructed to remain silent while the Queen entered, but the resplendence of the knights' gleaming armor caused a ripple of admiring comments. The two knights strode along—young and grinning self-consciously—between the lines of admiring robed men.

Once disrupted, silence could not be restored. When the

Queen, the Prior, and knights had passed, the community formed in procession behind them to follow to the community room. Low murmurings, sibilant whispers, and soft laughing blended with the scuffing of their sandals on the stone passageway.

In the community room, Prior Vincent escorted the Queen to the throne and then moved quickly aside so that the knights might step forward and offer their arms to the Queen. Queen Urraca took her place on the throne and waited while the community continued their procession into the room.

"You are from among all of my people, I know," the Queen said in a small, weak voice, "from among our nobles and knights, our freemen and serfs. But here at Holy Cross, all of you are nobles—no longer our nobles—but nobles of the King whose birthday we are celebrating."

It was her first visit as Queen to the community of Holy Cross. She had come before to visit the Prior and masters, but this was the first time many had seen their Queen, the first time more had heard her voice. An audible stir followed her words. Fernando knew she had won them completely.

When the greetings ended with Prior Vincent's address of welcome, they began the march to the throne. In his own turn, Fernando walked before the Queen; bowed slowly in the manner Dona Tereza had demanded of him; heard the Prior present "Fernando, a student;" straightened quickly; and turned away. From his place, he watched while the remainder of the community were presented until, at last, Ruggiero stood before the Queen and bowed. Fernando smiled because the two knights turned their heads perceptibly to look at the robed giant.

Queen Urraca motioned to the Prior and spoke to

him. Prior Vincent bowed and turned to the community. "Fernando!" he called.

The unexpected call startled him, but he walked again before the throne and bowed to the Queen.

"I understand it is not proper to address you here as Don Fernando?" There was warmth and humor in her voice.

Fernando's confidence deserted him. "No, Your Majesty," he whispered.

"Your parents were very dear to us, Fernando. I asked Prior Vincent to call you here that I might tell you that and to tell you that their son will also be dear to us in blessed memory of them. We will never fail to remember gratefully the family De Bulhom. You have put that name aside, I know. You have put aside all that other men prize and strive to obtain. That is extraordinary among nobles, but it is fitting for your father's son. God will bless you, Fernando."

He was not fully conscious of his bow nor the manner in which he turned away to resume his place. Queen Urraca's summons had frightened him; her forgiveness— if it should be termed forgiveness—had been so phrased that even an astute Prior Vincent would know nothing more than her words revealed. He was happy that she recognized his sacrifice, happy that she remembered his father's loyalty, happy that she extended to him the affection his father had earned.

Queen Urraca effectively abrogated Prior Vincent's instructions that the community continue silence until Her Majesty had departed. "There is little we of the world can do for you who are not of the world and who do so much for us. This afternoon, certain meats and provisions will arrive at Holy Cross as a present to the community."

An involuntary cheer burst from one; immediately

the others joined. Queen Urraca had touched a weakness not easily barred from monasteries. Prior Vincent's smile removed his restrictions completely, and the cheering increased proportionately.

When the Queen had gone, Fernando discovered that he had become a celebrated personage. The others surrounded him curiously. "Why did she call you? What did she say?" Fernando laughed. For days after, he had to repeat over and over the exact words the Queen had spoken to him so softly that others had heard only the sound of her voice.

Her visit, her manner, her present to them made Queen Urraca something more than the benefactor she had been in the past. The entire community held now a proprietary interest in their Queen. She had been gracious to them; in the explicable manner of human beings, they claimed her as their own.

Fernando sensed that his own position with the others of the community had changed as a result of the Queen's visit and her words to him. Stephen showed again that deference he had adopted when he first learned the family name of his fellow novice. Others were inclined to be silent when Fernando spoke during their group sessions in the community room or in the cloister garden. Still others, even some of the masters, tended to be in whatever group Fernando joined. He began to regret the Queen's visit and her kindness to him. He began to fear repetition of the incidents that had forced him from San Vicente.

It was February before he spoke of this development to the spiritual director. Master Matthew was sympathetic, but he was sympathetic also to the attitude of the others. "You may as well accustom yourself to your position, Fernando. The men here in the community are not here because they are saints, but because they want to become saints. Until they do, I'm afraid that any family name as famous as yours will impress them—it impresses me. Should that disturb you? We are not impressed by the name Bulhom because of what you have done; your father made your family name respected. You are living in his reflected light."

"But I want to be the same as everyone else at Holy Cross," Fernando objected. "I want them to treat me just as they treat each other—the way they treated me before this happened."

Master Matthew smiled. "Aren't you quibbling with God, Fernando?"

Fernando puzzled briefly. It was an unusual question. "Do you mean that God has made me Fernando de Bulhom, and I am quibbling because the community regards me as De Bulhom, and I want them to regard me as Fernando?" He laughed suddenly at the distinction he had invented without waiting for Master Matthew to reply.

The Master laughed with him. "There may be occasions in the future when you will be regarded as Fernando and will wish you were regarded as a De Bulhom."

His talk with the Master changed his attitude. If the presence of a Bulhom at Holy Cross proved so interesting to the others, that itself was of value. If the entrance of a Bulhom into the service of the Church was so extraordinary, it would serve to inspire others.

In June of 1217, Fernando and Stephen received major orders. Bishop Terello came to Holy Cross to ordain four to the priesthood, to raise six more to the order of deacon, to confer subdeaconship on six others, including Fernando and Stephen. Present in the chapel of Holy Cross for that ceremony were the relatives of those receiving orders at the altar. Present also, and standing in their position of privilege in front of the relatives, were two men, legates from the royal court. Fernando and the community knew, without inquiring, the reason for the unusual interest of the royal family. Fernando felt a new dismay.

Presence of the royal legates strengthened the proprietary interest of Holy Cross in Queen Urraca and in the entire royal family. A month after the ceremony—on a Sunday in the cloister garden—the Saracen announced what he expressed as "competition for royal favor. Some beggars— they call themselves religious beggars—arranged to gain the confidence and sympathy of Princess Sancha. The Princess brought them to the Queen. Now Queen Urraca has given them a chapel at Olivares and provides their food."

"Poor men of Lyons?" a voice inquired.

The Saracen grimaced his disgust. He struggled visibly to avoid detraction. "Whatever they are," he managed to say, "Rome should prohibit all religious beggars."

Fernando had no interest in the matter of religious beggars. The indignation of the others was amusing. He pretended innocence. "What are we to condemn—that they are beggars or that they have usurped some of our favor with the Queen?"

"They are beggars!" the Saracen exclaimed.

Fernando felt an immediate twinge of conscience induced by the violent answer of the Saracen. "The next degree of humility," a voice reminded, "is achieved when a monk speaks few words and in a quiet voice." He had violated both sections in one action.

Fernando's humor and the Saracen's indignation drew Ruggiero. "Then we are condemning them as poachers?" he asked the Saracen.

A storm of protests fell suddenly on Ruggiero. To the

sons of freemen and serfs in the group, no word was more hateful, none more odious than "poacher." There were few among them whose families had not suffered from charges of hunting game on the estates of nobles and knights.

Ruggiero looked helplessly at Fernando. His venture in innocent amusement had not only failed but had drawn down on him their half-formed resentment against the religious beggars. The big squire's helplessness was so comical, Fernando laughed.

At the very beginning of his laugh, all protests stopped. In a moment, the entire group was as silent as they had been noisy and abusive. It was Stephen who spoke—his voice sounded unnaturally loud in the shocked silence. "Poacher is not a humorous word, Fernando. You should be aware of that."

Fernando was astounded. "I didn't—" he began. He was hardly aware of what they had been saying. He had laughed at Ruggiero's discomfiture, but they thought he had laughed at them! He looked quickly around the group, but none looked at him; they directed their eyes above his head or in another direction. He was becoming angry that they misjudged him without cause. Then he heard a familiar voice that came not from without but originated and ended within himself: "The next higher degree of humility is attained when a monk is not readily moved to laughter."

Anger surged forward to obscure that voice. He thrust it back savagely. Time seemed to race away while the battle raged. Twice had he failed humility. His flippant comment to the Saracen had roused the anger of the other; his laugh had offended the rest. This, then, was the minute for which he had practiced and prepared as squires practiced and prepared for combat. Humility rose to overcome anger and pride—yet the actual enemy is always stronger and more savage than a practice enemy, more cunning, more desperate. Michael and Lucifer struggled before his eyes.

"I am very sorry," he said slowly and clearly. "I hope you will believe I did not laugh because of that word. I laughed because—." He stopped abruptly. If he mentioned Ruggiero, he would be excusing his fault rather than regretting it. "It does not matter why I laughed. I am sorry I offended you."

Elation filled his heart. The last trace of anger drained from him. His humility had been tested. Humility had triumphed.

His apology seemed only to lengthen their silence. He could read the cause, the thought that dominated them, the embarrassment that held them silent. A Bulhom had apologized to the sons of nobles and knights, but he had apologized also to the sons of freemen and serfs!

Arrival of Prior Vincent ended the impasse. The group rose as he approached; their silence was the customary indication of respect for him. "What subject occupies the minds and tongues?"

They turned as one to Fernando. He thought desperately. "We had started to talk about some group of religious beggars, Reverend Prior"—his mind raced before his words—"but I'm afraid we wandered from the subject." He smiled. "Who is the group that received a chapel at Olivares from Her Majesty?"

Fernando knew the Prior was not deceived. He watched the Prior's eyes dart around the group, measuring and appraising. Their momentary hesitation, their mute election of a spokesman, his own straining effort to answer the Prior—Fernando knew Prior Vincent had seen the evidences of conflict.

Prior Vincent took a place on a bench and waved them to resume their places. "There is a group of friars the Queen has befriended and they are beggars, but don't misunderstand the word. These friars work. They will work for those who will hire them. They want nothing more than their food for the day in payment for their work. If their employer won't pay them or if no one will hire them, they beg their food from others. They call themselves Friars Minor. In that way they distinguish themselves from the Friars Preachers." Prior Vincent spoke rapidly and precisely.

"Have they received—?" The Saracen faltered and then smiled. "I forgot the word." The group laughed in sympathy. Their tenseness disappeared.

"Approbation?" Prior Vincent paused. "There is some question at the moment. Pope Innocent III told the Lateran Council, the year before he died, that he had given his approval to the Friars Minor, but there is no indication that he wrote his approval nor of what he approved. The present Holy Father, Honorius, does not want to issue a Bull of Approval if one has already been issued."

Prior Vincent stood, but he motioned quickly that they should remain in their places. "There has been considerable opposition to these friars among some of the hierarchy because of the extreme manner of their life. Time will settle the matter." He smiled faintly. "But time will not settle matters for me. I must deal with them myself." He walked from them with his long, unhurried steps.

The Saracen looked at Fernando. "You have not yet expressed an opinion."

Fernando reflected uncertainly whether to engage in

this conversation that had already entrapped him; but he knew that the Saracen was trying, in his own way, to set aside their disagreement. He raised his shoulders in a gesture of indecision. "Prior Vincent associated them with the Friars Preachers. If they are similar, it would be a good group, just as the Preachers are good for the Church. If they are like the Poor Men of Lyons—and the Prior did say that some of the hierarchy objected to them—they would not be good." Even as he spoke, Fernando saw the others relaxing. They were restoring him in their affections.

Stephen revived the earlier basis of disagreement. "As long as there is any question of papal approval, it seems to me Queen Urraca would be more prudent if she withheld her support of them."

The group moved resentfully against resumption of discord. They knew Stephen's antagonism to all that was not of the Canons Regular of St. Augustine. Someone laughed derisively. "The Queen should be more solicitous of Holy Cross—is that what you mean, Stephen?" Stephen's answer was inaudible in the general laughter of the group.

2

HOLY Cross learned more of the Friars Minor during the summer of 1217. As information increased, community opinion turned steadily against the "religious beggars." Not only were these friars beggars, they acted at times like common minstrels, going into public squares and market areas and singing songs of God. They lacked dignity—they lacked stability, for anyone could be a Friar Minor. They had neither entrance qualifications nor novitiate. They did vow themselves to utter poverty (some wagged their heads meaningfully when that was mentioned). They had no houses; therefore, there was no order among them. And the Queen continued to befriend them.

Fernando had little interest in the friars or the attitude of the community toward them. During the intervening months he must consider the new order that would be conferred on him and the responsibilities attached to it. He must learn to read the Epistle and Gospel expressively so that the faithful would understand the Word of God. He must prepare sermons, and he must learn to preach. There was little time, he knew, before he would begin his active work for God.

In October, Prior Vincent called deacons and subdeacons together in his small office to announce a program of training in sacred eloquence.

"Bishop Terello has informed me that preachers are needed desperately in his diocese. There are not sufficient priests to preach. This year—beginning with Lent—deacons will also be required to preach in the churches of the diocese."

A startled gasp from the deacons in the group interrupted the Prior. "Reverend Prior!" a voice protested, "deacons have never been required to preach in the past."

Prior Vincent smiled confidently. "You are to be granted a privilege that, in the past, has been reserved to priests. If the prospect of preaching unnerves you, comfort yourself that it unnerves everyone; and console yourself with the thought that you will be prepared by systematic training.

"During the first week of training, subdeacons will read the Gospel and Epistle of the Mass each morning to the community; each evening, deacons will preach. During the second week, your duties will be reversed. Deacons will read the Epistles and Gospels; subdeacons will preach each evening. Each of you will be required to prepare a sermon and preach to the community once every two weeks."

The Prior did not tell them that he would also require them to preach without preparation. They learned that only when he interrupted Master Matthew's lecture the following morning, explained his purpose in his rapid precise manner, then summoned Fernando from the body of students. "Preach to us of God's mercy, Fernando." The Prior sat down on a bench with Master Matthew facing the dais.

Fernando stood uncertainly as the order penetrated through his fright, then walked to the front of the room. He tried to walk as though he were completely master of himself, but his legs trembled, his heart raced and pounded in his chest; when he turned and faced the others, his vision dimmed. "It is your pride that frightens you," he accused himself. "You are frightened because you are afraid of the opinions of these others before you." The accusation failed to strengthen him.

He tried to speak loudly, but his voice seemed to have lost all of its power. Sometimes his vision cleared and he saw faces looking at him—frowning, smiling, expression-less, critical, sleepy—then vision would obscure again, and his voice plodded painfully. One thought possessed him—to regain the haven of his bench. When he finished at last, he remembered nothing of what he had said.

"You spoke very well, Fernando," he heard the Prior say. He could not raise his head. He had not spoken well. In his heart, he heard the incessant accusation, "You fear the opinions of others. If your mind and heart were filled with the desire to teach the Word of God, you would not fear the opinions of others."

He prepared his first sermon. "Learn of me, for I am meek and humble of heart." He practiced the words, savored their softness and beauty as he pronounced them, antici-pated how effectively he would speak them; but his heart reproached him, "You are not meek, you are not humble. You fear the opinions of others."

When he stood before all of Holy Cross in the chapel, his whole body trembled. Instinctively his hands grasped the railing of the pulpit to sustain him. He had anticipated that his vision would dim again as it had before, but instead he saw faces clearly in the soft light from the olive wicks spaced along the walls. His courage mounted.

"Learn of me . . ." He heard the words, clear and soft as he had practiced them. And he had spoken them so that they would be heard by those seated in the far end of the chapel.

Courage mounted another step. His mind drew away from the faces turned up to him. He remembered the phrases he had prepared. His voice rose and fell, increased or softened as he had planned.

When he finished, he knew he had preached well. This had not been as the ordeal in the lecture room. He had prepared for this night. He had planned, had thought, had developed the phrases and sentences of this sermon. He enjoyed the relief that the test was passed but, more, the knowledge that he had achieved a great victory.

The entire community seemed gathered in the passage outside the chapel. Prior Vincent was the first to grasp his hand. "You spoke eloquently, Fernando. You have set a standard for the others." Masters, priests, and students crowded around him. Ruggiero beamed proudly above the others. Stephen had hardly waited until Prior Vincent moved away when he kissed Fernando on each cheek; then he stood possessively beside him while the others came forward to admire and compliment in their turn.

Happiness and excitement delayed sleep that night. This was not conceit or pride—that he enjoyed what they had said to him. They had not complimented nor admired him; they had complimented the talent God had given him. He was happy in the knowledge that he might use this talent for God's own purpose.

All improved as they gained experience and received advice from Prior Vincent. They became accustomed to standing and facing the others. Nervousness disappeared.

As he heard and watched the others, Fernando felt confirmation of his talent. Of the others, only the Saracen's talent equaled his, but the Saracen spoke words and thoughts that arose in his heart rather than in his mind, so that he was often reprimanded for recklessness.

During those months from October of 1217 to Lent of the following year, preaching became the major interest of Holy Cross. Priests gave greater care and attention to their sermons. Students—those who had not yet received major orders—attended to their own talents, their own abilities. Cloister garden groups assumed the status of informal forums where each in turn tried to express his thoughts in orderly sequence. Master Matthew began to admonish the Sacred Scripture lecture group that they were attending more to the manner than the matter of their speech.

A new measure determined prestige within the monastery. Masters, priests, deacons, subdeacons, and ordinary students either were acclaimed beyond the measure of their other accomplishments if they were preachers, or their other merits were ignored if they failed in this one. Preaching was the norm of all virtue. The Lenten season added impetus to the activity which Master Matthew condemned with increased frequency. Deacons returning from their assignments were questioned avidly. What had been the response by the people? How many had attended that church? What had the pastor of that church said of the deacon's sermon?

One of the deacons returned with information that a strange name was being heard on the lips of the people. "Zachary," the people acclaimed. "Zachary is the greatest preacher in Coimbra."

"Zachary?" There was no one of that name at Holy Cross. The people must have misunderstood a priest's or deacon's name.

Holy Cross received another explanation within a day. Zachary was neither priest nor deacon nor even of the Order of St. Augustine. Zachary was a religious beggar, a friar, but not a Friar Preacher. Zachary was a Friar Minor!

"The people are crowding to hear him," another deacon complained. "They are deserting the parish churches where they should be. They are pushing and struggling into that little church of St. John, that mean church in the center of the city, to hear this Friar Zachary."

There was but one possible explanation. This beggar could not be educated as were the members of Holy Cross; he could not be more talented; he could not be a greater preacher than their own. This Friar Zachary—of the group that had already bewitched the Princess and the Queen— was either heretic or fraud.

In the cloister garden, in the community room, at whatever place in Holy Cross where more than two individuals gathered, other than in the chapel or the refectory, Friar Zachary and the Friars Minor were denounced and deplored. His and their activities were both antagonistic to the interests of Holy Mother Church and a threat to Portugal.

Fernando could not conceal his own lack of resentment against Friar Zachary and the Friars Minor. Stephen knew it from his silence; the others sensed it from his manner and disinterest whenever the subject was again discussed.

His interest centered with increasing intentness on the order he would soon receive and the study of Sacred Scripture in which he must excel if the talent God had given him were to be employed properly in His service. He found more opportunities for prayer, more time for meditation. His visits to the spiritual adviser increased in number.

"Something continues to disturb me, Master Matthew," he complained. "This is not a question of my vocation. I'm sure of that now. I feel inside as though I'm not satisfied with myself; I'm not satisfied with what I am doing and the little progress I've made."

Master Matthew dismissed his complaints with successive explanations that he was physically tired from his intense efforts, that he was suffering "scruples," that he was being subjected to temptation. None of the master's explanations satisfied. March and April, Lent and Easter fled past. It was May, and they seemed no nearer a solution than before. Fernando frowned as another thought grew from his admission. "Could pride be involved in this, Master?"

The question surprised Master Matthew. "In what way, Fernando?"

Fernando had no clear idea himself how pride could be a factor. "I don't know," he admitted weakly. "But pride has tripped me so often before—and I never knew it was pride until after I fell."

Master Matthew disagreed. "St. Augustine had the same trouble you have, Fernando. He called it restlessness—restlessness for God. 'Our hearts were made for Thee, O Lord.' Do you remember the words? 'Restless must they be until they rest in Thee.'"

Fernando was silent. The casual manner in which Master Matthew compared this dissatisfaction of his with that of the Holy Doctor was embarrassing. It was uncomfortable to sit as a subject of comparison, but he could not devise an escape.

Master Matthew's next question relieved his discomfort. "What do you intend to do with your life, Fernando?"

Fernando smiled. He had answered that question before. "I want to work for God—be His priest, preach His Word. I want to lead people to God."

The answer pleased the priest. "You recited that as

though you had rehearsed it," he laughed.

"I did rehearse it. Prior Gonzalez made me memorize it so I could say it to him whenever he asked."

"Prior Gonzalez wanted you to be a saint, didn't he, Fernando?" Master Matthew's expression was serious.

Fernando paused. It was strange how this priest seemed to discern so easily and to understand what pertained to Prior Gonzalez. His mind seemed almost a counterpart of the Prior's. "Prior Gonzalez wanted everyone to be a saint." He smiled.

The priest nodded. "This may be the time, Fernando, for you to add something more to what you want to do with your life."

Fernando felt as though he were backing away from some challenge. Men could say they want to be priests, to work for God and preach His Word and lead people to God. But men did not raise their eyes heavenward and tell others, "I want to be a saint."

The dissatisfaction he had felt did not diminish even after Bishop Terello placed his hands on him and he was a deacon. It was not unpleasant, neither was it disturbing, Fernando decided. It was more of an urge to action without knowledge of what that action should be. Restlessness. It was that. Restlessness for God? He dismissed the question as quickly as it presented itself.

New duties, new obligations imposed on him during the summer of 1218. Prior Vincent gave the deacons a schedule of sermons they would preach in the parish churches during the last three months of the year. The number of sermons required was burdensome in itself, but the schedule given him included assignments to preach in the presence of the Bishop! Three of his twelve "parish sermons" would be preached in the Cathedral. He tried to hold his attention to the sermons themselves, but imagination persisted in putting the frightening picture before him. He was assigned to preach at the Cathedral first at Sunday Mass, next on the evening of the first Sunday of Advent, last on Christmas.

Rain fell steadily during the week preceding the Sunday of his sermon in the Cathedral. That was welcome: Those who came to earlier Masses would be discouraged from returning to the Solemn Mass. Rain would also prevent the long outdoor procession from the Bishop's palace; they would walk instead through the covered passage and not suffer the way past the eyes of the people.

Prior Vincent accompanied Fernando as he did all those who preached at the Cathedral. They left the monastery early Saturday afternoon—the overnight stay outside Holy Cross was the one compensation granted those who preached before the Bishop. The wet streets were empty; Coimbra was as a deserted city. Fernando reviewed his sermon for the Prior as they walked with their heads down in the pouring rain.

Bishop Terello received them at supper that evening. He was a big man. Fernando thought that he must have been strong and powerful when he was younger. The years had added flesh and had replaced physical strength with the more valuable strength and courage which is not of the physical part of man. There was about him a boldness and assurance that a bishop must have who would engage in disputes with kings. Fernando remembered that it was this bishop who had led the opposition against the avarice of King Sancho.

Prior Vincent presented him to the Bishop, and Fernando knelt to kiss the episcopal ring. "Deacon Fernando, Your Excellency," Prior Vincent said.

The Bishop grasped Fernando's hand and gestured that he should stand. "Deacon Fernando," he repeated. "Then you are Don Martinho's son?" Bishop Terello smiled at Prior Vincent. "I think that Fernando de Bulhom will enjoy having supper with the Bishop more than most of our deacons do." Prior Vincent laughed.

Fernando's mind had been so occupied with the sermon to be preached in the presence of the Bishop that he had forgotten this supper with the Bishop that other deacons seemed to think more important. He did enjoy the supper. He enjoyed the Bishop's comments and Prior Vincent's remarks while they ate.

"Is supper here similar to supper at Holy Cross?" the Bishop asked.

Fernando looked quickly from His Excellency to Prior Vincent, then back to the Bishop. He smiled. "I have forgotten how to answer such a question diplomatically, Your Excellency."

Bishop Terello laughed. "I would say you have forgotten not at all, Fernando. How long has it been since you left the life of diplomacy?"

"A little more than eight years, Your Excellency."

Bishop Terello glanced around their supper room. It was a small room similar to the trencher room where Fernando had eaten with his parents and Ruggiero. Over the fireplace was a crucifix; except for that, the walls were bare. "Do you enjoy having supper in this manner, Fernando?"

"Very much, Your Excellency."

Supper with the Bishop reestablished his courage. As many different opinions of Bishop Terello had been expressed by the deacons as there were deacons. Fernando was happy that Bishop Terello seemed not only a capable and strong administrator; he was a kindly man who was interested in the life of a lowly deacon at his table. Fernando recalled some of those who had been overawed by the Bishop.

In the vesting room before Mass the next morning, Fernando was surprised that even among the priests were those who feared the Bishop. The priest who was celebrant tugged nervously at his vestments. Fernando heard him tell one of the others, "He scolded me before because the alb touched the floor."

The line of procession formed; members of the choir stood near one door. Acolytes, censer bearers, servers, and officers of the Mass completed the line that curved within the room. "The Bishop!" a voice called softly. Bishop Terello stepped into the room followed by Prior Vincent, and the choir began to move slowly through the opposite doorway.

The sanctuary was bright with candles. Fernando turned his eyes carefully and glanced into the great cavern that was the body of the church. Faces reflected the light from the sanctuary. He genuflected before the altar and walked slowly to his place at the side. He glanced again into the great nave of the church. He had hoped the rain would thin the number; there were more here than had been in any of the parish churches!

His attention alternated from the Mass to the people. The celebrant chanted the prayers. Fernando felt a preliminary quiver run through him when the little group assembled to chant the gospel. Then he was walking slowly to the altar. In his mind, he had practiced over and over—genuflect— bow to the officers of the Mass—walk to the throne—kneel for the Bishop's blessing—turn and walk slowly.

Faces looked up to his. Deliberately he turned his mind from them as he had learned to do. "This is my commandment, that you love one another, as I have loved you." He fixed the sermon before his mind. Thought followed thought in order. Words and phrases rose to their places.

When he finished, he knew he had preached well. He knew it in the silence as he turned from the pulpit, in the rustle of movements that sounded from the body of the church as he returned to his place in the sanctuary. He knew in his heart that he had used well this talent for preaching the Word of God.

He had learned to expect the compliments of others. The priests at the parish churches had complimented him; he had learned that it was customary for pastors to compliment the deacons who preached in their churches. But he was not prepared for the sudden outburst of compliments when they returned to the vesting room. There was the usual silence until the officers of the Mass bowed to the crucifix; then voices sounded together their exclamations of praise. A hand grasped his arm firmly and turned him around. Bishop Terello was complimenting him! "One of the finest sermons ever preached in the Cathedral." Fernando knelt quickly to kiss the Bishop's ring; then the Bishop's hand urged him to his feet again. Prior Vincent smiled at him. "You preached the Word of God well, Fernando." Others crowded around. They clutched at his hands, some rapped smartly on his back. Fernando could no longer observe all that was happening. Their movements, their numbers, the torrents of words bewildered him. Their extravagance embarrassed him. Their enthusiasm made him feel alone and strange.

Prior Vincent brought the cloak for him; the Prior was already wearing his. He held Fernando's forward and waited while Fernando fastened it, then turned to the outer door. Those in the vesting room called their farewells in another burst of sound.

Fernando was happy. Their compliments had dispelled the doubts that had lingered even after his experiences in the parish churches. He could preach! God had given him this great talent! He need tremble no more when he stood in the pulpits. Confidence thrust aside the last of his fears.

3

CONFIDENCE increased rapidly in Fernando after his sermon at the Cathedral. He learned to use arms and hands in unison with his voice. He learned to stand straight and erect before his listeners without groping for support of the pulpit railing. He saw the crowds increase, slowly at first, then more rapidly, in the churches where he preached.

Holy Cross was proud of him, he knew. Priests and deacons related what people said of him. Ruggiero and Stephen delighted in each new report about "Deacon Fernando, the noble, the son of Don Martinho de Bulhom."

As his mind was freed from concern for the sermons he must preach, restlessness reasserted itself. Preaching would not satisfy it; prayer did not identify it. After each sermon, he heard the compliments of pastors, the Prior and priests, and thanked them absently. He cared nothing for the compliments of these who admired his technical proficiency. He wondered what those others would say—those who came to hear the Word of God even from a twenty-three-year-old deacon. Would there be one who would say, "You healed my heart"?

The question returned Christmas morning while he knelt in the sanctuary of the Cathedral and saw the number who approached to receive Holy Communion. They came forward as waves to kneel on the sanctuary step. Had he inspired some part of this fervor?

"Magnificent!" a voice whispered beside him.

Fernando had noticed without interest the two who knelt beside him. Their robes of rough gray wool marked them as representatives of some religious order unknown to him. He turned slightly at the sound and saw them smiling and nodding to each other as though they found some great personal pleasure in the groups surging forward from the depths of the Cathedral.

When the Mass ended, he had again to accept the compliments of the others for his sermon of the morning. Their words and his answers formed a familiar routine.

"Your heart must be very happy, Deacon Fernando."

The words penetrated slowly the screen that had warded off the customary compliments of the others.

"You are bringing many people to God," the same voice added.

Fernando recognized the religious who had knelt beside him during the Mass. The stranger was little taller than himself, but he was a stout man made stouter by the formlessness of his gray robe. "Thank you, you are very kind," Fernando responded. He did not know how to address this person. The robe he wore marked the man as a religious but his face—and the face of his companion—had the hard, tough skin of those who lived in sun and rain instead of in houses of religion. The one difference between their faces and those of serfs was their bright happiness that seemed to be more peacefulness than pleasure. When they left him, Fernando saw that they went to the door that opened into the street but that neither wore an outer cloak.

He thought of the two again when he followed Prior

Vincent through the same door. The movement of pulling his own cloak more closely about him reminded him of the two who had not worn cloaks. "Who were the two strangers in the sanctuary, Prior Vincent?"

"Strangers?" Prior Vincent repeated the word as though he had not been aware of any strangers.

"The two gray-robed men who knelt beside me," Fernando explained.

The description amused Prior Vincent. "They are not strangers, Fernando," he laughed. "They are Zachary and Michael, Friars Minor."

Friar Zachary! It was the great Lenten preacher whose words were so strange among the compliments of the others. "You are bringing many people to God," he had said, as though he also knew the emptiness of compliments. Had the man known the question that stirred within him? Had Friar Zachary also known a restlessness that Master Matthew termed a restlessness for God? It was not restlessness for God, Fernando knew. It was a hunger for souls.

He was disappointed when Master Matthew refused to share the joy of his discovery. The spiritual director seemed to find no reason for rejoicing that he would be hungry for souls. Master Matthew even frowned slightly at the conclusion of Fernando's explanation. "You have a tremendous zeal, Fernando," he said seriously. "All of your thoughts are centered on making the best use of this talent God has given you. But your very zeal can be a source of danger to yourself. There is always danger that zeal will become anxiety—even a sort of desperation. You can become so zealous for souls as to forget that the reason for zeal is God. You can exert yourself so much that the exertion, the work itself, overshadows the purpose of your work."

Fernando smiled at the master's gravity. "There is hardly danger of that. God never fails if we trust in Him."

"I'm not speaking of trust in God, Fernando. I am speaking of trust in ourselves." He shook his head. "For some reason, words always fail to distinguish the two."

Master Matthew's pessimism could not diminish the joy of his discovery. The purpose of his life was clear to himself even if he could not explain it so that it was clear also to Master Matthew. God had given him this talent of preaching. He would use it to claim souls for God. Ordination—the priesthood—would multiply his opportunities. As a deacon, he could preach; as a priest, he would still preach, but when he had preached, he would go from the pulpits to the confessionals, where he could finish the work.

At the beginning of Lent, Prior Vincent summoned the deacons together in his office to announce the assignment of each after ordination. "Fernando, Holy Cross guestmaster," he read. "Stephen, to the school at Paris to become a master as soon as one of the others returns." His voice continued through the list.

As the Prior read the other assignments, Fernando puzzled at his own. "Guestmaster of Holy Cross." There was no guestmaster at Holy Cross. Guestmasters were in monasteries to receive those who came to ask for food or haven from enemies or lodging for a night. Strangers seldom came to Holy Cross. The monastery was on the edge of the capital. Those seeking food would apply at the parish churches or even at the Bishop's house in preference to the poor fare they might expect at the monastery. Those seeking haven could claim it from the King. Those in search of lodging could find more comfortable accommodations at the inns of the city. At Holy Cross, Brother Gatekeeper was sufficient to direct occasional strangers to their destinations. Fernando waited for the others to leave that he might learn something more of this strange assignment.

Prior Vincent smiled at his comments. "It is an innovation," he agreed. "There has not been need for a guestmaster in the past. Circumstances change, Fernando. The past does not determine the future. Bishops and nobles visit Holy Cross; Friar Zachary and his companion come to us occasionally for food. It is not fitting that Holy Cross welcome visitors with a brother gatekeeper, whether those visitors be bishops or nobles or friars or whoever else may come. Not all come to monasteries to ask; many come to give. When some come to give, Brother Gatekeeper must seat them on a bench in the gatehouse until he can find me, and very often he must search for me. That is not proper, Fernando. We must have a guestmaster."

Fernando felt that a dream was being shattered. He had not thought that he would spend his life welcoming those who came to Holy Cross. In a vague, indefinite way, he had thought of the men and women he had seen in Lisbon, had remembered their manner of life, had remembered that their manner of life had so repelled him as to force him to think of the priesthood. They were the people to whom his life and his talent should be given.

Bitter thoughts thrust at him. He knew why Holy Cross must have a guestmaster. He was Fernando de Bulhom, the son of Don Martinho de Bulhom, the young man with the grace seen more often at court than in churches. He would still be permitted to preach; but his major duty would be to receive alms instead of souls.

The two legates from the royal court appeared on

ordination day. Fernando and Holy Cross expected them; as guestmaster, he must expect many more like them. He saw them standing, as protocol required, in front of all the others—in front of parents who had come this day to see their sons consecrated to God. The others had parents to rejoice in this ceremony; he had Ruggiero and two legates from the court. He was as a ward of the King; and he was Fernando de Bulhom, Guestmaster of Holy Cross.

He went to the outer garden after dinner. The others would be with their families this day, conducting them through the monastery, sitting with them in the refectory at tables apart from the rest of the community, or talking with them in the cloister garden. Even the chapel welcomed them. Ruggiero and the other lay brothers served them. Canon Fernando could enjoy for himself the outer garden.

He went to the gatehouse. Brother Gatekeeper looked up at him from his bench. "This is the day of days for you, Canon." Fernando smiled and retreated. He started back toward the building. The sun was hot; he could not stay in the outer garden, but he could walk slowly to the building.

A voice called from the gatehouse. Brother Gatekeeper was waving to him to return. Guestmaster Fernando! His duties had already begun. But he need not hurry. He could walk slowly to the gate as he had been walking toward the building. He could see others standing in the shadowed entrance of the gatehouse, but from his position in the bright, glaring sunlight, he could not distinguish them.

He lowered his eyes, half-closing them against the sun. When he neared the gatehouse, he raised them again. Instantly he quickened his steps. One of the two who waited was Friar Zachary; and the other was the companion he had seen at the Cathedral. They waited, smiling and patient, in their rough, gray robes, perspiration coursing down their faces. Fernando thought of the hot sun beating on his own summer-weight habit and scapular. These men who had worn no cloaks on Christmas wore the same heavy robe now as then!

They would not go to the building with him. Friar Zachary shook his head firmly. "We are begging, Canon Fernando, but we are not begging food today. The good God and Bishop Terello have already filled us with food. We beg your blessing, Canon Fernando."

Fernando was astonished. They knelt before him and he blessed them. "You walked out here under this hot sun for my blessing?"

Friar Zachary and Friar Michael laughed at his astonishment. "Brother Sun is God's great gift, Canon." Friar Zachary turned to his companion. "Tell Canon Fernando of Brother Sun."

Friar Michael looked toward the garden where the sun glared on ground and buildings. The gaiety vanished from his face, and he seemed to hesitate for a moment as though to pray.

> Praised be Thou, my Lord, with all Thy creatures,
> Especially the honored Brother Sun,
> Who makes the day and illumines us through Thee.
> He is beautiful and, radiant with great splendor,
> Bears the signification of Thee, Most High One.

Fernando remembered other voices like this friar's, voices that spoke each word in such a way that they seemed to be singing. He thought of the Great Hall at Castle de Bulhom when minstrels had come. This was the manner of the minstrels when they sang Roland's song. But Friar Michael had not sung a minstrel song. "That is a beautiful prayer for God's gift, Friar Michael. Is it your own?"

Friar Michael smiled and shook his head. "It is part of a much longer song, Canon Fernando. It is a part of the Sun Song our holy father, Francis, wrote."

Fernando felt that he was becoming involved in too many subjects he could not understand. They had come here for his blessing. They had walked in the hot sunlight, then sang thanks to God for His gift. Now they spoke of their holy father.

"Francis?"

Friar Zachary raised both hands in protest. "Not today, Canon Fernando. We came for your blessing and you have blessed us. Let us come some other day to tell you of our holy father."

In the weeks following ordination and his installation as guestmaster, Fernando came to realize that the two friars were, to him, the most enjoyable of all who came to Holy Cross. Nobles—great and lesser nobles with knights and squires—came to give of their bounty. Fernando recognized some names he had heard in the past, remembered a few as having been in the courtyard or at table in the Great Hall. All seemed to know him or were anxious to know him. Some regarded him curiously, and he knew they wondered what had brought Don Fernando de Bulhom to Holy Cross and the priesthood. A few could not conceal their thoughts that his mind was unbalanced.

Time weighed heavily. Occasionally, Stephen joined him in the visitors' room, which was made also the office of the new guestmaster. Stephen was even more bored and disconsolate than Fernando. "You know, at least," he complained, "that you will be busy after September with all the sermons you must preach. I have the privilege of celebrating Mass and doing nothing more and expecting nothing more until one of the others returns from Paris."

"Prior Vincent could appoint you as guestmaster," Fernando proposed.

Stephen grimaced with disgust. "I would be addressing knights as nobles and nobles as knights. You were born to that life, Fernando. The rest of us would be overwhelmed with the importance and fame of these men."

Ruggiero helped both of them through the hours when his own work permitted. He was not disappointed, as they were, by failure to achieve hopes and dreams. "Reverend Prior can find enough work for me without my suggestions. When he doesn't think of something, I sit down until he does."

Stephen looked up at the tremendous figure and shook his head sadly. "Someday, St. Peter will look at that big frame of yours and ask what you did for God with all that muscle. What will you tell him?"

Ruggiero grinned. "If heaven is as full of priests as you think it is, St. Peter will take every lay brother who applies. He'll need them to rebuild the place according to your plans."

Zachary and Michael returned in July. It was a hot day; their gray robes were spotted black with perspiration. Fernando lifted his shoulders in resignation to the madness of men who would come so far from the city on such a day. "At least you will come to the refectory today," he invited.

Friar Zachary's dark face was red with exertion and heat. "I hope it will not be comfortably cool there, Canon Fernando."

Fernando smiled. "Would your holy father, Francis, disapprove of comfortable coolness, Friar Zachary?"

The refectory was comfortably cool. Fernando sat with the two at the end of a long table. A brother came from the kitchen and took the bowls the friars had brought. "Don't fill them yet," Fernando cautioned. "The brothers must sit here for a time and rest before they eat."

Both objected to his order. They were not guests but beggars. The brother from the kitchen hesitated uncertainly.

"Ignore them, Brother," said Fernando, and smiled. "They told me they came to speak of their holy father, Francis, so they will do that." He could not permit them to eat immediately after their walk in the hot sun: There was a distinction between mortification of the body and mistreatment of it. "You have mentioned this Francis," he told Zachary. "Tell me about him. Who is he?"

Friar Zachary smiled delightedly. "That is the way of Francis, Canon Fernando. You and Father Francis are brothers." He stopped and looked critically at Fernando. "No! you are his son. You are not yet old enough to be his brother," he laughed. "But what you did is what he would do. Father Francis teaches us mortification; but when we suffer from mortification or when something is difficult, Father Francis has pity."

Fernando raised his hand. "Before you praise him more, Friar Zachary, tell me who he is."

"He is the founder of our Order, the Friars Minor—the little brothers." The friar opened his eyes very wide to indicate a discovery of unusual importance. "Again you are like him, Canon Fernando. You were rich. He was rich. You turned from riches to God. He turned from riches to God. You preach the Word of God. He preaches the Word of God."

"Is he a priest?"

The friar shook his head. "He said he is not worthy to be a priest. He is known as Francis, the Poor Man of Assisi."

Fernando frowned.

Friar Zachary did not see the frown. He would have continued with his words about Francis, but Friar Michael interrupted. "Canon Fernando is displeased about something."

Fernando was embarrassed. "I am sorry," he said. "I am not displeased. What you said reminded me of something else that is unpleasant."

Friar Michael smiled knowingly. "The Poor Men of Lyons perhaps, Canon Fernando?"

Fernando was more embarrassed than before.

Friar Zachary leaned toward him over the table. "Canon Fernando"—his voice pleaded for understanding— "Francis is not—we are not—like those devils! Pope Innocent blessed our order, and Pope Honorius has blessed it. We are subject to Holy Mother Church—not her enemies."

The pleading tone increased Fernando's confusion. He could have understood if they had resented his inference; but they did nothing more than explain to him. "I'm sorry," he repeated. "The words are so much alike that the one reminded me of the other. I did not mean that Francis or you were like them. And I interrupted what you were saying of Francis, Friar Zachary. You said he gave up his father's wealth, and yet he is not a priest. Why did he found your order?"

Friar Zachary drew back slowly. "To show others how God wants them to live."

"He could be a priest, Friar Zachary, and continue to show others how to live," Fernando smiled.

Both friars nodded their agreement. "There is one difference, Canon Fernando. A priest may show by example the life all should live. The people see his good life. Then they are only sorry that they cannot live as he does. 'The priest is stronger,' they say, or 'God gives the priest greater graces than He gives me.' They excuse their weakness, Canon Fernando, and pretend they cannot live a good life. Francis proves to them they can live as good a life as priest or anyone. They cannot say he has received greater graces, because then Francis points to his order and tells them that here are many others, men like themselves who are not in monasteries or convents but who live in the world." Friar Zachary looked at Fernando and a small smile of amusement wrinkled his face. "You do not think I am conceited in saying this?"

Fernando shook his head slowly and soberly. "You mean that you are men living in the world to show other men and women how they should live. You preach to them, Friar Zachary. Perhaps you, Friar Michael, sing to them." He smiled. "But you also live for them."

Friar Michael looked eagerly at the other across the table. "That is the way Father Francis expressed it." He turned to Fernando. "'Preach by example,' he told us, Canon Fernando. 'Live in such manner that your life will preach to others.'"

Fernando looked quickly from the one to the other, from the minstrel to the great preacher. "Live in such a manner that your life will preach to others." What a tremendous ideal it was! Did these two believe it, believe in it with as much enthusiasm as Friar Michael expressed?

Fernando called the brother from the kitchen. Zachary and Michael ate gravely all that was placed before them. When they had finished, he went with them to the gatehouse and stood watching them walk toward Coimbra.

"They are a queer pair, Canon Fernando," Brother Gatekeeper said and laughed.

Fernando nodded. They were queer: with the queerness of Peter and John rejoicing that they were thought worthy to be beaten for Christ's sake, or the queerness of Paul in many perils and suffering, calling on others to "rejoice in the Lord always." He hurried from the gatehouse before Brother Gatekeeper might be moved to more comments.

As he walked toward the monastery building, Ruggiero intercepted him and followed him into the visitors' room. "What do you think of them, Fernando?"

Fernando hesitated as though deciding just what he did think. "I think there is more good about them than most of us will believe, Ruggiero. They live that life as an example for others."

Ruggiero pretended to shudder. "Our Lord did say that we can enter into eternal life just by obeying the commandments, didn't He?"

Fernando shook his head. "Our Lord said, 'Be perfect.' The only way we can become perfect is by working our spiritual muscles—by practicing just as a knight must practice in order to become perfect."

Ruggiero seemed to regret that he had asked about the friars. His cultivated antipathy to exertion urged him firmly away from the subject. "Every man to his calling," he grumbled, and turned to the doorway. He looked back then and grinned. "My work is calling from the garden."

Fernando went to the window opening that faced the outer garden. He watched the big brother walking slowly but with long strides that carried him quickly over the ground. Why did people run away from the thought of perfection? Why did Ruggiero—and who lived a more perfect life than big Ruggiero?—why did he suddenly decide that his work in the garden demanded immediate attention?

The friars came again to Holy Cross late in August. Fernando expected to see the two, but from the garden as he approached the gatehouse, he could see the shadowed entrance filled with gray robes. Seven of them!

Friar Zachary appeared from among them. "Canon Fernando!" The tone of his voice made Fernando smile. It was as though Friar Zachary were welcoming him to their party—as though these others were guests who had arrived earlier than he. Their voices and laughing trailed away as he approached. They stood quiet and smiling when he entered the shade of the gatehouse.

Friar Zachary brought them forward and recited their names. "Berard." (A happy, handsome man, Fernando decided.) "Peter. Peter is a deacon, Canon Fernando. Brother Otho—Brother Otho is the first priest we have had with us."

Fernando regarded the man with interest. "Friar Zachary did not tell me that there were priests among the friars."

"There are not many, Canon Fernando," said Brother Otho, smiling.

Friar Zachary continued his introductions. "Adjutus," he said. "Then, Accursius. Adjutus and Accursius are lay brothers. And, last, Michael."

Fernando shook hands with the two lay brothers and Michael. "Is this your entire community, Friar Michael?"

Michael smiled. "Temporarily, Canon. But Friar Zachary is custodian." The group around them laughed readily.

Fernando smiled with them and glanced at Zachary. "Through you, then, Friar Zachary, Holy Cross extends the invitation to the refectory."

Zachary shook his head doubtfully. "We are too many. We came only to visit you, Canon Fernando. These others are our missionaries. They are going to Morocco. I brought them for your blessing."

"Missionaries to Morocco?" Fernando glanced at the group. "You will need more than my blessing," he smiled. "You need Brother Cook's blessing." He grasped Otho's arm. "We will lead the way, Friar Otho, as good priests leading the faithful." It was strange, he thought, how cheerfully he responded to the cheerfulness of these friars. They filled him with joy.

With Friar Otho beside him, he led the group in and seated them at an end of one of the long tables. He took the bench at the end for himself so that he could face all of them. Friar Otho he placed at his right. He gestured that the others should take whatever benches they wished. They lowered their voices, but their gaiety was not diminished. They laughed and talked as they had been doing when he first saw them in the gatehouse entrance.

"You mentioned there were not many priests in your group, Friar. Why do not more of the friars become priests?"

"There will be more in time, Canon Fernando." Friar Otho spoke with quiet assurance. "There are many who live this life who are not qualified to be priests. By their example, they will lead others to live a good life. Then, from those people and those families will come priests."

"But Friar Zachary could be a priest," Fernando said. "Or Friar Michael. And that Berard—" he nodded to the man at the end of the group. Berard sat erect and dignified, laughing and talking with the others.

Otho smiled. "None of them read or write—they could not read the Mass."

"They could learn."

Friar Otho agreed. "But is that important, Canon Fernando? There are many priests, many to administer the sacraments and celebrate Mass. Is it not more important that there be many who will be an example for people? You and I can preach to the people; Peter and all deacons can preach. These men live their sermons. Example is more powerful than advice."

"Do you expect example to influence the Saracens, Friar Otho?"

The priest lifted his head expressively. "God will decide that."

"Surely you have some plan, though. You are not leading these men to Morocco without some definite plan for them."

Friar Otho was amused. He smiled and leaned forward, pointing a finger toward himself. "I am not leading them, Canon Fernando. Berard is our leader."

"Berard? But you are a priest and he is not."

Otho nodded. "He is a leader. I am a priest, but he is a leader."

Fernando thought he had acquired some understanding of the friars and their purpose. Now Otho had introduced another puzzle. Priests were in a group, yet were not leaders. A layman was leader.

"Berard was a great noble, Canon Fernando. All of his life, he directed men. I never directed men. I am the son of freemen. So are these others. Is it not better that Berard direct us on our mission?"

They joined in the talk of the others. Fernando was conscious that his interest had fastened on Berard; he marked the noble's courtesy to the others of his group. He should have liked to talk to him, to ask what had led him to this life of the Friars Minor, whether others had been influenced to follow him, whether others had been influenced to improve their lives.

Even as he studied the other, a new vision arose before him. A new plan for bringing to God the people of Lisbon and all Portugal. He thought of the nobles who came to Holy Cross with their attendants and horses and other evidences of wealth and power. They were the great of Portugal, the leaders, the examples. What they did was imitated by all others through all ranks of society, even to the serfs! Bring the nobles to God, and all Portugal would follow them! And who knew these men better than Fernando de Bulhom?

In the days following the visit of the missionary friars—the visit of Berard—Fernando forgot that he had disliked his appointment as guestmaster. Carefully he began to prepare the sermons he would preach during the winter months; these, he determined, would be sermons that would lead great nobles to God.

4

IN whatever church Canon Fernando preached during the last four months of 1219, people of the capital crowded to hear him. They came to hear "the one who preached so well when he was a deacon."

Fernando did not disappoint them. The long summer hours had provided time for preparation, for revision, for practicing the sermons. He had thought of these nights, had prepared in his own mind what he must do, had added purpose to confidence. Yet from the beginning, he was disappointed. He looked down from the pulpit that first night and thanked God again for the talent that had brought these people before him.

His eyes searched over the crowd below him. Many were women. Most seemed to be of the tradesmen class, of the archers and men-at-arms. Far back in the church were serfs. Below him, immediately beneath the pulpit where nobles would stand, was a small group, so small he counted them in the slight interval before he started to preach. Six! Only six of those he must address, six of those who must hear him and must lead all of Portugal to God as they led them to war—or to worse destruction. The first misgiving settled in him. He could not inspire the leaders if they would not come to hear him. He determined that he would not be disappointed nor discouraged. The others would come. Those who were his own, those who were the leaders, those most difficult to attract would, with God's grace, come eventually.

Through the succeeding weeks, prayer supported him; but even prayer was not proof against the accumulating depression. Each night that he preached, he looked hopefully at the space immediately below the pulpit. Each night he saw the same evidence that those he strove to influence refused to interest themselves in him or his cause. He allowed his hopes to rise when he thought that the approach of Christmas would bring a change, and was depressed accordingly when he saw no change.

In January he appealed to Prior Vincent. "What is necessary to attract those people? The tradesmen and serfs come with all their families. What must I do to attract the nobles?"

Prior Vincent shook his head in rare admission that he had no answer. "Nobles and knights respond slowly, Fernando—if at all. It is hard for men to turn their minds from their wealth or power or comfort. Rich men are afraid to think about becoming poor in spirit. Proud men do not want to be meek. Comfortable men do not want to mourn."

Fernando refused to surrender. "There must be some means. God wants all men to turn to Him and to come to Him. Riches and position are not barriers."

Prior Vincent smiled wryly. "They are obstacles."

Fernando tried to put out of his mind the disappointment of the months. Lent would soon begin, and Canon Fernando would preach in the Cathedral. Of all seasons of the year, Lent should bring into the Cathedral those leaders who must hear him. He distracted himself by applying himself tenaciously to the matter of his sermons.

Brother Gatekeeper interrupted him early in February with the announcement, "The older friar is here." It was a peculiar message, but Brother Gatekeeper left before Fernando could question him.

Zachary was alone. "I sent Michael to Santarem," he explained in a voice that was a tired imitation of his usual tone. "I sent him to Santarem to receive the bodies of our missionaries."

Fernando was not prepared for the announcement. Zachary's unusual expression and the absence of Michael were indicative of trouble but not of tragedy. "Bodies?" he repeated.

"I should have said martyrs, Canon Fernando. Our brothers are holy martyrs now."

"Berard and Otho?"

"All five." Zachary breathed deeply. "God called all of them at one time to witness His name with their blood."

Fernando remembered suddenly the sight of a building, fire-blackened at the window openings, and a pillar of white smoke curling above it. He saw the brown earth of the courtyard of the village of San Bruno, and figures lying still and helpless. "Saracens?" he whispered.

"The Emir himself. Prince Pedro tried to rescue them, but the Emir acted so quickly." Zachary stopped abruptly. "Did you know that Prince Pedro was marshal to the Emir, Canon Fernando?"

Fernando felt revulsion sweep over him. Had Prince Pedro turned even against God? He had turned against his brother, against his friend, against his country . . .

Zachary interrupted his thoughts. "Berard reclaimed Prince Pedro. Prince Pedro had tried to protect all five because Berard was a noble. When the Emir martyred them,

Prince Pedro cried and vowed he would return to God."
A thin smile appeared on Zachary's face. "Berard lived his
example, Canon Fernando. He lived it so well that he influenced even a prince to change his life."

Fernando shuddered involuntarily. He could not share
Zachary's pious joy. Berard had paid a terrible price to
ransom a dissolute prince. "You must come with me, Friar
Zachary," he said, changing the subject. "You must give
this news to Prior Vincent yourself."

News of the five martyrs spread rapidly. The nobles
who came to Holy Cross persisted in retelling the story to
Fernando. Each related the particular version he had heard
or which his fancy had invented; successors contradicted
and related something different. In but one feature were all
these nobles united: Berard was their champion. The noble
Berard had led his men even to martyrdom; Berard had
reclaimed their prince.

The initial excitement dissipated. King Alphonso issued
a proclamation that the bodies of the martyrs would be
brought to Coimbra to rest forever at Holy Cross. Nobles of
the kingdom were commanded to appear in the capital so that
the martyrs would receive the homage of the entire nation.

Fernando awakened suddenly to the opportunity that
was being placed before him. He had not immediately connected the death of Berard, the presence in Coimbra of the
noble class, and the sermons he would preach during Lent.
When at last the three elements joined together in his mind,
he submerged himself in preparation for the task before
him. Berard had begun this work with his life; Fernando de
Bulhom would conclude it with his preaching. From early
morning until late each day, he toiled over his sermons.

When he mounted the pulpit in the Cathedral on the

night of Ash Wednesday, the sight startled, then inspired, him. His first glimpse was of a massive crowd, so large that even the great doors were not closed. People overflowed the church! He looked at the area beneath the pulpit. Tonight they had come! Tonight he would not be able to count them. The nobles of Portugal had responded.

His voice called the challenge of God. "If any man will follow me, let him deny himself, and take up his cross, and follow me." Fernando paused that they might hear and savor the challenge. Let them understand that these were not words of soft invitation! Neither were they a challenge to knightly combat to be pursued for a time, then abandoned for other interests. Let them understand the fullness of these words—the challenge to eternal life!

"For whoever will save his life, shall lose it: and whoever shall lose his life for my sake and the gospel, shall save it." He looked down on those immediately below the pulpit—the privileged, the leaders, those blessed with the goods of earth. "For what shall it profit a man, if he gain the whole world, and suffer the loss of his soul?" He raised his eyes to those beyond the nobles, to those less privileged, less blessed with the goods of earth. "Or what shall a man give in exchange for his soul?"

He knew he had never preached as he preached this night. Never before had he cried out the planned, ordered thoughts of his mind, joined with the power of his heart. When he descended from the pulpit, he forced his way through the crowd and took his place in the confessional.

"I want to confess my entire life, if I may," a voice spoke from the darkness.

Fernando recognized authority and command in the deep, smooth tones—the voice of a noble.

"How long ago did you confess?"

"Ten years, Canon. I am twenty-nine now. I want to start a new life. I want to be done completely with the old."

The man's confession was much as he expected: the story of the prodigal son with the few individualizing details, the story of the young man whose freedom in the world had become slavery to sin. But this confession was different in the explanation he had given—"I want to start a new life." An extraordinary grace had been given him; he must be made to know and appreciate this mark of God's goodness.

"Do you understand what moved you to repentance?" He waited. The man could not be expected to offer an answer until he had considered the question. Forced to think and to offer an inadequate answer, these penitents were more alert to the significance of the explanation he would give them of the grace of God.

"Berard, the martyr," the voice answered.

Fernando hesitated. He had almost spoken the first words of his usual explanation, but this answer was an opportunity to present something better. The man had not attributed his repentance to the grace of God in general; he had specified a particular grace of God in the person of the martyred Berard.

"Berard was a special grace from almighty God," he explained slowly. "He was put here by God to be an example to all nobles and knights. If he was an example to you in his death, he should be an example for you to follow in your life."

"He will be," the voice promised earnestly.

"You have received an extraordinary grace from God," Fernando continued. "You attribute it to Berard and that is well. But God stirred your heart to respond to Berard. Berard's example and sacrifice would not have been sufficient of themselves. God also moved you to respond to that example and that sacrifice and to cooperate with His grace.

"You must keep in your mind—in the very forefront of your mind—that God has conferred a signal favor on you. Berard was an example to all nobles and all knights, but not all have responded as you have. God has not yet stirred the hearts of others as He stirred yours."

The voice interrupted him softly in protest. "The others are stirred, too, Canon. They need only a little encouragement."

Those who followed repeated and confirmed what the voice of the prodigal had told him. Here in the confessional, as at the gatehouse of Holy Cross, Berard was the name on their lips. Berard was the model, the champion of the nobles. Even as he heard and absolved and counseled, Fernando knew that this had not been his victory. He had prepared his sermons with the view to having his words finish the work begun by Berard. But he could not claim a share of the fruit. This was not his work nor his victory. This was Berard's. The preaching of the noble Fernando de Bulhom had not been necessary. The example of the noble Berard was sufficient.

Fernando lay awake long hours that night in the darkened dormitory. His mind turned from the present, from the voices he had heard in the confessional, to race into the future. An impossible dream seized upon him.

On Friday of that week, the bodies of the martyrs arrived at Coimbra to be escorted from the gates of the city to Holy Cross by all the nobles of the kingdom and the people of the capital. The church, intended only for the monastery, could not contain the crowd.

Fernando knelt in the sanctuary where the community surrounded the bodies of the five. He wondered which of the shrouds concealed Berard, which Otho. Perhaps it was not important. All had sought perfection in life so that they would be examples in death. He thought of himself and the pulpits from which he preached—pulpits from which men had turned without interest. He thought of the pulpit of martyrdom from which these five had preached—pulpits from which men could never turn and never forget.

The Mass and burial ended. The stones of the floor were replaced over the five forms. Fernando looked about and found Zachary. "Come with me," he whispered. "Bring Friar Michael."

He thought quickly where they might go. The visitors' room would fill with visitors on this day. The refectory also would be a place of people and confusion. He had not much to say to them; he could say it as they walked together across the outer garden to the gatehouse. If that were not enough, they could return together to the building.

He led the friars to the outer door before others could call to him. None would suspect; they would see him walking to the gatehouse with these two as he had before.

"Do you believe in their sacrifice, Friar Michael?" He avoided Zachary deliberately. He knew what the superior's answer would be.

Michael did not hesitate. He had no need to prepare his reply. "They are worthy of Christ," he said.

Fernando had expected some different answer from this. "What of the effect of their sacrifice on others?"

Zachary answered him. "The people are following them already, Canon Fernando. In Coimbra and in the country to the south, wherever men learn of these holy five, they are crowding the churches and changing their lives. Prince Pedro was the first. Since that, many more have come."

Fernando had not thought of others in addition to Prince Pedro and the nobles gathered in Coimbra. The dream that had claimed him obscured all else. "There were others, then, Friar Zachary?"

Zachary almost shouted his answer. "Hundreds! Hundreds, Canon Fernando! Soon those hundreds will be thousands. God is generous to his martyrs."

"Would he be as generous to me?"

They were nearing the gatehouse. Zachary reached out his hand and laid it on Fernando's arm. They stopped together. The question stunned the two friars.

"You, Canon Fernando?" Zachary whispered. "You want to be a martyr?"

"I want souls, Friar Zachary—hundreds, thousands of souls." He had evaded the friar's question, but there was no need to answer that. "If God will give me those, what price could He ask that would be too great?"

Zachary's lips formed words he could not speak.

Fernando smiled. "Did you wonder, Friar Zachary, why I asked you to come with me and bring Friar Michael? I did that because I want to make a bargain with you.

"Your group—Friar Otho told me you have few priests. From his manner, I know the Friars Minor need priests. There is one priest you can have, Friar Zachary, if you will enter into a bargain."

The implied promise of his words and tone restored the friar. Zachary regained again his manner of peace and serenity. "You will agree to become a Friar Minor?" Delight tinged his words.

"Gladly, my brother, would I become a friar if you will agree to my bargain. Assure me that immediately after I become a member of your order, you will send me to preach to the Saracens."

Friar Zachary turned from Fernando to Michael. For moments the younger man returned his gaze soberly and without expression.

"Canon Fernando is required to preach throughout Lent in the Cathedral."

Zachary nodded agreement. "Your bargain is extreme, Canon Fernando. Only if your desire remains constant could I agree."

Fernando smiled the more as he considered the answer. "You wish to test the spirit; is that it, Friar Zachary—test the spirit to see if it is of God?"

5

SEVERAL weeks passed, and Fernando became conscious that his desire had weakened. For a time, he attributed the decline to the unexpected reluctance of Zachary and Michael to accept him; but as Lent progressed, the memory of the burned village of San Bruno returned more frequently, and the truth of his weakening desire refused to be denied: He no longer desired martyrdom; he was afraid.

Once recognized, fear insinuated itself more rapidly to claim him. It retreated readily before deliberate revival of his courage only to reappear immediately when he relaxed his efforts to repel it. Panic followed fear as his efforts to revive courage became more feeble. He must act, must announce his intention, must establish his course by the finality of action, or admit his cowardice and forego his purpose. Each day, each week, each month would turn him farther from the dream. He began to sense that life is a complex web men weave about themselves until they can no longer escape the pattern of their weaving. Those who weave well rest securely and peacefully in the fortress of their habits; those who weave badly thrash about vainly, only to ensnare themselves more securely in their evil.

He found Ruggiero in the outer garden. The big squire straightened from his work expectantly. "I want to tell you something confidentially," Fernando said.

They walked halfway to the gatehouse and sat on a bench. "I'm going to transfer to the Friars Minor, Ruggiero." Fernando watched Ruggiero's face so that he might see the reaction.

Ruggiero leaned forward, supporting his arms on his knees. He looked straight from them toward the open fields that bordered the garden and disappeared beyond a hill. His face was serious, and there was a trace of sadness. "I have expected something like this, Fernando. You've been unhappy for weeks."

Fernando felt as though something heavy had lifted from him. There was relief in the mere statement of his intentions after the weeks of indecision. There was relief, too, that Ruggiero had accepted his statement as he had. Ruggiero did not seek explanations, did not judge and condemn. Loyalty overshadowed curiosity; Ruggiero could be loyal even when he did not understand.

"People listen to me, Ruggiero, but they can find too many excuses to escape me. If I live my sermon, if I preach by example, they cannot excuse themselves or escape. A Friar Minor preaches in a way that all can understand."

"It's a life much different from the one you live here, Fernando."

Fernando thought of his bargain with Zachary. He would not tell of that. A different life it would be; Ruggiero did not know the full truth of his words. "This is a life much different from the one I lived before." He smiled. That much Ruggiero would understand.

Ruggiero smiled with him. "There has been one bit from the past that has been the same, Fernando. I have been with you. That bit will continue. If you transfer to the friars, I will go with you."

Fernando's smile faded. Ruggiero would go with him? That could not be; that must not be. Ruggiero did not know the sermon he was prepared to live nor the destiny he planned. He shook his head. "You must stay here," he said firmly.

Ruggiero twisted his big body on the bench. "You would go without me, Fernando?"

Fernando was uncomfortable. "This requires a different type of vocation, Ruggiero. Becoming a friar is not like becoming a canon or a brother of the Order of St. Augustine. God offers different vocations to different people. You have a vocation to be a brother here at Holy Cross."

Ruggiero's smile returned. "I'll tell you a secret, Fernando. The only vocation I ever had was to be a knight;that's why I was squired to your father."

"You had a vocation to be a brother. You must have had that, Ruggiero, or you wouldn't be here."

Ruggiero shook his head patiently. "You know more than I do about most things, Fernando, but not about this. Do you remember when you first saw me at San Vicente? I told you then that your father said I would be a better squire to you than to him. I didn't enter there because I wanted to be a brother. I went there because your father said I should. He knew that I was not happy at Castle de Bulhom after you left. Then I learned that life as a brother was a good life—better than life in the world. Maybe God gave me a vocation to remain—I wouldn't know. When you moved to Holy Cross, I told Prior Gonzalez he must send me also. If you move again, I'll move with you."

Fernando was helpless. Ruggiero's story was incredibly wrong, but no one could convince him of its wrongness. Ruggiero's attitude complicated his own problem, but it would be futile to challenge it now. He must seek time later for a solution.

The announcement to Ruggiero accomplished his purpose. Fernando knew that his fear did not diminish, but it could no longer turn him from his dream. Having admitted to Zachary and Michael his purpose of martyrdom and announced to Ruggiero his intention of leaving Holy Cross, shame would compel him to push forward.

Interest in his work languished. As Lent drew to a close, he knew that the fire had died from the words he preached. He hid the coldness, born of fear, behind the brilliance of technical perfection. That was sufficient. His words needed no warmth; they needed only to reflect the burning intensity of Berard. The fire of that heart surmounted the coldness of the preacher's words and struck fire in the hearts of others.

The necessity for delay ended with Lent. He had discharged the obligation Friar Michael had used against him; he had waited seven weeks to convince Friar Zachary. Immediately after breakfast on Easter Monday, Fernando went to Prior Vincent.

Prior Vincent had pulled a bench into the sunlight in the center of the room. "You appear to be recovering from your labors, Fernando," he said as he rose to greet him.

Fernando grasped the opportunity offered by the Prior's words. "My labors were not so strenuous that any recovery is necessary, Reverend Prior." He smiled. "A struggle inside myself was more tiring."

Prior Vincent's sharp eyes examined him briefly. "The war of the spirit," he murmured. "It can be exhausting; and your labors would intensify it." He pointed to the side of the room. "Bring one of those benches. We can enjoy this warm sun while we talk."

While he pulled a bench into place, Fernando groped for words that would turn the conversation again to his purpose.

"The Bishop did not expect such crowds," the Prior continued. "He hoped they would diminish. Then at the end of the fourth week, he thought of having someone relieve you, but the people were responding so well that he was afraid to interfere." Prior Vincent laughed. "During the last two weeks, Bishop Terello did not hear a word you preached."

Fernando looked questioningly at the Prior.

"While you preached, the Bishop prayed. He could see that you were becoming thinner, and he wondered where you found the power for your voice."

"My voice and the physical exertion did not trouble me, Reverend Prior. They were minor problems. Something more serious has occupied my attention. I have had it in mind for months. It began to form last summer, but it was during this past Lent that it grew sufficiently that it became important."

Prior Vincent watched every movement of Fernando's lips and every change of expression. "That was the internal struggle you mentioned?"

Fernando saw in his mind the outline of what he must say. "Master Matthew once asked me what I intended to do with my life. It is the answer to his question that has become clear to me. Not that I devised the entire answer myself. Other men were an example to me. Now I know what I want to do."

He paused, but Prior Vincent did not comment nor question.

"You may dislike what I have decided, Reverend Prior," he cautioned.

"I will know that, Fernando, when I know what you have in mind."

Fernando hesitated to arrange his thoughts. "The work I will do as a canon has become quite clear. I will be a preacher because God has given me a talent to be a preacher. But I have come to know that words alone are not sufficient to bring people to God. If I spend all of my life preaching brilliantly, I shall accomplish less than one man in the world who never preaches but who so lives his life that he is an example to others."

Prior Vincent penetrated beyond the words. His discovery was apparent in the surprise of voice and expression. "Fernando, you are outlining a manner of life somewhat like that of the friars." There was in his voice a trace of pleading that was alien to the Prior, an intimation that Fernando should deny his statement.

Fernando pressed forward to complete what was becoming repugnant to the Prior. "I am speaking entirely of the friar's manner of life, Reverend Prior. I said that I know now what I want to do with my life; it is to live a greater example than I have and than I can as a canon of Holy Cross. Only the friars live the example I want to live."

Prior Vincent recovered from his initial surprise. He sat quietly looking past Fernando to the window and the sky beyond it. "Did you discuss your thoughts with anyone else, Fernando, before arriving at this decision?"

Fernando faltered. "I didn't discuss it with anyone," he admitted. "I did tell Friar Zachary and Michael my intentions in order to obtain their agreement. I told Ruggiero, too, Reverend Prior." The memory of Ruggiero's reaction strengthened him. "Ruggiero wants to go with me," he added.

"Brother Ruggiero, too!" Prior Vincent said.

Fernando felt the implied accusation that he was not only engaging in a reckless venture himself but was leading another into danger with him. "I told him he shouldn't, Reverend Prior," he admitted weakly.

Prior Vincent ignored his admission. "You have given a full outline of your thoughts, Fernando. I will not question them. Perhaps you believe them as much as you indicate. Are you satisfied that you have expressed your entire reason? Is there a possibility that you want to change to the friars, not entirely because of the reason you have expressed, but because you do not like the duties given you at Holy Cross?"

Fernando shook his head quickly. "I've asked myself that question, Reverend Prior. I did not care to become guestmaster—you know that. But I am not leaving because I dislike that duty. I am leaving Holy Cross only because of the reasons I have explained to you."

Prior Vincent nodded as though satisfied. He sat silently, considering. "You will not leave today nor tomorrow, Fernando."

Fernando looked curiously at the Prior. The Prior had not asked a question. He had stated definitely that he would not leave.

"Are you aware, Fernando, that you cannot leave Holy Cross unless and until every member of the community agrees to your release?"

Fernando considered the Prior's question. The words stirred something in his memory. It had been long ago that he had heard that. It must have been at the time he came to Holy Cross from San Vicente and he had no reason to remember it at that time. "I had forgotten."

"Now that you remember, do you think they will agree?"

Fernando did not attempt to answer. He sat disconsolately waiting for the Prior to speak. He no longer held the initiative. Prior Vincent had seized it.

"I know they will not, Fernando. I could give you many reasons why I am sure they will not, but I will mention no more than one. They love you, Fernando. You are one man in Holy Cross that everyone loves. You have been an example to us because of the life you left. You seem to consider that of minor importance now. It is not to us. None of us gave up as much wealth or comfort or position or future as you did, and when we are inclined to mourn about our sacrifices, you are a living inspiration to us.

"That is one item, Fernando. There are others. You are already advanced in devotion—I might almost say sanctity. The community is conscious of that. They look to you as an example in that also. Men become discouraged in the spiritual life. Here at Holy Cross, you are an inspiration. The only way I can express their attitude in these things is by saying that the community loves you, Fernando. Because they love you, they will not be willing to release you."

Fernando was silent. He could say nothing to contradict the Prior—though it was unseemly that the community would become so attached to him. He could not say that.

"I will announce this in chapter, Fernando, if you are determined on your course. I will first tell you, however, that I will not release you for at least three months. I want to be satisfied that you are not acting impulsively or hastily. And I will not announce this in chapter until you discuss it with Master Matthew."

"He will oppose it, Reverend Prior."

Prior Vincent did not answer him. "I think, Fernando, you should also tell Stephen before I summon the chapter."

Fernando considered that his announcement had become a beginning rather than the end of trouble. He had expected that he would be exhilarated and joyful when he left the Prior, that now he would be free at last to pursue his own desire. Instead, he was dejected—it was almost a despondency, he acknowledged. Months of internal strife had ended only in a new conflict.

After dinner, he caught Matthew's arm as they left the refectory. "Are you free for a time?"

Matthew smiled. "Until lecture time, Fernando." He pointed toward the door that opened on the outer garden. "Shall we walk as we talk?"

The garden would be the better place. They would not face each other. It would be easier to talk where he would not see Matthew's reaction to his words and could conceal his own expression. Fernando was silent while they walked away from the building. He could dispense with a long introduction, he decided; but he did not want others to hear the announcement. He looked around to be sure that others were not near. "I am going to transfer to the Friars Minor, Matthew." He held his face forward. He knew that Matthew would look at him as quickly as the words were spoken.

"That would be a serious mistake, Fernando."

He had expected Matthew to oppose him. Fernando wondered whether he should attempt to justify his intention or whether the attempt would intensify opposition.

"You have excellent reasons, I have no doubt, Fernando. I won't ask what they are. They are not important. They are nothing more than excuses to justify what you want to do. How long have you desired this?"

"Since last summer."

"Did you discuss it with anyone?"

Fernando shook his head patiently. This was the same question Prior Vincent had asked. "I knew what others would say."

"That is the first and greatest reason against it, Fernando." Matthew's voice changed from sharp observation to intense persuasiveness. "Surely you value counsel. We can make terrible blunders, terrible blunders," Matthew emphasized, "when we depend entirely on our own judgment. And the first sign of weakness in any spiritual decision is refusal to ask the advice of another because we know, or think we know, he will disagree."

"We cannot let others make decisions for us, Matthew."

"Isn't there a difference, Fernando, between advice and decision? No one can make a decision for you, but you can make a better decision when you have the advice or the comments and reactions of others."

They had walked toward the gatehouse. They turned onto a path that circled through the garden and turned gently back to the building.

Fernando shook his head firmly. "I knew no one would agree. I would only become involved in arguments. Suppose I had asked advice of people in the world before I entered the service of the Church. What would their advice have been?" He waited, but Matthew's silence was sufficient proof that he had advanced a conclusive rebuttal. Let Matthew reflect whether there would ever have been a Canon Fernando if the son of Don Martinho had sought the advice of others! They walked a considerable distance, and Matthew did not speak; determinedly, Fernando persisted also in silence.

When Matthew spoke again, he ignored Fernando's argument. "The second reason against what you propose, Fernando, is that you have no vocation for that life; you lack the preparation that fits a man for that life."

"What preparation is that?"

"Physical preparation. That's a hard life, Fernando. I admire those two friars who are able to live it, but that is not sufficient reason to believe that I could live as they do. I couldn't do physical work as they must for their food. I couldn't sleep and live in the poor establishment they have. I can't do those things, Fernando, and you are not stronger than I."

Fernando was baffled. He could not answer Matthew unless he were prepared to speak the full secret of his heart. Living the life of a friar would not be difficult for him; he would have but a short time to live it. It was better, he decided, to let Matthew talk without opposing him.

Matthew talked until they neared the building. Either because of Fernando's silence or the presence of others, he also fell silent. They walked together into the building as far as the visitors' room. Matthew stopped as though to say something more, but Brother Gatekeeper came forward to summon Fernando to the gatehouse. Matthew walked away.

Stephen was the next obstacle. Fernando anticipated Stephen's reaction and his opposition. Stephen would regard his purpose as treason to Holy Cross and to the entire Order of Canons Regular. Stephen would object strenuously and violently. Because of the reaction he expected, Fernando waited until mid-afternoon when others of the community were in the lecture rooms or working at their assignments. He led Stephen to the visitors' room.

Stephen listened to the explanation only as long as necessary to understand Fernando's intention. His round face lost every indication of good humor as Fernando spoke. "I will not hear any more," he interrupted sharply. "Fernando, you are a priest and a great preacher. You cannot live the irregular life of those friars."

"You must hear my reasons for this change, Stephen."

"I will not! You want to waste yourself and your talents, and I will not hear any reasons for that. You were not intended to live in a mean hut or to beg your food. Have you thought how you will feel, Fernando de Bulhom, when you knock on someone's door and ask for the food they cannot eat? Or do you think that will make you a saint?"

Fernando did not answer. If Stephen would not hear more, he could not force him to listen. He had complied with the Prior's suggestion to tell Stephen; he could return to him now.

Prior Vincent did not seek refuge in delay. He summoned the community to the chapter room before supper. "I have summoned the community," he explained, "because two of our members, Canon Fernando and Brother Ruggiero, request that the community release them."

Prior Vincent had phrased his announcement bluntly and dramatically. A stunned silence followed the words. Then sound swelled through the room, sound that was both a cry and an expression of disbelief. Fernando turned his eyes to the floor. He felt the community staring at him.

"Canon Fernando"—the Prior's voice quieted the others—"has decided that he wishes to become a member of the Friars Minor. Brother Ruggiero wishes to accompany him."

An outraged cry broke from the community. Their first disappointment edged toward anger against the religious beggars who had first insinuated themselves into the affections of Queen Urraca and now had invaded Holy Cross. Prior Vincent made no effort to quiet them, nor did he reprimand them for the breach of discipline. He stood on the dais, allowing them to complain among themselves until curiosity turned their attention again to him.

"I have informed both men that, before they may leave Holy Cross, they must obtain the release of each individual member of the community. I have also told them that I will not agree to any release for them for at least three months."

*   *   *   *   *

A strange contest occupied Holy Cross through that summer of 1220 and even some weeks of the fall. It was a contest which one side could win by immobility—Holy Cross had but to hold firm and to refuse permission. On Fernando devolved the necessity for action that would persuade the community. Stubborn silence, avoidance of the subject, a fixed attitude of opposition was the community's weapon. They did not attack; Fernando's reputation and achievements had gained an esteem they would not put aside.

Fernando knew what he must do. He could not hope to overcome the opposition; he could do no more than pray that their stubbornness would diminish. In the beginning he avoided discussions; his visits to the chapel grew in number as they increased in duration. Not until there was evidence that their attitude was relaxing did he attempt to supplant their ideas with his own and win their agreement to release.

Prior Vincent's dictum, which had seemed excessively severe in the beginning, became an unexpected aid to the cause Fernando pleaded. "If the Prior considered three months sufficient, surely it should be sufficient for the others of the community," he argued.

A majority came slowly to agree with him. His determination sustained him. The three months stipulated by the Prior expired. Opposition dwindled. It was then Fernando began to think again of Ruggiero, and his determination flagged as he thought of him. Ruggiero should not go. Ruggiero should stay at Holy Cross.

Quickly he fixed his mind on his objective. He could not think of Ruggiero. That was a distraction inspired by fear. He could not risk that danger again. Then, too, Ruggiero had begun to join him in vigil in the chapel. Fernando wondered whether Ruggiero prayed because he himself had found a desire to join the friars or if he prayed only because of loyalty.

He avoided mentioning the matter again to Stephen, but as the number of opponents diminished, Stephen moved forward into greater prominence. What opposition remained grouped itself around Stephen. When Stephen surrendered, the others would surrender with him.

Early in September, Fernando made the first attempt to discuss his departure again with Stephen. Stephen waved his hands impatiently. "I will speak with you of anything but that, Fernando."

"Stephen," he pleaded, "you and a few with you are the only members of the community who refuse to release us. Surely, I should expect you to be more generous than the others." Stephen shook his head slowly and firmly.

"As long as conditions remain as they are, Stephen, the Prior cannot assign me to preach nor to any other work. You must know that. Of what value can I be if I cannot work?"

Stephen repeated silently his gesture of refusal.

In the weeks that followed, neither of them would change. Fernando was determined; Stephen countered his determination with stubbornness. "You will realize the folly of this, someday, Fernando."

Late in October their roles reversed. Fernando knelt in the chapel; another figure approached and knelt beside him as Ruggiero did so often. Fernando did not turn until a hand touched him. The other was Stephen. "Come outside," he whispered. Fernando saw the elation in his eyes. He followed him from the chapel.

"There is real news, Fernando," Stephen exclaimed in the passageway. "Prior Vincent has just told me that one of the men is returning from Paris. That means I will be able to go there soon."

Fernando smiled with him. It seemed impossible that anyone could be so elated at the opportunity of burying himself in books and study, but if Stephen yearned so much for that life, he could rejoice with him.

"I'm glad you are about to realize your dream, Stephen. Someday you will be a famous master."

Stephen smiled the more. "When you hear that, Fernando, you will have good reason to thank God."

Fernando discovered then a significance in this new development even greater to himself than to Stephen. His hand fastened suddenly on Stephen's arm. "Stephen, you cannot refuse me my request any longer." The words had rushed from him in the joyfulness of discovery. "You can be generous to me now that your prayer has been answered."

Stephen's smile changed to a frown. He turned his head away as though he would repeat again his refusal.

"Stephen," Fernando pleaded, "as soon as you leave

Holy Cross, I will no longer need your agreement. You can understand that. As soon as you go, I will be able to leave, because the others will agree to release me. Wouldn't you rather give me now what I ask?"

Stephen considered the plea doubtfully. He turned back to Fernando. "Why can you not become a saint here at Holy Cross, Fernando? Why must you go to those friars?"

Fernando could not answer. Stephen had led the way to a subject he did not want to discuss.

Stephen nodded his head slowly in agreement. "I will release you, Fernando, on one condition. My uncle wanted you to be a saint." The smile returned faintly to his face. "That is my condition, Fernando. You must be a saint. Go and become a saint."

Fernando laughed happily. "When you hear that, Stephen, then you, too, will have good reason to thank God."

6

FERNANDO felt conspicuous in the formless, gray robe of rough wool. He saw the people of Coimbra staring, saw the shock in their eyes at the sight of Canon Fernando in the robe of a friar, saw wonder as their eyes appraised the giant form of Ruggiero walking beside him, saw them look to Zachary and Michael as though to find explanation in those two.

He was happy; the elation of achievement filled him. "I will breach the walls of heaven," he exulted within himself. "There have been sieges of earth's cities and kingdoms. I will encircle and besiege the kingdom of heaven itself. I will burst my way through the walls of God's kingdom with the help of His grace."

When they had passed through the city, the road descended gently. Ruts and narrowness attested the unimportance of both the road itself and its destination. There was room for but one cart; two could pass only if one turned from the road into the olive orchards along the side. At the bottom of the hill was a small, unpretentious building almost hidden by the trees.

"St. Antony of the Olives," Zachary announced.

Fernando looked curiously at the tiny building they approached. He had not considered the kind of building these friars had received from Queen Urraca. Remembering the indignation of Holy Cross at news of the Queen's gift to the religious beggars, he felt like laughing.

It was a chapel. Some might call it a shrine, a tiny place by the road where travelers could interrupt their journey with prayer. He looked beyond the chapel for some other building, some house the friars might have received. He could see nothing but the trees clustered about the chapel.

"Where do you sleep?"

Zachary pushed open the door of the chapel. "In here." He pointed to a space on the stone floor. "Michael," he designated the space, then turned and pointed to another on the opposite side. "Zachary."

Fernando gauged the hardness of the floor. There was no evidence of sleeping pads or of straw. "Do you sleep on the hard floor?" There was more amazement than alarm in his voice.

Michael laughed softly. "When the weather is cold or there is much rain, then we use straw."

"But that is not the rule, Friar Fernando," Zachary added quickly. "You can use straw at any time if straw is available; and it is available to us because Her Majesty ordered that we may take what we need."

Fernando looked at the two who had led them here. They were not extraordinary, he decided. Michael was a little bigger than himself. Zachary was stronger, but he was older also, and the one offset the other. If they could do this, he could also.

Ruggiero had listened while the others talked. Alone he seemed to fill the tiny chapel. He had to bend to avoid the cross supports of the roof. He looked quickly at the bare interior. Disapproval radiated from him. "Where will we sleep?" he asked.

"In the stable," Zachary said with a laugh. He ushered them out through the doorway and led them around the building. Someone had attached a rude lean-to, some boards that sloped downward from the roof to shelter an area as large as the interior of the chapel. Two poles supported the edge of the roof. Beneath it was a great pile of straw. "Here you will sleep, Ruggiero. Here you have straw."

Ruggiero looked critically at his sleeping place. "Some animals live more comfortably," he grumbled.

A bell sounded in the distance, striking the Angelus. Other bells joined the first; the sounds blended as they came to them over the quiet country. Zachary turned to Fernando. "You are our priest," he reminded. Fernando recited the words of the prayer.

When the prayer ended and they returned to the front of the chapel, a serf was waiting to deliver food sent by his master. Friar Michael thanked the man, hurried into the building, and reappeared immediately with four bowls. Gravely Michael gave one to each. The incident proved to be the pattern for the days that followed. Men came regularly to St. Antony of the Olives with food for the group. Zachary and Michael accepted the presents gratefully, but their reluctance increased as the givers continued to come. The two senior friars wanted to work for their food; their patrons waived aside their objections and protests. "Friar Fernando is one of you," one donor answered. "His work and your work, Friar Zachary, is to preach. That will be work sufficient for all of you."

On the fourth day, the giver remained, sitting on the ground with them while they ate. Thomas, he said his name was. When they finished, he approached Fernando. "May I be one of you?"

Fernando looked at him without understanding. "One of us?" he repeated. Then he realized the import of Thomas' question. "Friar Zachary!" he called. He grasped the arm of Thomas and presented the youth to Zachary. "Thomas wishes to be one of us, Friar Zachary."

Zachary smiled his welcome to Thomas. "You are the first to follow him, Thomas. There will be many more."

"You should go into the city and preach," Fernando proposed. "Then more would come."

Zachary shook his head emphatically. "There will be more, Fernando—many more. I need not preach. You will draw them."

"You have not forgotten your promise, Friar Zachary?"

"But you need not hurry," Zachary protested. "You must stay at least a short time to help as these others come to us."

Fernando said firmly, "We have made a bargain, Friar Zachary. You and Michael agreed."

The necessity for demanding fulfillment of their agreement reminded Fernando also that he had not yet told Ruggiero his plan to go to Africa. He waited until night to tell him.

Ruggiero welcomed the news. "We can start immediately, Fernando." His eagerness reflected his impatience with the few duties he performed.

Ten more days passed before they could leave. Other candidates followed Thomas to St. Antony of the Olives, as Zachary had said they would. Fernando helped with them until the group acquired some measure of order. Some of the arrivals brought news that men were carrying the story through all of Portugal that Canon Fernando had abandoned Holy Cross and joined the Friars Minor to go to

Africa. "They say you are going to be a martyr," Ruggiero charged him.

"I will preach," Fernando said evasively.

"You can preach here in Coimbra," Ruggiero countered, "or anywhere you wish in Portugal."

"Ten days ago, Ruggiero, you were anxious to leave here. Now that we are about to leave, you are drawing back." The retort silenced but did not satisfy Ruggiero. Fernando hoped it would distract him and would serve to remind him that he was not happy with his duties at St. Antony of the Olives.

The information that the common people had perceived his purpose disturbed him more than it disturbed Ruggiero. Gossip had carried his name throughout Portugal; gossip would carry news of his purpose even more rapidly. If this gossip was carried to Bishop Terello, it was entirely possible that the Bishop would inquire and forbid departure from the diocese. Even if Bishop Terello did not interfere, there was danger that Queen Urraca would. He considered the possibility of being overtaken and arrested by knights of the royal house. On the following morning, after he had celebrated Mass and they had left the chapel, Fernando motioned to Zachary to fall behind the others. "We will leave today, Friar Zachary."

Zachary nodded dispiritedly. "I had hoped you would delay longer with us."

"I have already delayed too long, Friar Zachary. These last who came to us told us that people have already guessed why I am going to Africa. They have carried my name all over the country."

"They know your name because you are a great preacher, Fernando."

"They also know my father's name, Friar Zachary. That is the reason they talk about me now. That name has become a handicap. I must not be Fernando."

Zachary's face reflected his bewilderment.

"You know that even here, Friar Zachary, my name has interfered. Ever since I came here, people have sent food to us. We will not be friars if people will not permit us to work for our food—or to beg it from them. You and I must agree on a new name for me. It must be a name that only you, Ruggiero, and I will know. You must not allow others to learn it."

Zachary shook his head. "That is impossible. People will learn who you are despite your name. Prior Vincent— even the Bishop—will ask questions about you. What can I tell them?"

"They will not learn immediately. If they learn later, that is not important. A new name will hide my identity while Ruggiero and I travel through our own country."

Zachary considered momentarily. "It will do no harm. What name do you wish?"

"Antonio."

Zachary smiled with delight. "Antonio," he repeated. "You have chosen the name of our chapel."

Fernando did not contradict. Zachary's explanation was sufficient for any who inquired. But there had been another Antonio, another who had turned his back on wealth and honors, a man who had also sought martyrdom that he might be an example and inspiration to others. Antonio, Father of Western Monks—who had also sought martyrdom in Africa.

They progressed slowly toward the south. Those who hired them watched suspiciously as they began the work given them, marveled and rejoiced as the day progressed and they saw the work the big man accomplished with the small man's assistance, then watched them regretfully when they departed.

Ruggiero delighted in his new life. "I feel free again," he boasted. "I can break a horse to saddle, I can strike metal in a forge. I can work for those I like, I can refuse to work for those I do not like." Something in his manner disturbed Antonio. Ruggiero's exuberance had increased steadily since they had left the chapel at Olivares.

They entered Leiria at night and begged shelter of a parish priest. The priest looked at them doubtfully but opened the door to them. The inevitable questions followed, and they answered patiently, as they had learned to do.

"I am the priest, James," their host told them when they had satisfied his questions. "I probably would not have allowed you to enter here tonight, but my mind is filled now with Christmas. My people will criticize me for sharing their food with strangers, but I could not turn you away at this holy season."

"We will work for you and for our food," Ruggiero offered quickly.

The priest's smile was sad, Antonio noticed. There was sadness in every action of this priest, a sad resignation as though all of life was disappointing. His shoulders drooped forward, the cassock accentuated his sharp bones; his long, thin hands lay flat on the table, mute witnesses of hopelessness. "There is no work to be done for a parish priest."

"If you wish," Antonio volunteered, "I could help you in your parish. I am a priest also, James."

The priest's eyes widened with astonishment, and he glanced again at Antonio's rough robe. "You are a priest!"

Ruggiero leaned forward across the table. "Friar Antonio is also a preacher, James. Let him preach to your people. If you do that—if Friar Antonio preaches to them—they will like him—they will like both of us and will not criticize you for offering welcome to strangers."

The priest turned again to Antonio. "If you can preach, I will be grateful to you, Friar Antonio." His eyes glistened and he averted them. "The other, the one who was here before me, was removed because he adopted a heresy and taught it to the people. But the people loved him and have resented me. I cannot preach. I have not attempted to preach for months. I am discouraged. They have defeated me."

Few attended on the first night that Antonio preached. He looked down sadly on the few who gathered in the poor church; but he would preach no less eagerly to them, he determined, than he had to the thousands in the Cathedral. He watched carefully, saw their astonishment as he preached, saw their pleasure. On the second night, he saw that the number had increased. On the third and fourth nights, Antonio saw that the doors were held open by the press of the great number who had come. He rewarded them with the fullness of his talent.

James sang the Christmas Mass. His voice lifted in thanks to God for the miracle he had witnessed. In the church, the people crowded together, and some stood in the street beyond the doors.

In the room that was his house, James pleaded with them. "You must not leave; you must remain."

Antonio saw Ruggiero watching him; Ruggiero's expression told plainly his desire to remain. He weakened before the hopeful expectation; he had accomplished much in the week; he could accomplish more. Then he remembered that he had endured this temptation before. Slowly he shook his head. "We are appointed to Africa, James. We will stay with you this holy feast day, but tomorrow we must leave."

In the hour before dinner, Antonio went alone into the church. Father James's plea that they remain and Ruggiero's unspoken appeal had revived his fear. Never before had he felt the tremendous force of nature. Turn away, Antonio! Turn away from this path! The temptation swelled within him. He prayed.

James beckoned to him from the doorway leading from the church to the house. "It is dinnertime," he announced, "but I also have a message for you. One of my people has sent a horse and cart that I may take you to Lisbon."

Antonio felt the weakness assail him. Weeks would have elapsed before he and Ruggiero would have arrived in Lisbon in their manner of travel. The priest would deliver them there in three days.

Depression succeeded fear after they started. He concealed it for a time by joining the others in their gaiety, but he could not sustain the effort. Ruggiero and James enjoyed the journey; Antonio tired quickly, burrowed deeply into the straw bed of the cart, and withdrew from them.

Ruggiero called to him when they surmounted the last ridge. Antonio raised himself from the straw to look down on the city and, beyond the city, to the mountains. Fortress St. George gleamed brightly in the winter sunlight. His eyes lowered to the Cathedral, dark against the background of the mountain. Don Martinho and Dona Tereza were there. He forced his eyes downward to the gloomy, stone mass that was Castle de Bulhom. "It is too cold," he complained. He dropped back into the straw and gathered it around him.

James would have remained to help them. Antonio thanked him for the distance he had brought them, but they would find passage quicker if only two approached the masters along the river. They exchanged farewells: "May the Holy Virgin go with you." James turned the cart toward the center of the city.

They found passage. The master of the ship inspected the oddly matched pair before him in their strange garments. He shrugged his shoulders—the world moved through Lisbon. "You will be able to earn passage," he said to Ruggiero, then he looked contemptuously at the figure of Antonio. "Will you earn it for both of you?"

Antonio spoke quickly before Ruggiero could reply. "I am his helper," he motioned toward Ruggiero.

"Take up the lines," the master ordered.

Antonio drew in the lines wet from the river. The water was cold on his hands. He shivered. The straw of the cart had been warm. The heat of it was still in his body. The master called an order, and Ruggiero answered. Antonio followed him, but he could do no more than watch. Ruggiero leaned his weight against the ropes and pulled mightily, drawing them tight against the cargo. A cold wind blew on them, and Antonio moved toward the sheltered side of the ship.

They raised the sail together, and the ship turned sluggishly from the shore. The cold wind increased, and Antonio felt the shiver course again through his body. He huddled down in the shelter of the cargo.

Ruggiero joined him. "We have nothing more to do until we leave the river."

Antonio nodded. He did not raise his eyes. If he raised his eyes to Ruggiero, he would also see Lisbon. Ruggiero left him. Antonio slid his hands into the opposite sleeves and drew up his knees to hold the warmth in his body. Forgotten scenes rebuilt themselves before him; he discarded them. One scene he could not repulse—the scene of five men who knelt and bowed their heads willingly, even eagerly, before an emperor's sword. When the master bellowed again, he went forward unsteadily to the mast to set the sail with the others. The river was behind them. The ship turned slowly until the coast line lay to the left and the sea to the right. Little of the day remained.

For supper the master gave them each a portion of meat. Antonio was not hungry. He cut a small piece from the portion and gave the greater part to Ruggiero. "You can eat this." He tried to laugh a little to reassure Ruggiero. "I must do more work before I will be hungry." He crouched down again in his place against the cargo.

Stubbornly he fought the chills that shook him. Each morning he awakened exhausted; each day he watched the shore line moving past; each hour he crouched against the cargo when he could; each night he sank again into sleep that was not sleep. The ship held close to the land and turned at last toward the east. Fernando saw the great rock rising from the sea—the rock that marked the entrance to the inner sea and marked the approaching end of this voyage. Stubbornly he forced his body to its tasks. Stubbornly he refused to submit to sickness.

But sickness did possess him. On the third morning after passing the Great Rock, Ruggiero called him, but he arose with difficulty. Ruggiero saw his efforts and lifted him to his feet. "You are stiff," he laughed.

"I'm sick," Antonio admitted.

Ruggiero looked at him anxiously in the faint morning light. Antonio knew that the master came and looked at him. Sometimes he knew Ruggiero was near him. He knew little more. Someone carried him easily. When he was put down, something warmer and more comfortable than a boat deck was beneath him.

When he opened his eyes, it was as though he had been sleeping. His eyes traced the lines of rafters above him. He puzzled at them. This was some kind of building. He was no longer on the ship; he was on land. And he was warm with straw around him. He closed his eyes and slept again.

When he opened his eyes again Ruggiero was sitting by him. The big friar leaned toward him quickly with his finger to his lips. "Do not talk, Antonio!" Ruggiero left him but returned immediately.

Antonio saw the bowl in his hand and smiled weakly as though even the bowl were a friend. The great arm slid beneath him and raised him so that he could drink. He swallowed a hot liquid, then Ruggiero lowered him gently to the straw and he slept again.

"We were two days on the boat and seven more days here before you regained consciousness," Ruggiero told him later. "Two more weeks have passed since then, Antonio."

"Where are we, Ruggiero?" Antonio tried to point to the roof over him and the walls of the building, but his arm would not raise.

Ruggiero shrugged his shoulders. "I saw straw here, Antonio, so I carried you in here from the boat. No one has come since then. The building is abandoned."

"But where?" Antonio repeated.

Ruggiero smiled. "Ceuta, Antonio. Africa. We are in the port of Ceuta."

Antonio focused his eyes on the rafters above him. His dream had brought him this far. He had landed in Africa;

having landed, he could do nothing but lie here in this straw. He did not want to think why he had come. Later there would be time for that.

Two more weeks passed before he could rise from his straw. Ruggiero would not allow him to remain long away from that bed. Antonio protested but returned willingly. His legs would not support him. He noticed the thinness of his hands.

As he regained his strength, the depression returned. He had thought of that as the first indication of his illness. Now, as he recovered, it returned to press down upon him. When he recovered sufficient strength to walk outside the building, he sat in the warm sunlight to heal his body; but the sadness weighed heavily.

Ruggiero was in the room each morning when Antonio awakened. He left for a time after they ate but returned soon again. Each afternoon he left again to return with food a short time later.

Antonio did not know when he first noticed Ruggiero's short absences or the food he obtained so quickly and easily. He commented about the food, but always humorously, before he realized that it was of better quality and in greater quantity than they had received together for their work on the way from Coimbra to Leiria.

Ruggiero refused to divulge the source of this supply. "I will tell you when you are well." He laughed. "I am not stealing it, Antonio."

As Antonio's strength returned, he became interested in the new world that surrounded them. From the doorway, he could see Ceuta and the water that looked much like the sea itself. It was a great sea, he reminded himself, that lay between them and their homeland.

Ceuta was disappointingly small. He had thought to find the Emperor's port a city like Lisbon, but this was more like one of the fishing villages along the seacoast of Portugal. Rising above the mean, poor structures was one building, white and magnificent, but the rest were small and ugly. He pointed out the large building to Ruggiero. "Learn what that building is."

Ruggiero followed his direction casually. "I know already. That's the governor's palace."

When February ended, Antonio had regained his physical health. The depression and heaviness of heart remained, but be concealed it. Ruggiero examined him critically and agreed that he might walk short distances from their haven.

Antonio gauged the time of his first walk so that he would meet Ruggiero returning in the afternoon. He walked slowly along the road leading to the city. The fields that bordered the road were dotted with tiny marks of green where new plants pushed through the soil.

Antonio did not permit Ruggiero to evade his questions that afternoon. "You have brought meat—meat in good condition. You have oranges and melons. Not many people have food like this, and the kind of people who do are not inclined to give it to beggars. Now tell me where you get it."

Ruggiero turned Antonio to face toward Ceuta. "There," he pointed, "I get it at that big, white palace."

"But you told me that is the governor's palace, Ruggiero."

Ruggiero laughed. "The Governor and I are friends. The very first day that he saw me, he sent his captain of the guard to bring me to the palace."

Antonio looked doubtfully at Ruggiero.

"That's the truth, Antonio. There are few big men here,

and the Governor wants only big men in his bodyguard. He wants me to join the guard."

Antonio laughed.

Ruggiero did not share Antonio's amusement. "Why are you laughing?" he asked seriously.

The question increased Antonio's laughter. "I tried to imagine you, dressed in that robe, mixed in with all the shining armor in the guard."

When they arrived at the barn, Antonio lay down on his bed of straw while Ruggiero deposited his burden and began to prepare a fire in the chimney place. "How long will the Governor continue these presents, Ruggiero—or should I call them bribes?"

Ruggiero was blowing at some straw that had caught a spark from the flint. "Until you are well," he answered, and continued with his work.

Antonio frowned as he considered the answer. He raised himself until he sat facing Ruggiero. "Why is the Governor interested in my health?"

A small flame appeared among the twigs in the fireplace, but Ruggiero pretended to continue his attention to the fire. "Because I told him I would not answer until you have recovered."

"There is only one answer you can give, Ruggiero. You are a friar. You cannot join a governor's guard."

Ruggiero was silent. He was engrossed with the food and the fire, moving back and forth between the table and the fireplace.

Twice Antonio thought to ask other questions, but each time he suppressed the words. He lay back on the straw. He did not want to consider new problems. He had sufficient trouble. The depression deepened on him and engulfed him.

Now it became more than depression; it became in him a dread of something as yet unknown. The Mass! If only he could celebrate Mass, the trouble would end.

In the darkness of the night, the dread increased. A dull pain formed in his heart. He had no power to solve this conflict. Only God could help Ruggiero. God must help him.

Morning brought no relief. His dread did not diminish, nor did the pain in his heart. There was restraint in his manner toward Ruggiero; there was defensiveness in Ruggiero's attitude toward him.

Antonio asked the big friar if he could obtain some flour with which to make altar breads, and his companion agreed to try.

When Ruggiero left, Antonio walked outside the doorway and watched him striding along the road until the big figure disappeared. He felt the sun warming him and found a place where he could sit. Ruggiero had said he had no vocation to be a brother. "The only vocation I ever had was to be a knight," were his words. Antonio thought of their stay at the little chapel and of Ruggiero's impatience. He remembered Ruggiero's boast, "I feel free again," and his hopefulness that they might stay with the priest, James. Temptation had not overpowered Ruggiero here in Ceuta; he had been weakening over a long period.

Ruggiero brought the flour, and in the simple task of making hosts, they drew together again. Ruggiero waved his arm to indicate the whole interior of the barn. "It will not be like Holy Cross," he said and laughed.

7

WHENEVER he awakened during the night, Antonio consoled himself that the Mass would bring a solution to the troubles that depressed him. His hope endured through the Mass he celebrated and through breakfast; only when Ruggiero had gone did he admit defeat. He went out into the sunlight.

He felt none of the joy he had anticipated from the Mass; he felt only the heaviness in his heart. He could endure that—he had placed Ruggiero before himself in the Mass so that Ruggiero would receive God's help and grace. He had been generous, generous even to the exclusion of himself. He sensed something of smugness, a contentment in himself as though he had presented Ruggiero's need in a manner that denied any need for himself. He had felt that same smugness at the end of Mass when he had blessed Ruggiero. It was a smugness born of compassion and pity.

Antonio awakened fully in the sunlight. The force of self-accusation startled him. Pity! Pity was the province of almighty God! He struggled to recall that moment at the end of the Mass. It was as though he had placed himself beside God to pity Ruggiero instead of placing himself beside Ruggiero to beg God's blessing on them both.

His whole being was suddenly alarmed. His mind reached back into the past—how far must he reach to uncover the beginning? Where, when, had this course begun? He had thought often of Prince Pedro's steps to apostasy; had troubled himself about Ruggiero's steps that seemed turned in the same direction. How blind had he been to the course he himself had been following?

Ruggiero had not chosen to come here to Ceuta; he—Antonio—had led him here. Ruggiero had not chosen to leave the safety of Holy Cross; he—Antonio—had led him away. A new light shone in his mind. What had been the purpose of his preaching, and why had he enjoyed preaching? Because he loved God?—or because he had hoped to lift himself toward God on the souls who heard him? "Are you concerned about your spiritual progress because of your preaching or because of God?" Matthew had probed as though he saw a fault.

Memory's floodgates opened upon him. One by one, the incidents ranged before his mind. He had not consulted the others about his plans to become a friar; he had said that others would oppose him but the reason was clear in the new light of his mind. He had set his own mind and own desires above the advice and counsel of others.

The five who had come here before him had not come to be martyrs. They had come only to preach to these people; they had come only because Father Francis had sent them. Missionaries, they had called themselves, and had come to preach as missionaries. They had not taken to themselves the title of martyr. Only he, Antonio, had aspired to martyrdom, and only a man who was ambitious would aspire to such an exalted goal. "Charity is patient, is kind," St. Paul had written. "Charity does not envy, is not puffed up, is not ambitious, is not self-seeking." He knew that he was rushing toward a knowledge of himself and that some tremendous power was rising to distract him. It was a power that had concealed itself within his depths, hiding behind nobility of mind and nobility of thought and nobility of action. It was the power of pride!

His mind pushed past the barrier. He was Fernando, the boast of Holy Cross; he was Fernando, the forceful young man who preached so well; he was Fernando, who had brought his body to be destroyed—the Fernando who had given his possessions to the poor. Fernando had done all these. "If I speak with the tongues of angels," St. Paul had also written, "and if I should distribute all my goods to feed the poor, and if I should deliver my body to be burned, and have not charity . . ."

The words moved Antonio suddenly to his knees. The new knowledge of himself overwhelmed and overpowered him. A great sob burst from his heart, "Jesus Christ, Crucified, have mercy on me!"

He stood up weakly and went into the building. He must lie down; the new weight within him was insupportable. He must rest and regain strength.

Ruggiero returned. Antonio forced himself from the bed, forced himself to conceal his pain. They talked quietly as they ate, then Ruggiero was gone again. Antonio sank into the straw, satisfied that he had suppressed his thoughts until a more favorable time. The evening would be more appropriate.

That evening he began by saying to Ruggiero: "My sickness is more serious than I thought."

Ruggiero looked up anxiously from his food. "I thought you had nearly recovered."

"That was an illness of my body. I have recovered from that. I have a worse illness, Ruggiero, an illness in my soul."

Antonio had not known until then any difficulty of expressing his thoughts. What he knew was clear within himself—clear, not in his mind, but in his heart. He explained what he could, but that was little, and Ruggiero's expression showed that he did not care to understand.

"We cannot turn back, Antonio." Ruggiero's voice hardened as his words turned memory to the mean chapel at Olivares. "Go back to that wayside shrine?" he exclaimed. "We have had enough of that, Antonio. We are free of that now. We will stay free. Set up a group of your friars here, if you wish. We cannot go back."

"We will go back, Ruggiero." Antonio's voice matched the hardness of Ruggiero's.

Ruggiero's voice became harsh and contemptuous. "To what will we go back, Antonio or Fernando or whatever you please to call yourself? To the ridicule of all those who told you to stay at Holy Cross? To the humiliation of those who said you would be a martyr? Do you think that because you call yourself Antonio, they will not know that Fernando de Bulhom is a coward? You have led me into enough strange twistings and turnings, Antonio. You will not lead me into more!"

Antonio felt the pain swell in his chest. It would be easier to die beneath the Emir's sword than to face the past; but he could not retreat now. He knew the price of return, the sly laughs, the contempt of nobles and knights, even of freemen and serfs. Holy Cross and the friars, too, might join with the rest to humiliate him. That was the price of returning; the price he must pay if he were to return to the way of God. There could be no reluctance nor unwillingness. The price of God is total submission.

He leaned across the table. His voice lowered and

became the cold, confident voice of the commander. "Ruggiero, you said you came to San Vicente and to Holy Cross and even to the friars because my father sent you to be my squire. Did you mean what you said?"

Ruggiero breathed deeply to answer. He strained against the force of Antonio's question. Antonio waited. "I ask my release." Ruggiero spoke the formal request of a knight.

Antonio shook his head firmly in refusal. "I need your help to return. I will release you, if you wish, when we are in our own country—when we arrive at Olivares." Antonio knew he had won. He had forced Ruggiero to admit the bond of his service in his very request to be released. He had denied that release until they had returned to their own country as he was permitted to do.

Ruggiero stood up. "We will go when you give the command," he said savagely.

"Tomorrow," Antonio answered.

They found passage as easily as they had before. This master, Antonio decided, was less critical. The man seemed to have a casual good humor that accepted whatever befell him in life; he smiled as he admired the great mass of Ruggiero, but his smile was no different in warmth to Antonio. "Come aboard," he agreed. "She is not a big ship, and the cargo is light. Two men will be a full crew."

Antonio did not wait for the master's orders. He reached for the lines and brought them in wet from the sea. The water was cold, but he felt no shiver pass through his body as he had in the Tagus before Lisbon. Only the pain in his chest remained—he knew now that it was not a physical affliction.

Ruggiero did not speak. When they cleared the land and when they went forward together to raise the sail, Ruggiero continued his silence. He allowed Antonio to haul a lighter rope; Ruggiero himself handled the main rope. The master held the ship so that the wind could not fill the sail until they had made it fast.

The ship moved sluggishly. The sail filled, then hung limp as the wind gathered behind them and then failed. In the last hours of light, they could see Ceuta lingering in the distance. With darkness, the wind failed completely. Antonio lay on the deck listening to the water lapping softly at the side of the ship before he slept.

Near dawn, the master called them. "We must row back," he told them. "A storm will be on us soon."

Ruggiero rowed alone at one side. Antonio joined the master at the other oar. It was strenuous work; they did not seem to move, though there was nothing against which to measure. The stars disappeared. A gust of wind drove suddenly against the sail, and the ship lurched forward with the impact. "We will have some wind to help us now, Master." Antonio smiled into the darkness.

A steady wind rose, and the ship forged ahead. Antonio could feel the movement in the deck. The oar suddenly became heavier, and he realized that the master had left his place beside him. There was no need to row now, and he drew the great oar from the sea.

The wind increased. Antonio heard the master call in the darkness to lower the sail; the pitch of the master's voice indicated some danger. Antonio hurried to the mast, but Ruggiero was before him. The sail tumbled down at their feet. They gathered it together as well as they could in the darkness.

The wind sounded as it increased. Antonio wondered if they would be driven ashore. The boat rocked wildly as it rose and fell. They seemed to be moving at incredible speed with the sea. Antonio clung to the mast. "Ruggiero!" he called into the wind.

"I am here behind you."

Dull light of dawn marked the sky before them—they were rushing eastward directly toward the lighted portion of the sky. As the light increased, Antonio saw the water tumbling angrily, closing furiously against them, pouring onto the deck, tearing at the ship, then running before them. The ship was no longer bobbing and jerking. Antonio comforted himself for a moment that the sea was subsiding, then realized that he had mistaken heaviness for stability. Water was filling the ship, lengthening each roll, slowing each effort of recovery, dragging them deeper into the sea.

Antonio twisted his head. Ruggiero stood a pace behind him clinging to a stanchion. In the uncertain light, he saw that Ruggiero was sick and weak; his great body lurched drunkenly with the movements of the ship. Beyond, at the rudder, the master was almost indistinguishable against the blackness of the sky behind them.

The light grew slowly in the east. A great roar came from behind; the boat thrust wildly forward, then twisted suddenly across the wind. A scream of terror sounded above the storm, and Antonio swung his head around. Ruggiero still clung to his stanchion. Antonio could see no one at the stern. The rudder bar was turned sharply. He shuddered and lowered his head but raised it quickly again. He held tightly to the mast with his left arm and raised the other free to make the sign of the cross while he spoke the words of absolution.

Waves engulfed the ship. Fearfully, Antonio clung to the mast. He began to recite an act of contrition. The ship rose and staggered, then leaned farther and farther to the side. Soon he was in the water, flailing with his arms. His hand struck something and grasped it, holding himself above the surface. In the dim light, he saw Ruggiero's robe and caught at it frantically, drawing the big friar to his own support. Both of them held to the mast that had wrenched free of the ship.

Rain came to still the waters. Antonio's panic passed slowly. He saw Ruggiero's eyes clear; Antonio could see them focusing again as the sickness diminished. His own courage revived as the rain beat and leveled the sea. He saw their ship capsized but floating near them; when Ruggiero's strength returned, they would find some means to reach it. Day increased.

The rain ended abruptly. Over them spread a cloudless, blue sky; the sun appeared. Only to the east where the storm retreated was the sky obscured. "Thanks to God," Ruggiero moaned.

Long after, they pushed their way to the overturned ship. Water swirled across the hull, but they could lie upon it and rest. The sun climbed above them. Antonio felt exhausted, and the hurt had returned to his chest. He felt the water ripple about his face, but the gentle eddies held no threat, and he was not afraid of it. At times, he slept.

Ruggiero's shouts awakened him. Ruggiero was standing unsteadily on the rocking platform that was the hull of the ship, pointing and shouting, "A ship, Antonio! A ship!" Antonio stood up carefully. When he saw a ship, a long way from them, he forgot his caution and joined his own voice and movements to Ruggiero's. The ship turned toward them, but they shouted and waved until it was almost upon them.

A man reached toward him, and Antonio felt himself being dragged into the ship; he knew that another was pulling Ruggiero beside him. He knew little more except that the man helped him stumble across the deck. When he awoke, the sun was low on the water behind them. A stocky dark-skinned man at the rudder grinned at him cheerfully. It was the man who had lifted him into the ship. "We are grateful to you for saving us."

The stocky man shook his head sharply. "The good God saved you, Friar. He delayed us in port until that storm was past, so He saved us and He saved you."

Ruggiero joined them. He and the seaman were already friends, Antonio saw. He saw, too, that his status with Ruggiero had changed. Ruggiero spoke to him eagerly even though shyly; the night had rid him of his anger.

When darkness came, they sat together with their backs against the cargo. From their place, Antonio could see the man at the rudder, his figure outlined clearly in the moon-light. Stars filled the sky.

"God was good to me, Antonio."

Antonio did not answer. God had been good to him also.

"I realized last night," Ruggiero continued, "that I almost turned away from God in Ceuta. I realized that I have allowed myself to love the world all these years when I should have been loving God. I once told you that I had no vocation. I think now that I was pushing away God's offer of a vocation. I loved the things of knighthood, and I kept all those in my mind even during the years at San Vicente and at Holy Cross. God let me see that last night. And He saved me that I could show Him I no longer love those things."

Antonio smiled. He could share Ruggiero's happiness even though the pain in his heart suddenly increased like the stab of a great love. There were, in Ruggiero's words, the same thoughts that had been in his mind when he transferred from San Vicente to Holy Cross. There had not been question of his vocation—but he remembered how nearly he had surrendered to the allurement of his parents' home and the opinion of the world. He had thanked God then for inspiring him to demand transfer to Holy Cross as Ruggiero now thanked God for saving him from death.

There are two great steps to God, his heart told him. The first, when a man renounces the world and its pleasures as he had done at San Vicente; and there was this other step he struggled now to ascend, when a man relinquishes himself completely to God. This was the step that determined whether man's will or God's would prevail.

Again as at Ceuta the past returned to torment, to flame, to burn, to purge. He slid down until he lay full length on the deck and turned his back to Ruggiero. He suffered the full knowledge of his failings, the full knowledge of disappointment, the full knowledge of a man who knows God with the heart. Darkness protected him from Ruggiero and the others. He cried his anguish quietly in the night.

8

"YOU seem to know so little of our order, Friar Antonio."
Antonio smiled. "I was a friar only two weeks
when I went to Ceuta from Portugal. After we left Coimbra, we met no other friars until we arrived here in Sicily. I
have had no opportunity to learn more than the little I knew
when I became a friar."

The superior wagged his head in disapproval. "That
is why Pope Honorius has imposed a novitiate on all who
would become friars."

Antonio liked this superior, Giovanni. Giovanni was
not curious. He had asked nothing more when Antonio had
told him of their wanderings. Neither was Giovanni abrupt.
Not once had he indicated impatience or lack of interest.
Antonio thought he combined in one person the serenity of
Zachary and the decisiveness of Prior Vincent.

"A novitiate would have discouraged me," Antonio
objected. "I should not have asked admission if I had been
forced to wait a year before I went to Africa."

Giovanni agreed. "God has His own designs. He
allowed you to go to Africa, and there you learned something of His will. Then, when you would return to Portugal,
He sent you here to Sicily."

"Ruggiero and I must return to Portugal, Friar Giovanni.
Our superior is Zachary. We must return to him."

Giovanni nodded. "You are not troubled that I have assumed his duties temporarily?"

Antonio smiled. "You are the superior," he acknowledged. He pointed toward the water beyond the houses of Messina. "I would rather return to Portugal by land than by water—but I will do whatever you instruct," he added hastily.

Giovanni's eyes lighted with humor. "A seaman loves the sea, Antonio, and I suppose landsmen love the land. I will not tell you to return to Portugal by sea. Your superior, Zachary, may come to Assisi to attend the chapter. It will be better that you and Ruggiero go there with us and return from there to your own country. While you are here, I will teach you and Ruggiero what you should know of provincials and custodians and guardians, and whatever else a friar should know."

Friar Giovanni's words trained them to mingle with the others but did not prepare them against surprises at the great number of brothers on the road to Assisi. Each city contributed some number. When they arrived at Assisi, they found the great plain below the city crowded with brothers, clergy, nobles, and common people.

"They have come to see Father Francis," Giovanni explained. "He was away in Egypt, and we heard rumors that he was sick and other rumors that he was dead. These people and the brothers are happy that he has returned." Giovanni led his group confidently through the crowd to a grove of trees. "The Portiuncula," he announced.

Antonio strained to see the chapel of the Poverello. Ruggiero could look over the heads of the others and see without difficulty. Antonio saw astonishment in his expression, then delight. "Lift me, Ruggiero." Ruggiero lifted him, and he looked doubtfully and unbelievingly; then he also felt the astonishment and delight that had marked Ruggiero's expression. There was no explanation for the experience—the chapel was no larger than the one at Olivares, but there was about this little chapel of Francis an aura of peace.

The crowd pushed them slowly forward and into the tiny building. Antonio prayed for Pope Honorius. He remembered his parents and Ruggiero, Canon Joseph, Prior Gonzalez and Prior Vincent, Sir Thomas and Stephen. His mind recited names rapidly, and he tried to remember all for whom he should pray. Ruggiero tugged at his arm, and Antonio followed him reluctantly.

Outside the chapel, they waited for the others. They watched idly as friars came from the chapel in seemingly endless procession. They stood a long time before doubt stirred them. "They could not have been before us, Ruggiero." Ruggiero did not answer. They searched along the line of those pressing forward to the chapel. Faces looked at them curiously, but none called. The afternoon faded, and they admitted defeat: They had become separated from Giovanni and the others from Sicily.

Through the eight days of the chapter, in the short intervals when they had not to listen to sermons or to the Rule or attend devotions, they searched through the crowds. On Pentecost, when the chapter ended and the great plain below Assisi slowly emptied, they had found neither Giovanni with those of Sicily nor any from Portugal. Antonio and Ruggiero sat disconsolately, looking at all who passed. Clouds of dust hovered over the roads where friars were walking to their home communities.

One group yet remained, gathered near a grove of

trees. Antonio and Ruggiero approached hopefully until they recognized that these were provincials and custodians receiving assignments and instructions from General Elias.

A friar separated himself from the group. He walked with quick, energetic steps as a man of purpose and decision; his whole manner radiated a quickness of mind and will and body as he came toward them. "The chapter has ended," he announced brusquely. "Are you separated from your group?"

"We have no group," Antonio answered. "We are from Portugal, but circumstances brought us here, and we are not sure what we should do."

The stranger examined them swiftly. "I am Gratian," he told them, "Provincial of the Romagna. I will help you if you need help."

Antonio smiled. "We do need help, Father Gratian. We are subject to Friar Zachary in Portugal, but a storm placed us in Sicily. We came here with the friars of Messina, hopeful that we would find some of our own people. We have found none and lost even those we accompanied."

The Provincial smiled sympathetically. "You do need help." His smile broadened. "You are orphans." He looked approvingly at the great size of Ruggiero. "Are you brothers?"

"I am Ruggiero, a brother, Father Gratian. Friar Antonio is a priest."

Gratian was silent for a moment as though considering what help to offer them. "Do you consider it necessary that you return to Portugal?" he addressed Antonio. "That is a long distance from here—the end of the world."

"Nothing is necessary, Father Gratian, but the will

of God. We must return because we are subject to Friar Zachary."

"If the General releases you," Gratian persisted, "are you willing to come to the Romagna?"

Antonio did not hesitate. "That would be the will of God, Father Gratian."

PART III

1

THE fullness of the September moon lighted Monte Paolo and the country beneath. From the clearing that had become his place of prayer and repentance, Antonio could see all of the valley below, the river sweeping to the north, the town of Forli, unreal and illusory in the moonlight. Through many nights, he had measured the depths of the valley from the height of this mountain.

"You have traveled far," Father Gratian had told them. "I assign you, for a time, to the hermitage on Monte Paolo."

Antonio knew the value of these months. He had descended from the heights of self-esteem even as he had ascended the mountain of God. Knowledge of self had grown, had revealed him pitilessly to himself. That knowledge, begun as a lightning flash at Ceuta, had grown steadily during the months of retreat.

In the valley below, a light appeared—the tiny, squared light of an oil lamp framed by the window of some indistinct house. Other lights appeared, marking the end of the night. The first signs of dawn spread from the crest of Monte Paolo and reached across the sky. Antonio rose from the ground, stood for a moment to relieve cramped muscles and stiffened knees, then went down the path to rejoin the others.

He vested while Ruggiero and the barrel-chested Peter brought from the cave the planks that formed their altar, and Henry brought the cloth to cover it. None spoke. Peter grunted heavily as he worked, giving an impression of extreme labor, though he lifted the planks as easily as Ruggiero. Peter's gruntings seemed to compensate him for the silence he must respect. He grunted while he helped to erect the altar, became silent during the Mass, then resumed his gruntings as he and Ruggiero dismantled the altar and carried the planks back to the cave. Silence continued until the final word of Antonio's blessing of the bread that was their breakfast.

Immediately Peter began talking. Ruggiero and Henry joined him, but Peter's heavy voice rumbled louder than the others. "I will ask Father Gratian to assign me with brothers in a city; I want no more of this country life." His deep laugh followed. It was a voice fitted to the round, stocky figure of the man. "I was born to a big family, I was a soldier all of my life, I have lived always among crowds of people. There is no fate worse than this mountainside."

Antonio smiled at the conversation of the others but said little. Once Henry asked, "What assignment do you want, Friar Antonio?" but Antonio shook his head without answering. The others did not press the question; they were accustomed to his silence. Ruggiero alone looked at him as though he wanted to know what answer he would give.

When they had eaten, they started the descent to the valley. The trail was narrow and steep for a short distance. They followed one after another until they came to the wide path that sloped gently. Ruggiero waited until Antonio joined him, and they walked behind the other two.

"You did not answer Henry's question, Antonio. You must know what assignment to ask of Father Gratian."

Antonio shook his head. "I have no preference. An assignment is not important."

"Father Gratian will ask you."

"I will tell him what I have told you."

Ruggiero's long, casual strides carried him as quickly as the hurried paces of the others. "You cannot continue to hide in these mountains. You are a preacher . . ."

Antonio turned quickly to silence him. "You promised to say nothing of the past, Ruggiero. If God wants me to hide in these mountains, as you express it, what more could I ask than to do as He wills? And, if God wants me to preach, can anyone prevent His will? Leave such matters to God. We need concern ourselves only with coming to Forli and meeting Father Gratian because he has sent for us."

Ruggiero mumbled his dissatisfaction but said nothing more.

When they gained the road that skirted the base of the mountain, all four walked together. The road curved back and forth, clinging to the mountain; when it straightened from the mountain, Forli lay in the distance.

They had not to inquire the way to the church of San Mercuriale. The rough, gray mass of the church and the bell tower beside it bulked above houses and buildings. Approaching from the south, the four had only to pass through the gate of the city and continue forward to the square fronting the church.

Other friars were before them, gathered together at the steps of the church. Antonio recognized some who had been in the group Father Gratian had led from Assisi. Few seemed to know or remember him, though many remembered Ruggiero—the big friar was not easily forgotten. Father Gratian stood on the highest step of the church, calling his friars, one by one, to speak a few words to some and to engage in lengthy conversations with others. Once, Antonio saw him kneel to receive the blessing of a friar he had called, and Antonio knew that the friar who gave the blessing was a priest.

Antonio would have waited behind the others, but Peter pushed him forward. "You are a priest, Antonio; Father Gratian will speak first with you."

Father Gratian did call him individually from among the others. "Friar Antonio!" he called, and Antonio stepped quickly forward. Gratian knelt for his blessing. "God is good to bring us together again, Friar Antonio," he said.

"God was good to bring me before you at Assisi, Father Gratian."

Gratian considered him doubtfully. "I do not know what assignment to give you, Friar Antonio. I have many assignments for men like your big countryman"—Gratian nodded toward Ruggiero in the square—"but you are so slight. Can you preach?"

Antonio nodded without eagerness or reluctance. "I can preach, Father Gratian."

Gratian shook his head slowly. "You are so slender, Friar Antonio; I hesitate to ask permission for you to preach, and yet I should not return you to the hermitage—unless you wish yourself to return there," he added. There was a small measure of hope in his voice that this priest might settle the difficulty by his own choice.

"I will do whatever you wish, Father Gratian."

"I can do nothing today, Friar Antonio," Gratian

acknowledged slowly. "Tomorrow Bishop Albert will ordain some of the Friars Preachers and some of our brother friars. Remain here in Forli until then and pray that God will enlighten me that I may know your assignment."

Antonio went into the church as the others had and knelt while he waited for Ruggiero. His mind reflected doubtfully on his conversation with the Provincial. Perhaps he should have expressed himself more completely when Father Gratian asked if he could preach.

Ruggiero joined him. Antonio sensed displeasure in the manner that the other knelt and the manner of his walk when they arose to leave. "I am to be Father Gratian's messenger, Antonio—to Assisi or to Florence or wherever he wishes to send me from Bologna."

Antonio felt disappointment. He had not thought of the possibility, as they walked toward Forli, of their being separated, and the reality was painful. Ruggiero had come into the friars to be with him—but they had agreed that the past was gone and would be forgotten. They could not turn back.

There were other churches in Forli, and they visited all of them. In the late afternoon, they saw Friars Preachers walking also from church to church. There were few of them, and their white robes and scapulars distinguished them clearly. Antonio saw the respect and awe their brother friars accorded these learned preachers of Dominic's order. Late in the day, a large group of the preachers arrived in the square before the church.

Father Gratian was host to the assemblage. Antonio and Ruggiero went early next morning to the church, but they were required to remain at the back of the building. The sanctuary and front area was reserved to the Friars

Preachers, as befitted guests, and to the few Friars Minor who would be ordained. The same rule prevailed when the ceremony ended, and the company followed Bishop Albert and Father Gratian to a great building on the opposite side of the square.

The building they entered contained a single, immense room. "The Hall of the Podesta," someone said behind them. This, then, was the place where city officials met to rule Forli. Tables and benches filled the entire floor area. On the right, Antonio saw a platform with a small table and lectern where the chief of the Podesta might preside or a speaker could stand to address an audience.

The Bishop and Father Gratian had gone to the far end of the hall to the table designated for them and the friars ordained that morning. The rest of the company arranged themselves noisily in the great room; silence was not imposed on this festive gathering.

When they had eaten, their voices diminished gradually. Antonio saw them waiting expectantly for instructions from the Bishop or Father Gratian. He watched Gratian moving from one to another of some Friars Preachers. Antonio thought Gratian's expression betrayed increasing irritation as he spoke to them and each, in turn, seemed to disagree and explain something to the Provincial. Gratian returned to his table and spoke briefly to the Bishop. Antonio saw the prelate nod his head in agreement, and Father Gratian rapped on the table for silence.

Father Gratian thanked the Bishop, whose generosity had provided the dinner they had eaten. He spoke briefly of the young priests ordained that morning. "It is proper on such occasions as this," he continued, "that someone address us that our hearts and minds may be filled with good and godly thoughts. The friar who received that assignment yesterday pleads today that he had not sufficient time to prepare such an address." There was displeasure in Gratian's voice, and the room stirred uneasily.

"Is someone here present prepared to speak thoughts of God?" Gratian's manner clearly indicated that he had not addressed the appeal to those of his own order; he looked back and forth among the white-robed friars seeking a volunteer. None could misunderstand his gesture. It was a Friar Preacher who had failed to fulfill his assignment; Gratian looked for another from that order. A low murmur of voices filled the room. None volunteered. None dared in the presence of the Bishop and this group of friends and strangers.

"Yesterday," Gratian resumed, "a Friar Minor told me that he would do whatever I wished him to do." The Provincial paused.

Antonio started as the Provincial's words recalled to him his own promise of submission.

"Friar Antonio!" Gratian called. His eyes searched among his friars at the back of the room. Antonio arose from his bench at the table and stood to hear Father Gratian's instructions.

"Friar Antonio," Gratian said, "it is my wish that you speak to us whatever words the Holy Spirit inspires within you."

Again a murmur of voices, a sympathetic murmur swept through the room. Antonio knew what their sympathy indicated. All would dread such a summons to speak in the presence of the Bishop. Lack of warning, lack of preparation would multiply that dread.

Antonio turned to push his bench aside. His eyes fell on Ruggiero.

"I said nothing, Antonio," Ruggiero protested quickly.

Antonio smiled and put his hand on Ruggiero's shoulder as though to steady himself as he turned. He moved slowly between the lanes of men and benches toward the platform. Even in that distance his mind might formulate a theme and outline. When he stepped onto the platform, his mind had discovered neither.

He stood quietly before them. Resignation prevented the storm of panic that should have filled him. It was fitting, indeed, that he who had so loved to preach to men should now be humiliated by that same device. Peace filled his heart, peace was in his mind.

Theme and outline rose suddenly and together. "Christ became obedient unto death," his tongue recited slowly, "even to the death of the cross." A slight stir throughout the room, the thin sound of men relaxing answered him. They accepted those first words as assurance that he would speak fully to them.

Antonio bowed slightly. "My Lord Bishop!" he said, and Bishop Albert bowed his head in acknowledgment. "Father Gratian!" The Provincial's eyes seemed to widen slightly. "My brothers in Christ!" he said to the remainder.

Antonio forgot, from that moment, those who were before him; he was unconscious of time and of himself. He had not here the artistry that had swayed the crowds in Coimbra or enraptured James's parish in Leiria. He was not aware that he clasped his hands and cried out thanks to Christ for that obedience on which the whole redemption rested.

Gradually the pictures faded from his mind, his heart emptied, his tongue slowed and softened. He became aware again of Forli and the friars, of Bishop Albert and Father

Gratian, of men and earth and time. He bowed again to the Bishop and turned away from the platform. Bishop Albert seemed not to see his gesture of respect. None seemed aware that he was moving to his place. The silence of contemplation enthralled the room. Antonio heard his own footsteps sounding on the boards beneath him.

His ear was not alert to signs of their approval. He cared not that he had spoken well or ill. "Speak to us whatever words the Holy Spirit inspires within you," had been the command. He had fulfilled it. He felt a great peace.

Bishop Albert spoke the final prayer. Father Gratian joined him; others formed in procession behind them as they moved toward the door. As they neared his table, Antonio saw the Bishop walk toward him. Antonio knelt quickly to kiss the ring extended to him.

"The Holy Spirit speaks well with your tongue, Friar Antonio," Bishop Albert said loudly, and the words sounded throughout the room.

It was the signal they had awaited. His compliment dispelled the reverence Antonio's sermon had imposed on them. They cried out their own compliment, even more their thanks, in a steady roar of cheering. Father Gratian had followed Bishop Albert to Antonio's place. The gladness of a happy discovery radiated from him. On the one cheek and then on the other, the Provincial implanted on his friar the kiss of peace that was also the kiss of affection and respect, the kiss of a father and a brother.

Others crowded around when the Bishop and Father Gratian moved from him. He heard Peter's heavy voice; he knew that Peter remained possessively beside him as Stephen had done the night he had preached for the first time in the chapel of Holy Cross.

After a time, he was able to look for Ruggiero. The big squire had drawn away as the others crowded toward him. His wide smile proclaimed his pride and happiness. A friar summoned both of them that afternoon to Father Gratian. The friar led them around the side of San Mercuriale, past the front of the Bishop's residence, and into a passageway beside the residence. He rapped sharply on a door, then stepped back. "Go in," he told them. "Father Gratian is waiting."

Father Gratian still retained his manner of surprised delight. His smile was a mixture of admiration, pleasure, and confusion. There was in his smile, also, the pleasure of a religious superior who has suddenly and unexpectedly encountered virtue in one of his subjects. "You astonished me, Friar Antonio," he said by way of greeting. He glanced at Ruggiero. "I think you astonished me with your sermon more than Friar Ruggiero's size astonished me at Assisi."

Antonio smiled faintly. He felt like a small boy who had been discovered in some good action that had brought the praise of an elder. He wished that Ruggiero would put an end to the smile of pride that had been a part of him since the morning.

Father Gratian gestured to the benches. "I must know something about you, Friar Antonio. Bishop Albert asked me about you, after you preached, and I was embarrassed that I could tell him only that you were a priest from Portugal. I must also write something about you to Father Francis that he will give his permission for you to preach to the faithful."

Antonio felt himself tense uneasily. He could tell readily of his education at San Vicente and Holy Cross, of his success as a preacher—even his presumptuous ambition

for martyrdom; but he guarded carefully against revealing Ruggiero's trial and weakness at Ceuta. He felt relief
that Gratian seemed interested principally in his preaching.
Even before he finished, the Provincial drew paper from a
pocket, smoothed it on the bench beside himself, and wrote
quickly. When he finished, he offered the paper to Antonio.

> Father Francis, Greetings in the peace of Our Lord,
> Jesus Christ. Among the friars of this Province, I
> have found a priest, Antonio, trained among the
> Canons Regular of Saint Augustine, who preaches
> as one inspired by the Holy Spirit both in word
> and thought. I ask permission to appoint him as
> preacher in the Province of Romagna. While await-
> ing your permission, Lord Bishop Albert, who has
> heard Friar Antonio preach, has appointed him to
> preach within his diocese.
>
> Gratian

While they awaited the return of Ruggiero, Antonio
preached each night in one of the churches of Bishop
Albert's city. Each day, he knelt long in San Mercuriale to
declare his love, to consider God's love for him. He knew a
great change had occurred in him; he knew the change was
not yet concluded. It was as though he was at some mid-
point of a journey.

Ruggiero appeared quietly beside him in the church late
one afternoon to summon him again to Father Gratian. The
big squire did not volunteer information about the answer
he had brought from Assisi; Antonio had no curiosity to
know it.

Father Gratian's face clearly revealed disappointment.
"Father Francis is more generous than I asked—more

generous than I want," he complained. He offered a paper to Antonio.

> Greetings to my brother in Christ. Having considered your words regarding the priest, Antonio, and the action of Lord Bishop Albert, I wish you to appoint him to preach throughout Italy.
>
> Francis

It was a puzzling message. Antonio looked up at Father Gratian as he returned the paper to him.

"Do you understand the meaning of this, Friar Antonio?"

Antonio shook his head. "It is permission to preach, but Father Francis extended his permission to preach in all of Italy."

"So few can preach, Friar Antonio! We have many friars; but some have not the talent, some have not the learning to preach. Now, Francis has released you from my province and has appointed you to preach wherever you will in the whole country." The Provincial endeavored to conceal his disappointment. "There are sections of this province where heretics have led many of the people from the true Church. Their leaders are wicked and deceitful. I had hoped to send you into those sections to tell people the truth and love of God."

Antonio heard the disappointment in the Provincial's voice. He heard also the love of the man for his people. "I will go wherever you wish, Father Gratian." He smiled lightly. "Father Francis said all of Italy; the Romagna is part of Italy."

Gratian's expression brightened. "I had hoped you would say that, Friar Antonio. Whatever heresy is found in Italy flows from this Province of Romagna. And all the heresy in the Romagna originates in Rimini. Start in Rimini, Friar Antonio." He arose from his bench as though to terminate the discussion. "You must have a companion," he remembered. His eyes measured the great size of Ruggiero. "Rimini is not friendly. Ruggiero, you will accompany Friar Antonio."

2

A freeman with a cart carried them through the last day of their journey. "Those people will not welcome you," he warned when he learned their destination. Neither Antonio nor Ruggiero were interested in the reception to be expected, and the driver said nothing more of Rimini until he stopped to let them climb down in the city. "All these are heretics," he whispered. "The few who are still faithful to God will not welcome you because they are afraid of the politicians who are pledged to the Emperor. The priests are hiding."

Antonio thanked him and nodded absently. The people he had seen entering the city had shown no hostility. None had seemed friendly, but he and Ruggiero had not come to test their friendliness; they had come to restore these people to friendship with God.

They slept that first night in a church. No sanctuary light relieved the darkness. The place was dark and cavernous—meaningless without the Presence of God. To Antonio, the darkness of the Church symbolized the darkness of mind of these heretics who denied that Our Lord was truly present in the Blessed Sacrament.

In the morning, Ruggiero found employment to provide food; together they found a stable owner who agreed that their presence each night in the stable would afford some protection against fire. Ruggiero laughed exultantly at the ease with which they had completed arrangements for the necessities of life. "These people are not bad," he told Antonio. Antonio shook his head wonderingly. Certainly these people were not revealing the hatred and enmity he had expected.

He began immediately the work he had been sent to accomplish. The central square of the city was obviously the best site for his sermons, and the southern end against the stones of the Palazzo dell' Arengo the best position from which to preach. Everyone in Rimini must enter the square at some time and be aware of his sermons; but the part of the square in front of the noble Arengo's was less noisy.

Six men formed the first morning audience; two women and an elderly man the afternoon group. Day after day, the number increased. Not all were completely attentive; some stood half turned from him as though dividing their interest between the sermon and the activity at the other end of the square in front of the Hall of the Podesta. Antonio watched the number of his listeners increase until more than a hundred stood regularly before him.

On an afternoon near the end of October, the group suddenly stirred, and the greater part walked briskly away while Antonio was preaching. Their abrupt departure was so startling and inexplicable that his words halted.

"Bononillo," a woman whispered to him.

The word was meaningless. Antonio looked at the woman for explanation.

"Bononillo, Friar Antonio," the woman repeated, then pointed to a figure standing motionless some distance away in the square. Antonio saw a man, no longer young, with a stocky, powerful body. "He is a leader of the heretics and chief of the Podesta, Friar Antonio," the woman added.

Antonio remembered that many who had stood to hear his sermons had remained half turned from him. The woman's words explained their peculiar manner—they had been alert to some danger. This Bononillo was the danger they had feared.

He could not continue. The incident had shaken him as it had startled and distracted his listeners. "Pray!" he said to the few who had remained. "Pray!" Then he dismissed them and returned to the stable to await Ruggiero.

In the days that followed, Ruggiero adopted the practice of appearing irregularly at Antonio's side, to stand for a short time, examine those who listened to Antonio, then return to his work. The appearance of the big friar beside the preacher served to increase the number who stopped to hear Antonio. Slowly and steadily, through November, the crowd grew. Bononillo did not reappear, but the half-turned position of many among the listeners was sufficient evidence that the man might come at any time.

At the very end of November, the crowd again suddenly stirred and most walked away. Antonio looked out into the square expectantly. Bononillo stood as he had before, looking at him and the few who remained. Antonio knew he had expected this as he must expect it to recur in the future.

"What has happened?"

Antonio had not noticed the approach of Ruggiero. He pointed to the stocky powerful figure turning away from them. "Bononillo," he explained simply.

Impulsively Ruggiero started toward the retreating enemy. The handful that had remained of the crowd fled as they realized the giant friar's purpose. Antonio ran after

Ruggiero and caught his arm to restrain him. "That will do no good, Ruggiero."

"He will stay away from here."

Antonio held firmly to Ruggiero's arm. "Nine plagues were leveled against Egypt, but the Pharaoh would not release the Israelites from bondage. God will act, Ruggiero, when and in whatever manner He decides."

Ruggiero looked down at him uncomprehendingly, but his body relaxed to indicate abandonment of his own purpose. "You can't continue this way, Antonio."

Each morning and afternoon, Antonio returned to the scene of the contest. News of the disturbances in the square had traveled through the city, adding another inducement for attention to the small preacher whose actions defied Bononillo. Antonio saw that the crowds increased more rapidly than they had after the earlier encounters. Before Christmas, the crowd was larger than it had been at any time previously.

Bononillo struck again the day before Christmas. Antonio watched the crowd scatter. Perhaps this scene must also be repeated nine times before Bononillo would be struck down by God and forced to release the people of Rimini from the bondage in which he held them. "Pray!" he told the few who remained.

After hearing of the third reversal Ruggiero said, "We will be here forever, Antonio, if this man is allowed to interfere as he has." He shook his head slowly and seriously. "I was hoping that Christmas would change these people and make them listen to you. If they haven't sufficient courage to oppose Bononillo now, they will not obtain it later."

Antonio heard the discouragement in Ruggiero's voice. The big friar's words undermined his own confidence.

A small doubt insinuated into his mind and would not be dislodged. Once before he had led Ruggiero almost to destruction. How long could he justifiably remain in Rimini?

They went together to the square on Christmas afternoon but the great open area was deserted. The Hall of the Podesta was closed as though even heretics could not ignore the Nativity of the God they pretended to ignore. At the other end, the Palazzo dell' Arengo was blank and silent, as were the buildings facing the square on either side. Aimlessly, Antonio and Ruggiero continued through the narrow and deserted streets to the gate of the city that faced the sea.

A park-like strip of earth lay between the wall of the city and the sea. Others were there—a few individuals who wandered aimlessly and parents who had brought their children to escape from the narrow streets and crowded homes. Antonio and Ruggiero approached the sea and turned to walk along the bluff above the water.

"Do you realize how long we have been here, Antonio?"

"Three months," Antonio acknowledged.

"How much longer shall we stay?"

Antonio delayed answering. He could not offer an exact length of time; he must not increase the other's discouragement and his own doubts by stating a definite length of time.

They had come to a grassy knoll where the bluff formed a point into the sea. The air moving gently from the water was cold, but the sun countered the coldness. Some parents talked and laughed loudly a short distance from the bluff. Children ran about, shouting as they played. Antonio and Ruggiero stopped and sat on the ground facing the sea.

"There must be an end to unproductive efforts," Ruggiero resumed.

Antonio folded his arms around his knees and closed his eyes. "God will make known His will if we do not allow discouragement to overwhelm us, Ruggiero."

Bitterness tinged Ruggiero's voice. "When does courage become foolhardiness?"

Antonio did not answer. He held his eyes closed. Under the spur of Ruggiero's bitter question, the doubt within himself grew larger. Courage could become foolhardiness. Our Lord had warned His own twelve against that straining which was pride and vainglory: "And whosoever shall not receive you, nor hear your words: going forth out of that house or city shake off the dust from your feet." He must not . . .

"Antonio!"

Antonio opened his eyes. Ruggiero leaned toward him. There was an amused smile on his face that held something also of wonder.

"Look, Antonio!" Ruggiero pointed to the sea around them. The surface of the water had been calm and smooth, undisturbed by the minor breeze. Now the area before them and on either side puddled and rippled. At each of the puddles, a fish lifted its mouth from the water then slid gently back beneath the surface. On every side, fish thrust through the surface, then quietly retreated.

Antonio stood and approached the edge of the bluff. Hundreds—thousands—of fish thrust their heads above the surface, but now they did not retreat. They seemed to wait. How quiet they were! How much their ordered ranks reminded him of people! People who had stood quietly before him to hear the word he preached. The resemblance fascinated him. His heart lifted within him. These fish were as people who had come reverently to hear the Word of God!

"Then hear the Word of God!" Antonio cried out joyfully. "O fishes of the sea and of the river, hear the Word of God these infidel heretics refuse to hear!"

Antonio looked down on them curiously. They did not fly and scatter as their nature would direct. They remained quiet and motionless before him. Antonio knew a great, overwhelming joy.

While he preached to the creatures in the water before him, Antonio heard sounds behind him. Whispers and murmurs carried to him. Patiently, joyfully, he continued to extol to the dumb creatures the mercies of their Creator. Let these people who had hardened themselves against their God witness the adoration even the fishes of the sea paid to Him. "Blessed be God Eternal," he cried out, "since the fishes of the waters give Him more honor than do the heretics!" He raised his hand in blessing over the water, then watched the fish disappear beneath the surface.

Fright was in the faces of those who had gathered behind him. He saw fright that approached terror in some, fright that might become stubborn, willful malice against God in the faces of others. The families who had been laughing and talking were silent; the few had become fifty—fifty who might open the path for the Word of God to all the people of Rimini, or who might place such obstacles on that path that none would ever surmount them.

"You have seen the wonder, the glory, the majesty of God," he said to them softly. "I will preach tomorrow in the square." He turned about quickly to face the sea, then knelt on the ground. When he stood again, the crowd had disappeared; only Ruggiero remained beside him.

A   childlike   smile   of   wonder   had   replaced

discouragement in Ruggiero. "What is the meaning . . . ?" he began uncertainly.

Antonio shook his head. He could not trust his new lightness of heart to his voice.

All of Rimini seemed crowded into the square when he stood before them. He waited in his accustomed place, resting against the great hewn stones that formed the wall of the Palazzo dell' Arengo. Ruggiero stood beside him. People who came first stayed some distance from the two, but the press of others drove them forward until hardly more than an arm's length separated them. Protests sounded from those farther back in the square. "We cannot see him, we will not be able to hear him."

"Climb up to this window, Wonder-Worker," a voice taunted from above.

Antonio turned and looked up. From an open window of the palace, a maidservant looked down on him. Antonio smiled. "I cannot climb, but some others might lift me there, if that is permitted." The maid vanished suddenly. In her place a massive head appeared. Antonio knew the man was the Duke Arengo.

"Lift him up," the Duke ordered. The Duke himself leaned down to help as Ruggiero lifted Antonio.

Antonio stood on the broad sill of the window and faced the square. A low murmur of satisfaction from those in the back of the square greeted him. "If the grass of the field," he began to preach, "which is today, and tomorrow is cast into the oven, God doth so clothe: how much more you, O ye of little faith?"

From his vantage point above them, Antonio saw the crowd stir. They had not expected this. Perhaps they had expected some reference to the fish who had heard his words so attentively. Perhaps they had expected him to attack their heresy and defend the true Presence of Our Lord in the Blessed Sacrament. Ignore their heresy, he had decided during the night. Men and women do not turn their back to the Church of Christ because they do not understand God's mysteries. Men and women turn from that Church only because they will not live the lives God demands of them. "Seek first the kingdom of God," Our Lord said; but these people sought first the comfort of their bodies, for sense pleasure, for fine food and drink, for wealth and riches. Only their own weaknesses stood between them and God. Their yearnings for wealth and pleasure turned them away from Him who would give them whatever they needed, if only they had faith.

"Ask, and it shall be given you: seek, and you shall find: knock, and it shall be opened to you. For everyone that asketh, receiveth: and he that seeketh, findeth: and to him that knocketh, it shall be opened. Or what man is there among you, of whom if his son shall ask bread, will he reach him a stone? Or if he shall ask him a fish, will he reach him a serpent? If you then being evil, know how to give good gifts to your children: how much more will your Father who is in heaven, give good things to them that ask him?"

The words that closed his sermon penetrated close to their hearts. Epiphany neared, and on that day that would take joy in the gifts they gave to their children—heresy would not stop them from that. Their minds were filled now with the thoughts of those presents, with love for their children and the love of their children for them. Well might they think of their own loving Father and the love they denied Him.

Antonio bent down and motioned for Ruggiero to help

him descend. Before the other could move, he heard the voice
of the Duke Arengo in the window behind him. "Come this
way." Antonio straightened and turned to enter the palace.

"A moment!" the cry came from the square.

Antonio faced about and looked among those below
him, trying to find the one who had called. Bononillo!

"You have avoided the question of your Eucharist," the
heretic challenged.

"I did not avoid the question of the Holy Eucharist,
my brother. There is no question pertaining to the Holy
Eucharist."

A ripple of laughter came from the crowd. They had
liked this young man who had told them of God's love.
Now they liked his wit that could turn a question against a
challenger.

"You claim to believe that God is present in your
Eucharist," Bononillo persisted.

"All who believe in God believe He is present in His
Blessed Sacrament."

"I believe in God . . ." the heretic began, but Antonio
interrupted him.

"You do not believe in God," Antonio shouted with all
the power of his voice. "You believe only in yourself. You
are your own god."

The square was hushed. Fear returned among the crowd
for the manner in which this young preacher accused a man
that he did not believe in God.

"Prove that He is present," the man shrilled. "Prove that
He is present, and I will believe."

Antonio looked carefully at the man. Some note in the
voice of this challenger exposed him. This was not a challenge that he cried; this was the cry of a man entrapped in

some manner and begging now to be released. Pride? Had this man so attacked the blessed Presence of Our Lord that pride would not now allow him to recant? This man did not want proof; he wanted an excuse to profess openly the belief that was smothered within him and which demanded admission.

"What proof do you want, my brother?" Antonio's voice was calm and sympathetic. He saw wonder among those in the square that he would treat this challenger with such kindness.

Bononillo hesitated. Another beside him spoke rapidly to him. Antonio waited. The challenger shook his head repeatedly in disagreement but submitted at length to his adviser. He raised his head again to Antonio. "The proof is this. I have a donkey. I will not feed that donkey today. Tomorrow I will bring him here and I will bring feed here also. You will bring the Eucharist. If my donkey will bow down and adore the Eucharist before eating the feed, I will believe."

A shocked murmur from the crowd greeted the boldness of the challenge. Heretics they might profess themselves to be, Antonio reflected, but they were not heretics in their hearts. He looked down on them, men and women who had permitted themselves to be persuaded or terrified. In one way or another, all had become entrapped as had Bononillo. "You have not challenged me; you have challenged God," he answered. "Tomorrow we will see if God will give you the grace to believe." Antonio turned and stepped through the window into the presence of the Duke.

"You are very kind, Your Highness."

"And you are a reckless young man," the Duke

answered angrily. "You have stirred up all the beasts in Rimini with that agreement. It has been difficult to be faithful to Holy Mother Church and remain in Rimini; after tomorrow, it will be impossible." The Duke drew his breath in noisily. "Because God sent fish to hear you preach, do you think He will perform miracles whenever you desire?"

"That would be presumptuous, Your Highness."

Duke Arengo seemed about to continue his tirade, but the unexpected agreement surprised him.

"Bononillo challenged God, Your Highness. If God chooses to grant faith to this man and to these people, have I the right to say that I will not be His instrument?"

Duke Arengo looked at him blankly. The thought seemed to penetrate slowly. "Instrument?" he repeated wonderingly. As though perceiving, at last, the import of Antonio's question, he walked to the door and opened it. "Summon Friar Antonio's companion," he said to a servant. "The friars will remain here tonight."

Antonio and Ruggiero slept little that night. The manservant who led them to their room showed them also the tiny chapel of Palazzo dell' Arengo. When the palace stilled, Antonio went through the darkened building and knelt in the chapel. Minutes later he heard the chapel door open softly. He turned. The flickering vigil lights were sufficient to identify Ruggiero.

The next day the crowd gathered early. The square and the streets beyond filled with an expectant, roistering mass. Antonio and Ruggiero watched from the window of their room. They waited until they saw Bononillo struggling through the crowd, then hurried to the chapel.

The Duke and two manservants attended the Mass

Antonio celebrated. The Duke's face was impassive, but the servants did not conceal their alarm at the trial of the morning. Occasionally as he read the Mass, Antonio heard shouts and cries from the crowd in the square. They did not distract him; this was between Bononillo and God, between Rimini and God.

Duke Arengo and his servants received Holy Communion. Antonio nodded to Ruggiero and followed him from the chapel. A shout greeted them as Ruggiero opened the door into the square. Then silence fell suddenly on the crowd as Antonio followed, holding before him the Host of the Blessed Sacrament. Bononillo, grasping the halter of the donkey, stood close to the doorway. A basket of feed was on the ground. Antonio stopped before the heretic, holding the Host high while Ruggiero knelt on the stones of the square beside the donkey. A hush that was part reverence, part awe, gripped the crowd. Antonio bent to place the Host on Ruggiero's tongue. Awkwardly, the donkey bent its forelegs and knelt beside Ruggiero. A startled gasp arose from those who could see. On the other side of the donkey, Bononillo dropped heavily to his knees. Antonio stepped back, then followed Ruggiero through the doorway of the palace to complete the Mass.

Antonio remained that day in the chapel of Palazzo dell' Arengo. At times, he was aware that the Duke or Ruggiero knelt beside him; at other times, he knew that he was alone. He was not conscious of time. One of the manservants interrupted him. "His Highness must speak to you, Friar Antonio."

Duke Arengo smiled as a victor. "The whole country around Rimini knows the wonders of the fish and of the donkey, Friar Antonio."

"What news of Bononillo, Your Highness?"

Duke Arengo laughed. "Bononillo left his donkey eating the feed before my door. He went—he ran—to confession." The Duke stopped abruptly and became serious. "I did not laugh that he ran to confession, Friar Antonio. I laughed because he knew where to find a priest, and I laughed because he left his donkey eating feed before the door of the Duke Arengo." The Duke's face brightened again. "Everyone in Rimini followed Bononillo. All of them claimed they hated Holy Mother Church and hated the priests." The Duke laughed. "But all of them knew where priests were hiding. They made the priests come to absolve them just as they had forced them into hiding."

Antonio smiled. Awkwardly perhaps and, at times, blindly and blunderingly, he had done God's will.

"I spoke harshly to you, Friar Antonio, when you accepted Bononillo's challenge. You are not angry?"

Antonio wanted to deny again that he had accepted Bononillo's challenge. "Bononillo's conversion began when you helped to lift me to that window, Your Highness."

He found Ruggiero in their room, standing at the window that overlooked the square.

The big squire turned as Antonio entered. He was smiling, but it was a strange smile—as though he had been frightened and made timid by the events of the three days. He motioned toward the square below. "Your friends are waiting to greet you. They have been crowding the square all day."

Antonio had started toward the window but stopped as he realized the significance of Ruggiero's comment. Something of Ruggiero's timid smile transferred suddenly to him. He shook his head slowly and firmly. "Our mission here is finished, Ruggiero."

They returned slowly over the road they had come. News of the events at Rimini had spread far beyond the walls of the city. At each village, people welcomed them as "the friars who converted Rimini," and demanded that Antonio preach to them. All of January and half of February were gone when they came within sight of the mean huts that sheltered Gratian and the friars of Bologna.

"Father Francis also learned of the marvels at Rimini," the Provincial told them. He drew a paper from his robe and gave it to Antonio.

> Brother Francis to Brother Antonio, Greetings. It is my wish that you teach theology to the brothers, but in such manner that study will not extinguish the spirit of holy prayer and devotion, as contained in the Rule.

Antonio studied the message. As short as the other that had commissioned him to preach, this was even more puzzling. He offered the paper to Gratian, but the Provincial refused it.

"I know the message. Father Francis has appointed you to be teacher to the brothers."

"But I know nothing of teaching, Father Gratian."

Gratian laughed shortly. "The brothers know little of learning." He became serious again and pointed to the paper in Antonio's hand. "That is a great honor, Friar Antonio. Less than two years ago, another friar organized a school in this very city. Father Francis denounced him and closed the school. He wanted no schools of learning for the brothers. Now he has reversed himself. You must establish your school in this same city and justify Father Francis' confidence."

"The Rule prohibits us from owning buildings," Antonio objected.

Gratian shrugged his shoulders; the problem was not his. As an afterthought, he suggested, "Ask Jordan, General of the Preachers. He knows about such things."

3

THROUGH that year and the next and into the first part of 1224, Antonio taught the brothers and preached to the people of Bologna. "I will provide a room for your school in our House of Studies," General Jordan had told him, "if you will preach once each week in our Church of San Nicolo."

In the latter part of 1223, rumors came from the South that the Emperor Frederick had pledged again to join the Crusade. The people of the North heard but did not believe. In 1224, His Imperial Majesty proclaimed his intention to march northward, meet his son to arrange for the ruling of the Empire, then depart on the Crusade. None in the North believed the proclamation. Under whatever pretext the Emperor proposed to come with his army, the people saw but one purpose—renewed attempts to subjugate the cities of north Italy. The cities prepared for war.

Antonio watched the number of students in the lecture room diminish. One by one, students told their desire to return to their own communities before war prevented them. A message from Father Francis completed the dissolution.

> Brother Francis to Brother Antonio, Greetings.
> God permits war to close the school of the brothers
> at Bologna. It is my wish that you go to France—to

> Toulouse, the center of the heretics. Teach the
> brothers; preach to the people. When your work
> there is finished, return to me for instructions.

Father Gratian did not conceal his disappointment when Antonio told of the new assignment; the information delighted Ruggiero. "If we were here when the Emperor came, I might be tempted toward soldiering again," he grinned.

The welcome of the brothers in the country outside Bologna surprised Antonio. He recognized some who had attended the school at Bologna, but all—in Piedmont and Liguria and even the brothers in France—seemed to know his name; and their manner made him conscious that they esteemed him. Not until they arrived at Montpellier was there any change. There also the brothers welcomed them, as had the others, but their manner changed suddenly when Antonio announced his assignment.

"Toulouse is a place for missionaries," Guardian Louis said coldly, "not for reading Sacred Scripture."

"I shall also preach, Guardian Louis," Antonio emphasized. "My assignment is to preach and teach."

The answer did not satisfy the Guardian. He was confident in his opinion as in all else. "I know the conditions of this country and what is necessary. Father Francis would not have assigned you to teach in Toulouse had he been informed of conditions." The Guardian indicated the other brothers seated around them. "This entire community originated in Toulouse. The Perfecti, the leaders of the heretics, drove us from the city. Do you, Friar Antonio, and your giant companion expect to do better than the men of this house?"

Antonio tried to turn the conversation to subjects more pleasant to the brothers of Montpellier, but Guardian Louis refused to be distracted. The Guardian interpreted Father Francis' assignment of Antonio as an insult to the men of Montpellier and would not be diverted. Antonio became silent, and his silence finally discouraged the Guardian. "At least you will take a guide with you," Louis proposed ironically, "or do you know the people and country so well that you need no advice?"

"We will be happy to have a guide," Antonio answered. He and Ruggiero did not need a guide, but he grasped eagerly at the opportunity of placating the belligerent Guardian.

Louis pointed to one of the friars, a small, thin-faced man. "Brother Monaldo will be your guide."

The brother he designated paled visibly. His eyes enlarged and his mouth opened as though to protest.

"You, Brother Monaldo, will guide these brave friars," Guardian Louis said sharply.

Monaldo's mouth closed again. If he feared this assignment, he feared Guardian Louis even more. Antonio glanced at Ruggiero. The big friar moved his head slowly back and forth in token of sadness or disgust or both.

However defective his courage, Monaldo knew the country and the people. He described Toulouse, told of the crusade against the city, recounted the destruction of buildings and loss of life. "The King's army conquered Toulouse and the province," he observed, "but an army cannot drive out heresy. The heretics still control the city and the province." So well informed was Monaldo that, before they arrived at Toulouse, Antonio had completed his plans.

In the streets of the city, people looked at them without

interest. Antonio watched an old couple approach, each bearing a bundle of fagots. Their poverty and expression of sullen hopelessness epitomized the misery of all in the war-ravaged capital of the heretics. Monaldo led the way to what had once been a stable and which no one had considered worthy of use since the brothers of Toulouse had been driven from it.

Ruggiero pointed to the roof through which light sifted. "When does the rainy season begin, Monaldo?"

Monaldo tried to smile. Desperation or the company of the big friar had lifted his spirits since they left Montpellier, but he was not able to enjoy Ruggiero's humor.

Antonio preached twice each day. He avoided the great square in the center of the city but visited regularly each of the smaller squares. In the beginning, a few stopped curiously, then remained to hear all that he preached. In the last months of 1224, the number of listeners increased steadily.

A message from the brothers at Limoges, asking him to teach them, interrupted the work at Toulouse. When he returned, with Ruggiero and Monaldo, Antonio discovered that the crowds, so laboriously attracted to hear him, thought he had fled the city. He began the work anew.

Late in 1225, a plea from the brothers at Bourges again interrupted the work at Toulouse. Ruggiero and Monaldo remonstrated, but Antonio would not refuse. "I was not commissioned to convert Toulouse," he endeavored to explain. "Father Francis assigned me to teach and preach. At Bourges, I can do both."

When they returned and Antonio went to one of the squares to preach, he saw again the cost of his absence. A few came to hear him—a few more than had listened when he had appeared before them as a stranger fifteen months earlier. For the first time, Antonio was conscious of uncertainty. Twice he had attracted followers in Toulouse; twice his followers had dissolved during his absences. Even while he preached, the thought tormented him that he could be successful among these people or he could fulfill the dual assignment given him; he could not do both.

Listeners reappeared readily in the squares during the early months of 1226. In March, two youths approached the house of settlement with another problem. "We are no longer three wandering friars," he smiled. "We have established a community here in Toulouse. I have been temporary guardian but a guardian cannot leave his community and remain away from them for indefinite periods. Ruggiero and I will start tomorrow for Nevers. Of the rest of the community, only Monaldo is experienced in the order and in the Rule. You, Monaldo, must become guardian."

Monaldo's eyes opened wide, and he seemed stricken. "I cannot be guardian, Friar Antonio," he whispered hoarsely. "I . . ." he looked around frantically. "I am a follower, not a leader."

Antonio rose to his feet as a signal that the supper and the discussion were ended. "Do as much as you can, Monaldo."

Antonio and Ruggiero returned to Toulouse in June. A guard lounging by the city gate nodded recognition and smiled self-consciously. Antonio and Ruggiero returned the greeting and continued along the open space between the gate and the first house of the city. "He never did that before," Ruggiero observed.

Few people appeared in the street where houses of the

city began to border the road, but some spoke a greeting or nodded. Greetings increased as the number of people increased. The greeting by the guard had not been an isolated incident; it was representative of Toulouse.

They came to one of the small squares and Antonio glanced toward the corner, which was his usual place of preaching. A crowd was gathered—not as large as the crowds that gathered when he preached—but a crowd sufficiently large to attest interest in a speaker. Antonio strained anxiously to see who held their attention, but the press of people effectively screened the speaker.

None of those on the edge of the crowd seemed to notice their approach. Antonio saw in their unmoving concentration a tribute to the unseen speaker. Voice and words could be heard only faintly at this distance—absolute quiet was necessary to understand.

"Two hundred pennyworth of bread is not sufficient for them," the speaker could be heard, "that everyone may take a little." Antonio recognized the gospel of St. John, then recognized the voice of the speaker. Ruggiero was straining higher to see over the crowd; he leaned down to tell his discovery at the very moment Antonio announced it to him. "Monaldo!"

The whispered exchange distracted a man in front of them and he turned. His frown disappeared, and a smile of pleasure replaced it. "Friar Antonio is here!" he announced loudly, unmindful of Monaldo's voice and the attention of the others. "Friar Antonio is here!"

The cry disrupted the audience. Listeners turned away from Monaldo to look in the direction of the interrupter. Then the news sped swiftly through the crowd: "Friar Antonio is here."

A lane opened between Antonio and the place where

Monaldo stood. Antonio walked forward doubtfully, but Monaldo rushed toward him with a glad cry of recognition. Antonio heard the crowd laugh sympathetically as Monaldo embraced him and Ruggiero.

"Let Friar Antonio speak," a voice demanded. Others repeated the demand. Monaldo recovered himself and turned hurriedly toward the place where he had stood, drawing Antonio after him. "Preach, Friar Antonio! Preach! the people have been waiting for you."

Antonio climbed upon the box which served as his pulpit. He could see that the crowd had increased in the few minutes since he and Ruggiero had arrived. More people were coming from different sections of the square and others from the streets leading into it.

He had not time to consider the phenomenon of the crowd. He was conscious of the extraordinary fact that there was a crowd despite his long absence. He put aside the thoughts and conjectures that thrust themselves into his mind and continued, where Monaldo had stopped, the story of the five thousand Our Lord had fed. When the story ended, he preached the goodness of God. While he preached, he saw the crowd expand.

A murmur of satisfaction marked the end of the sermon. Antonio puzzled at the continuing demonstration of goodwill and friendship, puzzled also at the number who greeted them in the streets between the square and the house of the brothers.

The house was empty. Ruggiero sank immediately to the floor and stretched full length on the bare earth. Antonio sat on the floor beside the doorway, resting against the wall. Monaldo moved about restlessly, unable to repress his joy at their return.

"You should have remained here, Friar Antonio. You saw today that the people want to hear you."

Antonio smiled. "You were telling them the story from the Gospel when we arrived, Monaldo. They were there to hear you, not me."

"They did not come to hear me," Monaldo disclaimed. "They came to hear the story of Our Lord. They like those stories. I remembered that, when you went away before, you had to start your work all over again when you returned. I only wanted to keep some of them in groups in the squares until you returned. That is why I told them the stories of Our Lord."

Ruggiero lifted his head from the floor as Monaldo finished and watched the other curiously. "Monaldo, not many men have the courage to tell stories of Our Lord to heretics." The big friar sat up to emphasize his words. "You have lost your fear, Monaldo!"

Monaldo smiled with pleasure at the admiration of Ruggiero. "I was frightened," he protested. He looked uncomfortably and admiringly at Antonio. "Friar Antonio was obedient when he went away from Toulouse to teach at Nevers. He told me to do here as much as I could, and I wanted to be obedient like him."

Ruggiero leaped to his feet with an exultant shout to embrace the startled Monaldo. "There is no greater courage than that, Monaldo—to be obedient in the face of fear is the greatest bravery of all. Do you know a braver guardian, Friar Antonio?"

A shout outside the house interrupted him. Ruggiero glanced through the doorway. "Visitors," he announced.

Antonio arose as a group of friars arrived at the door. Not all were visitors, he saw. He recognized the four he had left with Monaldo. When he had greeted them, Monaldo introduced the others.

"These are new members of the community, Friar Antonio," said Monaldo, smiling. "These four joined the brothers while you and Ruggiero were away. I did as much as I could."

4

DURING the supper and after, Antonio talked with Monaldo about the crowds that had attended the Gospel stories in the squares.

"Thanks to your work, Monaldo, we can begin the great assault," Antonio decided. "I will preach once more in the small squares. I will tell the people that, beginning next week, I shall preach each week in the great square of the city. Let us ask God to bless our work there as He has done in the past."

They went early to the great square on the evening of the first sermon and waited in a silent group around a cart while people gathered. Ruggiero watched over the heads of the crowd. "Very few more are coming from the streets," he announced finally. Antonio climbed up to the platform of the cart.

Antonio preached that evening on the obedience of Christ to His parents, of the reverence of Christ for His parents, of the reverence due all parents by their children. Coldly and professionally, as in the days when he had strained to bring the men of Coimbra to God, he measured the effect of his words.

A cry from the crowd interrupted him. "Children do not ask entrance into this world."

Antonio looked down from the cart at the one who had hurled the challenge. The man's robe identified him as one of the Perfecti. Deliberately, Antonio raised his head to look at the crowd. "Let the hearts of mothers and the dreams of fathers answer this monster," he cried. "Answer with the words of your suffering hearts!" He watched the crowd stir as he continued his appeal.

Antonio marked the expression of anxiety on Ruggiero's face when the big friar helped him down from the cart. "Worried, Ruggiero?"

Ruggiero wagged his head slowly. "I prefer to hear you preach God's love than God's hatred," he grumbled. "I never saw you deliberately turn a crowd against anyone before."

Antonio saw Ruggiero's uneasiness mirrored in the faces of the others. "It is better that they hate God's enemies than that they hate God."

The incident of the first sermon swelled the crowd at the next. He looked at the section of the crowd nearest him and saw that the Perfecti had appeared in greater numbers. Four stood together to challenge him.

"Are you come to hear the Word of God or to interfere with those who would?" Antonio demanded loudly so that the whole crowd would know the presence of the Perfecti.

The four looked uncomfortably to each other as though not prepared to answer the direct attack.

"Pharisees! Men of uncleanness! Do you stand in the front ranks to hear the Word of God?"

Antonio heard the crowd rumble as they tried to see the four he addressed. The Perfecti heard the rumble also and seemed to realize it would become a threat unless they answered. "Preach!" one of them called back defiantly.

"Hear them!" Antonio cried out. "Hear the authority of their commands! The world is evil, marriage is evil, children are evil—all is evil except the Perfecti," he ridiculed. "Now they come and say, 'Preach—we would hear the Word of God.'" He watched the crowd straining to hear the exchange of words with the Perfecti. "I preach the Word of God to men, not to devils. Leprous souls! Stand apart from those God loves!" Antonio gestured to those nearest the Perfecti. "Make room," he commanded. "Do not become infected by their uncleanness."

Automatically, those nearest the Perfecti drew away from them. The Perfecti looked around, humiliated by the action. One of them plunged suddenly into the crowd, deserting the others, pushing his way to escape.

"Follow your weakhearted brother," Antonio called to the three that remained. The crowd had started laughing as the first fled; they began to call out their own insults to the three that stood irresolutely. Antonio stood laughing at their discomfiture, his action encouraging the crowd to greater taunts. The three could bear the ignominy no longer and fled after the first.

On the second Sunday of July, Guardian Louis of Montpellier arrived at the house of the brothers of Toulouse. All of the community were present in the house when he entered; he stopped on the threshold as though recovering his sight after entering the relative darkness of the house. His expression of surprise showed that he had seen the number of brothers who were present.

"Guardian Louis!" Antonio moved forward quickly to welcome the guest. His quick movement brought the rest to their feet.

Louis responded to Antonio, then looked around the

room again at the others. "Have you formed a community?" he demanded.

Antonio drew Monaldo in front of him. "This is not my community, Guardian Louis. Monaldo is guardian at Toulouse."

Guardian Louis was already shaking hands with Monaldo when he realized the import of Antonio's words. He released Monaldo's hand and glanced quickly at Antonio. "Monaldo? Monaldo is your guide, Friar Antonio," he protested.

Ruggiero interrupted the exchange to greet Louis. "The guide you gave to the brave friars has become the brave guardian." He grinned down disagreeably on Guardian Louis.

Antonio presented the other brothers. Louis acknowledged each of them, but his poise had been shattered, and he mumbled to the new friars. Only when he had met all of them did he recover his mind and strength of voice.

"Your work in France has caused a crisis in our order," he said to Antonio. "You have been teaching the brothers and preaching to the people. You have stirred up the bishops against us."

"Friar Antonio did not stir up the bishops," said Monaldo. His voice shrilled as though contradicting Guardian Louis revived the fears that had been long dormant. He swung around to Antonio. "The bishops have disliked the brothers for a long time, Friar Antonio. They think we may become heretics like the Poor Men of Lyons."

Ruggiero's laugh relieved the tension of Monaldo's strident voice. "Poor Men of Lyons and Poor Men of Assisi are all the same to the bishops. Is that what you mean, Monaldo?"

Louis ignored Monalda and Ruggiero. "The bishops

have instructed me to carry a summons to you. They require that you preach before them, assembled in council at Montpellier, on the feast of the Holy Virgin's Assumption. They also require the Assumption to be your subject."

Antonio felt alarm as Louis announced the subject. "But Holy Mother Church has not defined the Assumption as a dogma of faith," he objected.

Louis nodded. "That is why they have assigned that subject. They will use your sermon as a means for expelling the order from France."

Antonio measured the time remaining to him. He was not disturbed by the ordeal before the bishops. He regarded the summons as the others—a summons to preach, but a summons also that interrupted the work in Toulouse. "This will be the end," he announced. "I cannot teach and preach in this country. After the sermon on the Assumption, Ruggiero and I will return to Father Francis for instructions."

"Leave Toulouse?" Monaldo exclaimed. "Friar Antonio, you cannot!"

Antonio did not answer. Father Francis had said to return for instructions when he had finished his assignment in France. He had not finished, but he could not continue against both bishops and heretics.

Louis refused to remain with them. Having delivered his message and received assurance that Antonio would comply with the summons, he left immediately. Ruggiero's manner indicated plainly that he considered the Guardian's visit to have been excessively lengthy.

When Antonio went to the great square the next time to preach, a tremendous crowd filled the entire square—a noisy, good-humored crowd eager for whatever incidents might enliven the evening. Antonio could see none among them wearing the robes of the Perfecti. He was disappointed; he had injured those leaders of the heretics but had not yet crushed them.

He began to preach; he could see that the crowd was not attentive. An air of expectancy hovered in the square. Many had come to see a continuation of his struggle with the Perfecti. A disturbance to the left attracted him, and he turned about in time to see two of the Perfecti appear. They burst from the forward edge of the crowd, leaped forward, and began to climb onto the cart. A shout rose from the crowd as they saw, at last, the beginning of the struggle they expected. Antonio turned to meet the first of the aggressors; but the man who had already gained the platform was suddenly arrested by Ruggiero's great hand on his robe. With one mighty tug, Ruggiero swept the man from the cart to the ground.

Antonio glanced toward the other side of the cart where the second man should have appeared, only to see the Perfecti still endeavoring to climb the cart, hampered by Monaldo clinging to his back! In a moment, Ruggiero joined Monaldo to end the encounter. The big friar lifted the man, carried him around the cart, and dropped him on the ground beside the first. The crowd shouted their delight and cheered Ruggiero's exhibition.

In the corner to the left, another commotion arose. The corner seethed and milled about as men pushed through the crowd. There were not two now—at least twenty of the Perfecti were approaching. Antonio called a warning to Ruggiero and the brothers around the cart just as the Perfecti emerged from the forward edge of the crowd.

Antonio saw the first four hurl themselves directly at Ruggiero. Their combined weight drove the big friar backward. The crowd near the cart cheered and shouted as Ruggiero withstood the attack, then their cheers died as two more Perfecti added their weight against the big friar, and he fell to the ground. Other attackers fought their way through the brothers around the cart, and the first of them started to climb to the platform when a new sound arose from the crowd. It was a low sound, an angry, maddened roar that grew steadily in volume as more and more of the crowd joined their voices to it. Even as the roar started, those in the front ranks leaped forward. Antonio felt the cart tremble and turn about as some of the crowd pushed against it; then he saw men grasp the robes of those climbing the cart. The Perfecti collapsed under the unexpected attack. In a moment, all were subdued, some inert on the ground, the others angry and sullen captives. A short distance from the cart, Ruggiero arose to his feet and looked down at three of the Perfecti who remained on the ground. Men milled about the cart, shouting and laughing. Many of them looked up eagerly to Antonio, proud that they had helped him. More surged around Ruggiero, hitting his broad back appreciatively and admiringly; the big friar grinned his thanks for their assistance.

Long after the brothers returned to the house, they talked excitedly of the incidents in the square. They alternated between admiration of Ruggiero and rejoicing at what they considered Antonio's victory against the heretics. Monaldo was happiest—he had shared both the victory of Antonio and the victory of Ruggiero. Even when the others had quieted, Monaldo continued to exult. "You have won back Toulouse, Friar Antonio; you have won back our city to God and to Holy Mother Church."

Antonio lay awake looking into the darkness. "We have

not yet won the victory, Monaldo," he replied.

"Tonight!" Monaldo persisted. "Tonight you won the victory, Friar Antonio."

"Tonight, Monaldo, you saw nothing more than these people using the hatred the Perfecti taught them against the Perfecti themselves. That is not a victory for God." Antonio saw clearly what had been gained, what yet remained. "At first, these people listened to me in the small squares; they listened because of the talent God gave me. Then they listened to the stories of the gospel that you recited to them, Monaldo. They loved those stories because no one can help loving the stories of Our Lord. Tonight, you saw them turn against their leaders; but that does not prove they have turned to God. They no longer hate God as their leaders tried to teach them, but neither do they love Him and want to follow Him. The last step remains. Toulouse must love God, must realize that the gospel is much more than a series of beautiful stories—that it is the life they must live and that Holy Mother Church will teach them to live as God intends. Do not think that the victory is won. All must pray, must ask God to grant that my sermons will separate these people from me and from my words and turn them to others and the words of others who will lead them to God."

There was silence for a time. Then Monaldo said sadly, "You speak of others, Friar Antonio. We cannot continue your work."

"I was referring to the Friars Preachers, Monaldo. Tomorrow you must send a message to the nearest priory of the Preachers; tell them what has been done here and what remains. Ask them to send men to continue this work. Our brothers—those who are here in this room—must preach by the example of their lives while the Preachers exhort with their words. Pray that the people will turn to the Preachers and hear them; show by your example that the Preachers are the teachers the people must hear."

While he talked, his plans clarified. He could preach two more sermons before leaving for Montpellier. The Perfecti would not interfere again. He would be free to strengthen the people of Toulouse in their new attitude, to turn them toward the Preachers so that the Preachers might turn them fully toward God. There would be no miracle in Toulouse as there had been at Rimini; there would be, instead, the slow miracle of God's grace working in the hearts of the people.

All of Toulouse seemed crowded into the great square for his next sermon. From his place on the cart, Antonio saw that even the streets opening onto the square were crowded; he saw, too, that the people were quiet and attentive and without the boisterous air of expectation. They had come, not to witness another encounter with the Perfecti, but to hear the Word of God.

In the two sermons, he did not press them. When he told them, at the close of the last sermon, that he must leave Toulouse, there were cries of protest from the crowd. "I will not forget you," he promised. "In return for that promise, I will exact a promise from you." He smiled and waited for their answering cries of agreement. "You will come here each week and hear my brothers, the Friars Preachers."

The crowd did not respond. He saw them stir restlessly, reluctant to agree. "If you love me," he prompted, "you will grant me that. Give your promise."

A reluctant agreement arose from them. Antonio smiled.

"Louder! Louder!" he demanded. His demand destroyed their restraint. They laughed good-naturedly, and the roar of agreement swelled. Antonio leaped down from the cart as the sound increased.

5

MONALDO led the way along a poorly defined road that threatened often to disappear in the tangled mass of wild growth. Antonio and Ruggiero stumbled after him. On the crest of the hill above them, they could see Montpellier and the twin towers of the Cathedral marking the site of the bishops' assembly. The road they followed, Monaldo had assured, was the shortest way to the house of the brothers at the foot of the hill.

From a distance, they could see figures moving about in the area near the house, and Monaldo slowed at the sight. "There should not be so many present at this time of day," he noted wonderingly. Antonio recognized Guardian Louis standing with another gray-clad figure. "They are not all brothers of Montpellier," Monaldo announced. "The one with Guardian Louis is Provincial Gregory." Something of disappointment sounded in his voice.

"Is the sight of a provincial so disagreeable?" Ruggiero laughed.

Monaldo began to announce other names as they neared the house, and his task of recognition was made easier as the others saw them approach and stood watching them. Antonio counted fourteen in addition to Guardian Louis.

Only two came forward to meet them—the smiling, gray-haired Guardian Jean of Limoges and the young guardian of Bourges. The others waited near the house. Guardian Louis was reserved; Provincial Gregory, a solid, thick man, was proper and polite; the others varied between the warmth of Guardian Jean and the coldness of Gregory.

"The brothers in France are distressed and fearful, Friar Antonio," Guardian Louis said, explaining the presence of the others. "Provincial Gregory and these guardians of the brothers have come to discuss the ordeal imposed by the bishops."

"This is a serious matter, Friar Antonio," Provincial Gregory added ponderously.

Antonio looked around at the group. Their faces reflected the anxiety of Louis and Gregory. "I will preach as well as I can, my brothers. God will determine what follows."

"What follows, Friar Antonio, is more important to us than to you," Provincial Gregory answered. "Guardian Louis has informed us that you intend to return to Italy. We do not have such an escape. To us is entrusted the welfare of our order in France; we have come to advise you the course that must be followed if we are to remain in France." Gregory started walking toward the house.

Antonio glanced quickly at Ruggiero. The big friar's eyes followed the person of Provincial Gregory; his lips were pressed together. Ruggiero could not remain in the group. "You will want to find an employer, Ruggiero," he suggested.

Ruggiero looked down resentfully. His whole manner expressed unwillingness to do anything that required separation from this group. But his face cleared gradually, and he shrugged his shoulders. Without answering, he walked toward the road that led to Montpellier.

Antonio followed the others through the doorway of the house. He noticed that all moved to places without confusion, indicating that this was not their first meeting. Provincial Gregory stood at the inmost end of the house, the others stood against the walls, giving to the dilapidated house the appearance of a chapter room. Antonio leaned against the wall beside the doorway; Monaldo stood beside him.

"Friar Antonio," Gregory began immediately, "we presume you are familiar with the arguments of those who support belief in the Assumption of the Holy Virgin, the arguments of those who oppose such belief, the arguments of those who advocate a neutral position?"

Antonio drew himself forward from the wall. He had almost answered the Provincial's question before realizing the significance of answering. In itself, the question was harmless; but to answer without qualification would be accepted as submission to the group. "I will answer your question, Provincial Gregory. I must first state that I am not permitted to recognize this council as having authority." He saw heads turn quickly to Gregory as the others looked to the Provincial's reaction as a guide for their own. "I am familiar with the arguments relating to the Assumption of the Holy Virgin," he added. He saw that the blunt statement rejecting Gregory's pretense of authority had disconcerted the Provincial.

"Your attitude is discouraging, Friar Antonio," Gregory temporized.

Antonio looked around at the group. "My brothers, all are aware that I am commissioned by Father Francis and answerable to him. Father Francis has not given me permission to subject myself to others; if now I pretend to recognize the authority of others, I should be acting contrary to the commission he gave me."

"Well stated," Guardian Jean commented.

"His commission, however, does demand that I seek and accept gladly every assistance from my brothers and from all who love God."

"Your commission," Gregory answered, "also demands that you contribute to the welfare of the order, Friar Antonio. We have assembled here precisely because that welfare is endangered. We have agreed that circumstances require you to conform with Dom Usuard's *Martyrology*. To depart from that is to risk the future existence of the entire order in France."

Antonio frowned. "I do not agree, my brothers, with Dom Usuard's comment in the *Martyrology*."

"Do you consider yourself superior to the author of the *Martyrology*, Friar Antonio?" Gregory demanded. "Dom Usuard stated the position of Holy Mother Church."

"He added words of his own, Provincial Gregory."

"But you stated, Friar Antonio, that you do not agree with him."

"I agree with that part of his comment which does no more than state the attitude of Holy Mother Church. Those words are, 'As yet the Church has given no definitive decision upon the bodily Assumption of the Holy Virgin, exercising a prudent reserve.' I refuse to accept the remainder of his comment. The remainder represents his own antagonism."

"The words you quoted are sufficient, Friar Antonio, to warn you to follow the same course as Holy Mother Church."

Antonio did not answer. He leaned back against the wall. Gregory's purpose was becoming apparent.

"Prudent reserve, Friar Antonio," the Provincial continued, "can have but one meaning in this crisis. Prudent reserve demands that you neither support nor oppose belief in the Assumption of the Holy Virgin. Some of the bishops do not want preachers to refer to the Assumption because heretics seize on it to make trouble. Others want it preached in order to encourage the Holy See to define it as a dogma of faith. All of them are prepared to use whatever you preach as an excuse to expel the order. You may only review the arguments of antagonists and protagonists while you hold yourself with those maintaining a position of neutrality."

Antonio heard the words almost resentfully. It seemed impossible that the bishops so disliked the brothers that they would seek opportunity to expel them. Yet he could not doubt the anxiety of these guardians and the Provincial. And he remembered Ruggiero's comment that the bishops did not distinguish between the Poor Men of Lyons and the Poor Man of Assisi. He felt a depression settle on him; a feeling of distaste filled him. He had wanted to preach the love of his heart for the Mother of God; he must preach as a philosopher. He had three days in which to prepare a reversal of his life.

"Are we permitted to know your reaction to our suggestions?" Provincial Gregory prompted.

Antonio considered, then shook his head. "The sermon itself must reveal it, Provincial Gregory."

Tediously and stubbornly, Antonio labored that day and the next. He could prepare a sermon which neither affirmed nor denied and which made of her Assumption a philosophical debate without breath of life or beauty. He knew the statements of those who denied her Assumption; he had heard the empty mouthings of vain men who chose to glory in the wastes of philosophy rather than in the glories of God. As he recalled them, he revolted that he must repeat them.

"This is a trial of your brothers," he reminded himself to find strength to continue his efforts. The argument paled and the effort slackened. "It is the will of God," he drove himself. "It is not your will that you preach to the bishops; it is the will of God."

When he had completed his outline, he felt no joy of accomplishment; there could be no pleasure in her displeasure. He felt like a coward, like a traitor to the Holy Virgin he professed to love. He would preach badly, would preach without conviction, would preach monotonously. He would express himself laboriously and methodically. He had been summoned to preach, and he would be prudent; but prudence does not inspire as love. Depression weighed more and more heavily on him as the hour of trial approached.

On the eve of the Assumption, he left the house of the brothers after supper. Ruggiero and Monaldo looked up hopefully, but he gestured them to remain where they were. Slowly and heavily he mounted the hill to Montpellier. There was the church of Sainte Marie where he might kneel and pour out the sorrow that afflicted him.

For a time, he stood far back in the shadows, leaning against a pillar. He was like an intruder in this church of Mary, one who should not approach her church. Obedience was his only excuse—obedience to the bishops who summoned him, obedience to Mother Church who cautioned against reckless assertion, obedience to prudence enjoined by his brothers.

He moved forward to the sanctuary railing and knelt. Shadow was there also to conceal him from any who might enter. He wanted to be away from men, away from the eyes of men, away from the necessity of this sermon he must preach. He closed his own eyes against the reality of life and bowed his head. He should have returned to Assisi when the thought had occurred to him earlier in the year. He would not have become involved in this dispute, this—

"Antonio!"

His name sounded with strange beauty. It seemed almost as though someone had spoken his name in the dim vault of the church—spoken it with the soft tones of a mother's love.

"Antonio!"

The sweetness of heaven was in the voice that called, a sweetness that was not of earth unless it were of dreams. But he was not dreaming. His mind was filled with her whom Gabriel had recognized from the light of God that filled her with grace and to whom he had said, "The Lord is with thee." His heart was filled with love for her who had so loved Christ and who now loved him because she was his mother as Christ's gift. He thought he must lift up his arms to heaven, as his mind and heart had lifted, in a gesture of longing toward the heaven where now she reigned as Queen of angels and saints.

"Antonio!"

In such voice as that would the Mother of God speak to him if only he were free to preach to others as he could speak his soul to her! If only for the one day he might be free from restraint and tell men the glory of the Mother of God! If he might raise his voice before men, as now he raised his arms in this darkened church, and raise men's hopes to Mary!

"Antonio!"

He opened his eyes. His head had turned upward while he prayed. His whole being had striven upward to pierce the sky—that he might see the Mother of God. He opened his eyes, and the Mother of God smiled on him.

"Be assured, Antonio, that I was assumed, body and soul, into heaven. Mankind has not honored that day in vain; tongues have not continued that tradition in vain. The world does not hope in vain for the promises of their God. He has fulfilled them in me that all might increase their hopes and strength and courage in my fulfillment. All generations shall call me blessed, Antonio. Is not that sufficient for the peoples of earth? Antonio, I will bless the words you preach of me."

The words of the Holy Virgin impressed on mind and heart. Desire replaced dread of the ordeal. He knew an impatience to stand before the bishops, not as one they would test, but as one who would tell the mercy of God and the glory of God's Mother. For short moments, he was aware of the present—of the guard at the city gate who grumbled as he pushed back the heavy bolt, of Ruggiero and Monaldo joining him outside the city wall to walk beside him down the slope to the house of the brothers, of tense silence among the brothers when they ate their breakfast in the morning, of people in the streets of Montpellier, of the brothers entering the Cathedral with the people through the great doors, of Ruggiero walking with him along the side of the church and following him into the vesting room where bishops looked at him critically.

Expectation became reality. Before him were bishops and priests, nrothers and lay men and women. Far to the left he saw Gregory and the gray robes of the Minors. White-robed Preachers dotted the crowd. Immediately beneath the pulpit, the bishops of France waited to hear and to judge him.

He preached softly at first, as a man who saw a vision. Words and voice strengthened until they became the trumpeting of Isaiah. His mind searched back through the glories of Israel, while his voice gained slowly the measured cadence of the psalmist. He cared no longer that he had been summoned as to a trial; he cared only that the Mother of God so loved her children of earth that she would send him to sing her glory. "O most exalted dignity of Mary! O ineffable sublimity of grace; O inexhaustible fountain of mercy! Hail, Queen of Angels! Hail, Queen of Saints! Hail, Mother of God!"

In the fleeting instant as he turned to descend from the pulpit, he saw one bishop smiling rapturously. In the vesting room, he saw the bishop's smile mirrored in Ruggiero's. He sat on a bench to await the summons to return for the questions of the bishops. Ruggiero paced nervously from the window to the sanctuary door. His tension increased as the minutes passed; frequently he stopped at the door to look into the church.

A priest of the Cathedral came long after to release them with the announcement that the bishops would not question the Friar Antonio. The priest delivered the message in a monotone as though not entirely certain that he had heard or delivered the message correctly. He confided wonderingly, "A few wanted to question you, Friar Antonio, but the council would not permit them. That has never happened before."

They walked along streets virtually deserted on the feast day of the Holy Virgin and descended the road that led to the house of the brothers. Antonio felt Ruggiero glance at him several times, but the big friar remained silent.

None of the brothers were visible near the house.

Antonio and Ruggiero were only a short distance from the house before they heard voices. Without understanding the words, Antonio heard the precise tones of Guardian Louis, then the authoritative voice of Provincial Gregory. After them, as though answering, he heard another, high-pitched, trembling, loud with indignation and fright. "You are prejudiced," the voice shrilled. "The others no longer agree with you. Only you two continue to attack Friar Antonio. You, Provincial Gregory, because Friar Antonio obeys the will of Father Francis instead of yours; and you, Guardian Louis, because Friar Antonio appointed me as guardian of Toulouse."

Ruggiero's steps quickened and lengthened. Antonio had to run to remain beside him.

"I will have you deposed and disgraced," Gregory threatened. "You will be wise to escape to Italy with your Antonio."

Monaldo's voice broke with the fury of his effort to subdue his fear.

In the house, Monaldo stood defiantly in the center of the room facing the Provincial and the Guardian of Montpellier. For a moment, Antonio's view was blocked as Ruggiero walked through the doorway before him. Then he saw the others turn suddenly as they became aware of their entrance. Monaldo swung around—tears of anguish and fear marked his face. "Friar Antonio! Friar Antonio!"

"You—" Gregory began.

Antonio saw the Provincial's face stiffen as the one word escaped. He saw Monaldo's eyes raise higher as though looking at the top of the doorway. Ruggiero swung around and looked too. Antonio saw that all the others had turned their eyes above him.

"Father Francis!" someone cried impulsively.

Monaldo's voice shrilled more loudly than before, and his face lighted with joy. "Friar Antonio! Father Francis! Friar Antonio! Father Francis!"

Antonio looked wonderingly at Monaldo and the others whose voices took up Monaldo's cry.

Ruggiero pointed almost fearfully to the top of the doorway. "Father Francis blessed you, Antonio." The big friar's eyes lighted with a great happiness. "Father Francis appeared above you, Antonio, and blessed you," he repeated.

6

CECINA was a negligible place—a firm beach and a few poor houses—but the master of the ship explained that they would find brothers there and would be as near to Assisi as his ship could carry them.

A man on the beach told them where they would find the huts of the brothers, then added, "But the brothers have gone to Assisi." He looked at them expectantly, as though they would understand the absence of the brothers.

Antonio felt a premonition. "Were they called by Father Francis?"

"There was no call. There was only news that your Father Francis was dead."

In each town through which they passed, Antonio and Ruggiero sought the huts of the brothers, but all were deserted until, at Poggi Bonsi, they found a sick brother with another who had remained to care for him.

The sick man smiled weakly when he learned their names. "Father Antonio," he repeated, using the title Antonio had thought proper only to Francis and the superiors. "Father Antonio of Forli and Rimini. We know, too, about Montpellier." The smile faded and an expression of intensity replaced it; the man's thoughts seemed to revive his strength. "You must not continue to Assisi, Father Antonio. Join those who will try to keep our order as Father Francis gave it to us."

Antonio glanced at the friar seated by the sick man to enlist his aid in quieting the man, but the other merely nodded his agreement. Antonio took the sick man's wasted hand into his own. "The spirit of Father Francis will not die from our order, my brother."

The sick man would not be placated. "General Elias will destroy our order. He keeps horses; his table is filled with delicacies. Father Francis restrained him, but now Father Francis is dead. General Elias will neither obey the Rule himself nor listen to those who desire to keep the Rule unchanged."

Antonio avoided answering. The sick man's strength deserted him as quickly as it had come, and he lapsed into sleep. Antonio beckoned to Ruggiero. They waved farewell to the companion friar and went from the hut.

At Siena, they met the first of the brothers returning from Assisi and encountered others regularly as they continued on the road. Those they met spoke but little of Father Francis' death and burial; all seemed desirous of discussing General Elias. Mingled with their observations of the General were frequent allusions to the Romagna.

Among the brothers at Cortona, they met the youthful Henry, who had been with them on Monte Paolo. "Father Gratian died," Henry reported sadly, "not long after you left Bologna. General Elias appointed another provincial, and that provincial appointed Peter as guardian at Bologna. That provincial also died, but the General will appoint another like him. Five of us left the house at Bologna and went to other places."

His reference to Peter puzzled Antonio. Antonio remembered the barrel-chested, deep-voiced Peter who grunted as he worked, but Henry's reference was clearly intended to be unfavorable.

"Why did you leave?"

Henry raised his hands and let them fall as an indication of helplessness. "General Elias wanted to make the brothers of the Romagna the core of all opposition to the Rule. Those who wished to preserve the Rule were forced to go elsewhere. Father Antonio! You must hear the pleas of the brothers who want to save our order! God has made you a superior among us."

When they had left Cortona, Ruggiero, for the first time, added his voice to the pleas of the others. "You cannot continue to Assisi and ignore the brothers, Antonio. The brothers need you."

"The brothers need only God," Antonio answered shortly. "One way to God is through obedience to superiors."

"You are not required to be obedient to a superior who wants to destroy the Rule that imposes obedience," Ruggiero retorted impatiently. "Antonio, if you would give the slightest indication of agreement, the brothers will depose Elias and elect you as General."

Antonio frowned. "Does the Rule authorize the brothers to depose the General?"

"The Rule does not—" Ruggiero began. He did not complete the sentence.

"Cardinal Ugolino is Protector of the Order, Ruggiero. If the General seeks to change the Rule and the brothers oppose, Cardinal Ugolino must settle the matter."

Ruggiero abandoned the project reluctantly. "We need not go to Assisi," he proposed.

"We are going to Assisi, Ruggiero, just as we would have gone if Father Francis were still living. General Elias is our superior and will give us our instructions. As long as he is superior, we will obey him."

Ruggiero grumbled unintelligibly but did not object again. Before they came to the battlements of Perugia, he had regained his carefree interest in the towns through which they passed and in the people. Only when they found their way through the streets of Assisi did his opposition revive. He pointed to the stone building to which they had been directed. "Father Francis lived in a hut," he commented.

Antonio pushed open the heavy door but found that they had gained entrance only to the smallest of rooms, bordered with benches except where two doors led into the interior of the house. A brother who was sitting on a bench beside one of the doors arose immediately. Something in his manner reminded Antonio of the Brother Gatekeeper at Holy Cross. Antonio recited their names, and the brother disappeared but returned almost immediately.

"General Elias wishes to talk first with Friar Antonio."

Antonio walked through the doorway while the brother held the door open for him. The room he entered was many times larger than the tiny visitors' room, but all the benches in this room were grouped about a table near a large and ornate window. General Elias was standing behind the table but came forward smiling affably. "It is a pleasure to see you, Antonio."

Antonio felt the importance of the man. In the General's manner and in his ease were the marks of the successful, assured leader. He was not tall but broad and heavy; he spoke and moved with dignity. He was attentive while Antonio explained the assignment Father Francis had given, reported his efforts in Toulouse and the conditions that prevented fulfillment of the dual assignment. "We returned to ask new instructions, but when we landed at Cecina, we learned that Father Francis had died."

Antonio saw sadness appear when he mentioned the death of Father Francis. The man was not pretending grief; the slow disappearance of his smile was not contrived. Whatever faults the General had, whatever complaints the friars uttered against him, Elias loved Francis.

General Elias straightened on his bench as though physical movement would banish loss and sorrow from his mind. He did smile, and a challenge was in his voice when he spoke. "Now that you have returned for instructions, Antonio, and our Father Francis is not here to give them to you, what are your plans?"

Antonio shook his head slowly. "I have no plans, General Elias. If you give me no instructions, I will continue to teach the brothers and preach as Father Francis instructed me." He saw that the General regarded him appraisingly. For a brief moment, Elias' eyes reflected something like disbelief, but the expression disappeared immediately, and his smile returned.

"Your obedience is exemplary, Antonio," Elias began. "I must admit I am not prepared to give you instructions. Allow me to consider tonight, and I will talk with you again tomorrow." While the General talked, his smile increased steadily. "Another friar is with you. Bring him in that I may meet him."

Antonio called Ruggiero from the outer room but did not need to present him to the superior. Elias identified him immediately by his great size. "You are the greatest of all the friars," the General said, laughing pleasantly. Ruggiero smiled uncertainly. Antonio could see a struggle rise between Ruggiero's opinion of the General formed on information supplied by others and his own opinion formed on the evident abilities of the man.

In the morning, Antonio went alone to the house of the General. The General did not advert immediately to the reason for Antonio's presence. He talked lightly of the days when he had first joined himself to Father Francis, of the growth of the order during the years that followed. "Now I am left in charge of Father Francis' order and have the task alone of developing it." The General's voice was steady and deliberate and without trace of lightness. "There are such serious problems, Antonio, that I can only hope that all the brothers will be as obedient as you."

Antonio said nothing. He wondered what subject General Elias was approaching with such caution.

"One of our most pressing problems is lack of preachers. A second is lack of men qualified to be superiors. You must continue to preach to the people as you have in the past; you must also be a superior."

Antonio shook his head slowly. "I know nothing about directing the friars."

Elias leaned back from his table. "We learn such things, Antonio. I knew nothing of directing the order when Father Francis named me as General."

"Am I permitted to decline appointment, General Elias?"

Elias moved his head in emphatic denial. "I require this of you, Antonio. I appoint you Provincial of the Romagna."

Antonio heard the words as he might have felt a blow. Some men desired to hold office among the brothers, and their very desire conferred on them the ability; he had neither desire nor ability. He wanted only . . . His mind faltered. He had said he wanted to do the will of God and that obedience to superiors was one way to accomplish that. "As you wish, General Elias," he said, submitting.

Ruggiero was waiting for him in the street outside the General's house. Antonio tried to think of phrases that would lessen the shock of the announcement to Ruggiero, but he was so shocked himself that he was forced to the simple declaration, "I am appointed Provincial of the Romagna."

The blunt statement stunned Ruggiero. "No!" he protested. "You cannot be Provincial of the Romagna. Antonio! The brothers in the Romagna will resent you because you support the Rule. The rest of the order will despise you because they will think you have agreed to support Elias. Antonio!" he pleaded. "If you will not join those who oppose the General, you cannot let others think you have joined him."

A tired smile touched Antonio's lips. "St. Benedict once wrote that 'if hard and contrary things are done, or even injuries, while a man endeavors to follow the orders given him, he must accept everything patiently and not become discouraged.'"

Ruggiero would not oppose the pronouncements of a saint; but the pronouncements could not reconcile him. Even when they walked the road from Assisi to the north, Ruggiero continued his pleas. Antonio endeavored to discourage him by silence.

Bologna remembered them. Antonio saw the people look first at the great friar striding along, saw them glance at his small figure made smaller by the great bulk of Ruggiero. Some bowed gravely when they recognized him or smiled shyly; others stopped him to take his hand and welcome the return of the preacher of San Nicolo.

They had drawn near the site of the brothers' huts when a Friar Preacher told them the brothers were no longer at the place. "They have begun to live like other friars. They live now in a house in the city." Antonio and Ruggiero followed the directions of the Preacher to a house close to the church of San Nicolo.

The brothers welcomed them noisily. The friar who opened the door led them to the others, calling out loudly as he walked, "Friar Antonio and Friar Ruggiero are with us, my brothers." The friar led them into a room which seemed to serve as refectory. The six brothers seated around the table had risen to their feet to surround the new arrivals and add their own noisy greetings.

Antonio smiled but wondered at the noisy confusion of their welcome. The brothers had not greeted visitors in this manner when he had lived among them. Then, a visitor had been welcomed quietly as in other communities of the order. Peter stepped forward, as befitted the Guardian, to welcome them with a voice louder than the others and to invite them to remain with them and share their supper as brothers.

The food on the table was also different from the plain fare the brothers of Bologna had eaten while Father Gratian was superior. Antonio saw a large cut of beef with vegetables, bread, and a bottle of wine. He looked around at the brothers smiling their welcome. He knew that, behind him, Ruggiero would be glowering at the scene.

"We will remain, Friar Peter. We will remain with the brothers." Antonio looked about to include all in his announcement. "I am appointed by General Elias to be Provincial of the Romagna."

Peter's smile had widened as Antonio accepted the invitation; it collapsed as Antonio announced his appointment. The noisy laughing and talking died suddenly among all of them. Their faces sobered as they understood fully what Antonio had said. Peter seemed as a man stricken; his face stiffened. He could not speak. He looked vacantly at his place at the table and again at Antonio.

Antonio scraped a bench across the floor to the table; he motioned to Ruggiero to put a bench next to his. "Shall we ask God's blessing, my brothers?"

It was a quiet supper. Antonio filled his glass one fourth with wine and the remainder with water; the others followed his example. He cut a small piece of meat for himself, and each of the brothers took a piece no larger. He broke bread from the loaf and each of them copied him. He did not take vegetables; nor did they.

Antonio felt their resentment build against him as they ate sparingly and silently what they would have eaten generously and noisily. They resented the discipline his example forced on them. They resented his authority. Antonio felt a new disappointment in this assignment the General had imposed on him.

In the morning, Ruggiero walked beside Antonio as they returned from Mass; the others followed silently, even morosely. Breakfast was depressing as the previous supper had been. They ate the meat and bread remaining from the meal of the evening. As each finished, he arose quickly as though eager to escape to his work of the day.

As the group dwindled, Antonio realized that Peter was eating with deliberate slowness in order that he would remain after the others. Antonio slowed his own movements that he would also have reason to remain. He saw that Peter was angry, not with the furious anger of weakness, but with the calculating and cold anger of a man who has appraised an obstacle and determined that he has not power to surmount it.

"Peter, who is owner of this house?"

Peter seemed to return slowly to the present and to his surroundings. "Cardinal Ugolino," he muttered in reply. "General Elias told us that we should live here rather than in the huts."

The last brother went from the room. Peter looked at Ruggiero, but the big friar seemed unaware of his wish to be alone with Antonio. Peter gestured to the one other doorway leading from the room. "That is the room reserved for the Provincial, Father Antonio."

Antonio looked questioningly at Peter. Of all the brothers, only Elias and Peter had addressed him familiarly by name. From the one extreme of familiarity, Peter had changed to the opposite extreme of formality. "I should like to see that room, Peter." Carelessly, he put his hand on Ruggiero's arm as he arose from the table so that the big friar would remain where he was.

The room was small, barely large enough to contain the table and four benches that were the furnishings. A door in the wall, opposite the door through which they entered, opened onto a street. A leaded window, formed of glass ovals, admitted light.

Antonio seated himself behind the table and looked expectantly at Peter. Inexplicably, Peter seemed suddenly without desire to speak. The Guardian merely sat on a bench and looked at Antonio.

"Did you wish to speak to me, Peter?"

"You wish to speak to me," Peter declared coldly.

Antonio looked wonderingly at the other.

"Where will you assign me?" Peter asked.

For the first time, Antonio realized the import of Peter's actions. "Are you guardian of this house?"

Peter nodded. "The Provincial appointed me."

Peter's composure surprised Antonio. Yet it was in keeping with the man, he realized. Peter, the soldier, had learned to appraise objectively; Peter, the friar, must continue to appraise objectively. It was a virtue rare among men, for most men refuse to accept facts as they are, and this one virtue might be the key to the discovery and development of others.

"You are a realist, aren't you, Peter?"

Peter's eyes lighted with interest at the analysis of himself. "Only weaklings refuse to face facts," he retorted disdainfully.

Antonio shook his head in disagreement. "Not all are weaklings, Peter. Sometimes a man refuses to face a fact because he is not conscious that it is a fact. You are not a weakling; but there is one fact you refuse to face."

Peter leaned forward belligerently. "What is that?"

"Your vocation," Antonio challenged. "You have a vocation or you would not be among the brothers of Francis—would not have remained among them as you have. Yet you refuse to devote yourself to the development and cultivation of that vocation. You were successful as a soldier because you faced the facts of military life. You will be successful as a spiritual man only when you face the facts of spiritual life."

Peter relaxed, but his expression gave no indication that he understood.

"Peter," Antonio continued, "when a man pledges himself to the cause of a military leader, he pledges that he will die, if necessary, to defend that leader's interests. When a man pledges himself to God, he makes the same pledge; he pledges that he will die to himself, to the world, to his family, to riches, to power, to honor, to ambition, to pleasure—to all that is not God."

"I am not a priest," Peter objected.

"I am not speaking of priests. Priests are consecrated, not pledged to God."

Ruggiero interrupted them. The big friar moved noisily in the next room to warn them of his approach. "General Jordan has come to see you, Antonio."

Peter arose hastily from his bench and walked to the door opening onto the street. "If you can explain your meaning more clearly, I will be glad to talk with you," he said and disappeared into the street.

Jordan was smiling, and his eyes were bright with pleasure when he came into the room with Ruggiero. "Our friars brought reports of your work in the Languedoc, Friar Antonio. This morning, they reported that you were here. I came to welcome you back to Bologna, to San Nicolo, and to your lecture room."

Antonio smiled. He noticed Ruggiero standing in the doorway, uncertain whether to remain or to leave. Antonio motioned for Ruggiero to join them. "I have come back to Bologna but not to San Nicolo nor the lecture room, General Jordan. I have returned as Provincial of the Romagna."

The General of the Preachers sat very erect on his bench. Delight enlivened his whole body. "Excellent!" he exclaimed. "Excellent, Friar Antonio!"

Ruggiero had moved into the room and was about to seat himself when the General's exclamation burst in the small room. Abruptly, the big friar left the room.

Jordan looked around at the doorway through which Ruggiero had vanished. "Your big friend, Ruggiero, seemed to disagree. Did he prefer some place other than Bologna?"

Antonio hesitated. He did not want to discuss difficulties of his order with those in or out of it. "He is not entirely happy," he admitted.

There was a moment of silence, then the General seemed to discover something that had not been clear to him. "Of course! Of course!" Jordan became serious and his voice was sympathetic. "I think I understand your situation. I know of the trouble among the friars of Francis, Friar Antonio. I know, too, that many of the friars hoped that you would be the General. Instead, you have been appointed here."

Antonio shook his head. "I have no desire to be General of the Order," he said.

Jordan gestured impatiently. He leaned across the table toward Antonio. "Neither did you want to be appointed to a place that would indicate opposition to the wishes of your brothers."

Antonio did not want to continue this conversation. He did not want to discuss either his own difficulties or the difficulties within the order. He said nothing.

Jordan, too, seemed to lose interest in the subject. He straightened from the table and regarded Antonio. "There was a time, Friar Antonio, when Our Lord told the Apostles to 'come apart and rest a while.' Your brothers in the Romagna have been among the people for a long time. You may have noticed that this community is much smaller than it was when you lived here. Worldliness became so firmly fixed in this province that the brothers who were anxious to avoid worldliness transferred to other provinces after Father Gratian died. Those who remain—I will be blunt, Friar Antonio—those who remain are those who do not understand the dangers of worldliness. Perhaps they should separate themselves from the world for a time."

Antonio remained in the room after Jordan left. "Come apart and rest a while." This, then was God's purpose—to turn eyes from the world to the Leader, to remind these friars of their Father.

God had not pushed him nor shouted commands. God had required obedience—obedience that humbled him among the brothers but obedience that had returned him to Bologna. Only here had God made known His will through the words of Jordan and the actions of the brothers.

7

ANTONIO saw the suspicion of the brothers as he approached each group—saw their efforts to appraise him and to discover what he had promised General Elias. He saw their suspicion disappear and worldliness diminish as they separated from the world to rest and pray. He saw the heavy-voiced Peter respond at last to his vocation and saw Peter's response inspire others. He discovered that not all of the Romagna had been infected, but that isolated groups had maintained the spirit of Francis.

The work progressed slowly through December of 1226 and the early months of 1227. Wherever Antonio appeared among the brothers, he was detained to preach to the people and to receive into the order more who wished to live as Francis. He was retarded also by a growing reluctance of his body to respond to the work required of it. As Lent neared, he and Ruggiero had progressed no farther than Padua.

The guard at the gate of the city pointed along a road to a building on the farther side of a canal. "That is the place of your brothers. They call it Santa Maria Mater Domini." The building the guard designated was of rough stone and ancient, set in fields where they could see some brothers at work. Beyond it was a church; beyond the church was a cluster of buildings that marked the edge of the heavily populated section of the city.

Guardian Giuseppe welcomed them while the brothers returned hurriedly from the field. When Antonio had greeted and blessed them, Giuseppe led the way into the house.

Antonio saw that the whole interior was one large room with benches and a few tables, with twigs for the beds of the brothers, and cooking pots heaped near a fireplace that held only dead ashes. Whatever faults the brothers of Padua might reveal, they were not seekers of comfort and luxuries.

Giuseppe walked ahead of them through the room to a door that opened into a smaller room hardly large enough for the bed it contained. "Bishop Rainaldo learned that you are not well, Friar Antonio. He sent this bed with the command that you are to sleep in it."

Antonio looked doubtfully at the bed. The other brothers had followed and grouped behind him. He did not want to disturb the simplicity of these brothers with comforts even when commanded by the Bishop. He turned to the group. "What do my brothers think of a provincial who would sleep in such comfort?"

No one answered immediately. In the smiles of some was amusement, as though he had indulged in some pleasantry. Others showed surprise that their provincial would ask their opinion. Still others revealed a pleased and happy admiration that their famed father would value their opinion. Guardian Giuseppe spoke for them: "That he is obedient to our Lord Bishop, Friar Antonio."

Either the question or the necessity for answering ended the reserve that had characterized the Guardian. He was not old, but he was sufficiently advanced in years to understand the revolt of the body against hardships and discomfort. His sunken face assumed a hesitant smile. "Bishop

Rainaldo wishes you to recover your health, Father Antonio, so that you will be able to preach the sermons for Lent at his church. He has instructed his doctor to attend you."

Bishop Rainaldo's doctor, Signor Lancia, came that same afternoon. Antonio lay on the bed while Signor Lancia questioned him. Ruggiero pressed his great bulk into one corner of the room.

Signor Lancia motioned Ruggiero forward to the bed. "Remove Friar Antonio's robe from his chest," he instructed.

Ruggiero followed the order and returned to his corner. The doctor stood motionless above Antonio for a moment while a frown of disapproval gathered. "My Lord Bishop sends me to treat your body, Friar Antonio. You have no body," he exclaimed. "You have bones and a little covering of skin and a great robe to hide what is left of your body." The man of science rocked his head back and forth while he scolded the man of the spirit.

The man of the spirit smiled at Signor Lancia's gesture of despair.

"Bring milk!" Signor Lancia ordered Ruggiero curtly.

Ruggiero looked wonderingly at the doctor. "There is no milk in a house of the brothers, Signor."

Signor Lancia raised his hands impatiently above his head. "Bring food, then, any food!" Ruggiero hurried from the room.

Lancia leaned down over Antonio to press the skin of his shoulders and chest. His voice held a gentle sorrow when he spoke. "Friar Antonio, why are you so ungrateful to your body? This body carries you all through our country to preach to the people; this body gives you strength to preach. You have repaid it with nothing but labor and more labor. Now, you have punished it more than it can bear. You have burdened it until it can bear nothing more."

Antonio looked up curiously at the doctor. "Will I die?"

Signor Lancia hesitated before he answered. "You will if I do not prevent you, Friar Antonio. But I will not permit you to die. I will make you well," he concluded defiantly.

Ruggiero returned with bread. The doctor looked at it critically, then handed it to Antonio. "Eat this," he commanded. He sat on the bed at Antonio's feet. "I will wait to see that you do eat it."

Antonio chewed obediently at the loaf. He felt remorseful that he was causing this good doctor evident anxiety. When he had eaten most of the loaf, he said, "I am much better already, Signor Lancia," and smiled.

Lancia looked from Antonio to the loaf, but he did not answer nor move from his position. Antonio returned to the task of eating the bread. When the last fragment had disappeared, the doctor arose and turned to Ruggiero. "You will be responsible that Friar Antonio eats as much as he should," he instructed.

"Signor Lancia," Antonio called quickly. "I cannot have you think I do not eat."

"You are wasted," Signor Lancia returned. "I have seen others like you."

"My body suffers only from illness—perhaps work, Signor—but nothing more."

Lancia turned gravely to Ruggiero. "You will also be responsible for seeing that Friar Antonio works very little."

Ruggiero glanced from one to the other as though he were happy with the authority given him.

Signor Lancia returned regularly to examine Antonio

and to question Ruggiero. He examined more diligently when Antonio began to preach in the open square of San Nicolo because the church would not contain the crowds. "I am to heal you," the doctor grumbled, "but you exhaust your strength because all of Padua insists they must hear you."

Before the middle of Lent, Antonio was no longer able to pray or to meditate. Paduans came to Santa Maria Mater Domini to assist with the brothers at Mass and continued to come through the day. Signor Lancia scolded, but Antonio remained in the confessional until Ruggiero summarily ended each day by telling all who remained that they must return another day.

During Holy Week, papal messengers arrived in Padua to announce the death of Pope Honorius and election of the aged Cardinal Ugolino as Pope Gregory IX. "General Elias is secure in his position," was Ruggiero's interpretation of the news.

A message from the General, in the wake of the papal announcement, seemed to confirm Ruggiero's observation. "Bring all friars of your province to the Pentecost chapter," Antonio read.

"General Elias is exceeding his authority," Ruggiero grumbled. "Only superiors should attend the chapter."

"All from the Romagna will attend," Antonio answered.

"You have not the strength to lead them," Ruggiero objected.

Antonio nodded his head in agreement. "The custodians can gather the brothers and lead them."

Signor Lancia gave permission to Antonio to depart on Easter Monday. Antonio knew that the Lenten stay in Padua had strengthened him, though his body still responded sluggishly. He was glad to walk in the warm, spring sun after weeks in the cold dampness of Santa Maria Mater Domini. At times, he was aware that Ruggiero was studying his slow movements.

The pleasure of the season terminated as they entered the Province of Tuscany; the brothers of Tuscany demonstrated a desire to avoid them. Antonio had forgotten the unrest in the order and widespread opposition to General Elias; the brothers of Tuscany reminded him of it—some by their reserve, others by indications of actual dislike. Antonio and Ruggiero began to avoid the huts of the brothers and to seek shelter with the people. When they arrived in Assisi, they saw that they were unwelcome among those who opposed General Elias but welcomed eagerly by those who supported him; to avoid both groups, they remained long hours in the churches of the city. Soon they were as distrusted by the General's friends as by his enemies.

Late on Thursday, the friars of the Romagna arrived in a great body. Antonio greeted them and led them across the plain below Assisi to a grove of trees. He was conscious of the stares of others as the group passed and knew the reason—of all lesser friars of the order, only those of the Romagna had been invited to this chapter, and none knew whether they were friends or enemies.

On Whit Monday, Assisi's hall of the magistrates was well filled when the friars of the Romagna entered. The room was square and not large, designed both for assemblies to propose laws and for the hearing of trials. At the front of the room, General Elias sat at a desk raised two steps above the floor. All others in the room were arranged on long rows of benches, interrupted only by a narrow aisle from the door to the judge's desk. Three rows of benches remained at the back of the room. Antonio drew Ruggiero aside while his friars filled two of the rows; he sat in the last row with Ruggiero.

"The friends of the General are at the front of the room," Ruggiero whispered.

Antonio saw for the first time that the brothers had grouped according to their sympathies. In the forward rows were a great number of custodians and guardians, adherents of Elias. In the rows behind them were John Parenti, Provincial of Tuscany, two other provincials, and a lesser number of custodians and guardians, opponents of Elias. The General's friends were more numerous; his opponents older both in years and in religion.

Few were talking. Remembering the joy and elation of other gatherings of brothers, Antonio knew that this assembly was waiting tensely.

General Elias seemed contemptuous of opposition among the brothers. He smiled pleasantly from his place without indication of strain. When he began to speak, his voice was even and confident.

"I need hardly remind you of the difficulties His Holiness Pope Gregory is encountering as a result of the Emperor's plottings, the mental sufferings he must endure because of Emperor Frederick's boundless ambition. Yet in the midst of such torments, His Holiness, who was cardinal protector of our order, has not forgotten his friend and our Father, Francis. My brothers, we may now rejoice because His Holiness has ordered inquiry into the cause of Francis for canonization."

His announcement was so unexpected, their minds had been so attuned to dispute, they sat for a moment in stunned silence. Father Francis had died only eight months before, and already his name was proposed for enrollment among the saints! A tremendous roar of happiness burst suddenly from all of them. In their love for Francis, there was no difference, no disagreement. In their love for Francis all were brothers of his order.

The General smiled benignly while waiting patiently for quiet. "We can anticipate the findings of the prelates who are examining the cause of our holy father. We must work quickly that our preparations will be completed when His Holiness proclaims Francis a saint. I have already designed and am now gathering funds for erection of a church to contain the body of our saintly founder."

Again, cheers greeted the General's words; but Antonio saw that only those in the forward rows cheered announcement of a church. Reaction followed immediately. Even before the last of the cheering died, a new sound was heard—a voice of accusation. "You have violated the Rule, Brother Elias."

Antonio saw that it was a guardian who stood in the center of the group opposed to the General and hurled the challenge. "You have violated the Rule because we may not own churches nor have money."

The benign smile of Elias vanished quickly. He looked sternly at the brother who had presumed to cry out against him. "No brother may speak in chapter without permission," he answered coldly.

A roar of fury burst from the group surrounding the guardian. Instantly a greater roar of denunciation by those in the front rows answered. No voice, no word was distinguishable from others. Antonio felt some of his friars turn and look questioningly toward him. Elias quieted his adherents in the rows nearest him. The opposition group stilled slowly and distrustfully, sensitive to any effort of the General to utter another rebuke. Elias waited almost disdainfully.

A provincial, a tall stately man, arose and stood quietly until his friends noticed him and became silent. "It is the consensus of the superiors of the order, Brother Elias, that your term as General has expired. Therefore—"

An angry roar from the brothers who supported the General smothered the voice of the speaker. Some of them jumped from their benches and started toward the group around the Provincial. Elias made no effort to quiet his supporters. There could be but one result from the unequal contest, and the General was content to await that result.

Antonio moved swiftly forward from his own bench. The others from the Romagna arose with him, but he motioned that they should remain where they were. Ruggiero, alone, ignored the order and moved forward with him.

In the instant before actual physical combat could begin, a new voice sounded above the shouting and noise and tumult. The novelty of a voice so powerful as to transcend the roar was itself sufficient to distract all those within the hall. "Return to your places!" Antonio commanded. "Return to your places!" The authority of his voice drove most of them back to their benches; the sight of the massive Ruggiero moved the more reluctant.

Antonio stood in the narrow aisle while the noise and confusion gave way to quiet and order. Elias, too, who had half risen from his place, settled slowly to his bench. Antonio glanced at Ruggiero, and the big friar returned to his place among the friars from the Romagna.

None but Francis could soothe their angry hearts, could

dissipate their rancor, could turn their minds from their own pursuits. In the tense silence, they heard the voice of Antonio but heard the words, the heart, the very prayer Francis himself had taught them.

> Lord, make me an instrument of Your peace!
> Where there is hatred, let me sow love;
> Where there is injury, pardon;
> Where there is doubt, faith;
> Where there is despair, hope;
> Where there is darkness, light;
> Where there is sadness, joy:
> O Divine Master, grant that I may not so much seek
> To be consoled as to console,
> To be understood as to understand,
> To be loved as to love; for
> It is in giving that we receive,
> It is in pardoning that we are pardoned,
> It is in dying that we are born to eternal life.

Antonio paused. The room was still; tenseness had fled. "If we are brothers of Francis . . ."

General Elias interrupted him. "We are grateful to you, Antonio, for recalling Father Francis to us. Now return to your place."

Antonio's footsteps sounded clearly in the shocked silence as he walked along the narrow aisle to his own place. Faces turned to see his reaction to the order, then turned incredulously to the General.

Antonio saw Guardian Giuseppe rising and motioned to him to be seated, but Giuseppe seemed not to see him. "We are witnesses of perfidy, of ingratitude, of disgraceful conduct by our General," he began.

Elias arose hurriedly from his bench behind the desk of the judges. "You will be disciplined," he said.

Peter arose. "You have exposed yourself this day, General Elias," his heavy voice rumbled. Elias' face flushed angrily, and he shouted a reply, but his voice could not be heard against the heavy voice of Peter. "With favors and flattery, you ingratiated yourself among the men of the Romagna and led them away from the way of Father Francis. You led us almost to destruction before Father Antonio came among us to lead us back."

"I will discipline every man who speaks," Elias raged.

"You will have no power to discipline," a new voice countered from the foremost bench. "Father Antonio has opened the eyes of all of us." The brother turned to speak to those grouped about him. "Do I speak for all?" he demanded.

Elias' eyes ranged along the brothers before him who had come as his friends and adherents. Their shouted "Yes!" to their brother's question was declaration that they were no longer friends of the General. He banged his closed fist on the desk before him. "This chapter is suspended," he declared. Before any objection could be spoken, Elias walked quickly from behind the desk and along the narrow aisle to the door. Five of the brothers in the front of the room followed him.

Nervous excitement permeated the room. Some stood to relieve their tenseness, some laughed uneasily, all looked about uncertainly as though waiting for someone to volunteer leadership. More and more of them turned toward Antonio.

John Parenti arose among the provincials, and the room stilled. The Tuscan Provincial turned slightly that he might look back toward Antonio while yet addressing all in the

room. "In thoughts, in words, in actions," he began precisely and slowly, "I have been extremely unkind to you,
Father Antonio. I grieve to the depths of my heart that I did
not sooner recognize the spirit of God, moving and guiding
you away from the morass wherein I myself foundered and
into which I led so many of our brothers. I need not ask for
your forgiveness, for I know that you forgave even as I was
offending."

Parenti turned and addressed the entire gathering. "All
of us know of the miracles by which God has approved the
work of Father Antonio. Here in the birthplace of our saintly
founder, we have witnessed a new and even more wonderful miracle in the love which has been rekindled among us.
Some of us came here determined to elect a new general of
our order; some came to oppose that action. Father Antonio
has mended our hearts as he has mended hearts wherever
God's will has directed him.

"The Holy Father, Pope Gregory, must solve the difficulty that besets our order. We must send a number of the
brothers to him so that he will know our unity. But to present the case to the Pope, we must send the one brother who
will plead no cause but the cause of our saintly founder.
Our spokesman must be Father Antonio!"

The chapter roared approval. As one, they arose to their
feet, cheering and shouting. Some climbed upon benches
so that they might better see the small figure at the back of
the hall. A new madness seized them—they would propose
Antonio as successor to Elias!

Within himself, Antonio shrank from their expectations
and the burden of responsibility they would impose on him.
If the Holy Father asked their choice of a successor, it must
be one stronger in body and more capable than himself.

He walked quickly to the front of the hall and they quieted to hear him. Fervently he pleaded. They would not hear when he disclaimed ability; they surrendered reluctantly as he pleaded the weakness of his body. Protests diminished, and at last they released him: He must be their spokesman before the Holy Father, but they would accept Parenti as general.

The journey from Assisi to Anagni, despite willingness of the others to slow their pace, was a physical ordeal; summer heat of the lowlands slowly drained Antonio's strength. Before the delegation arrived at the summer palace of Pope Gregory, Antonio knew that the gains realized during the period at Padua had evaporated.

The delegation gained admission readily, but the aged Pope received them as though he knew the purpose of their extraordinary request for an audience without presence of General Elias. He held his thin body sternly erect and nodded to them to state the purpose of their visit.

Antonio knew the conflict that must occur within the heart of this Pope. Gregory respected and admired General Elias; he would not withdraw his support from the General, whose abilities he knew, merely because some of the brothers complained. Antonio related the unrest of the order and the fears of the brothers following the death of Francis, told of the chapter at Assisi and the events that led to submission of the difficulty to His Holiness.

Pope Gregory's eyes fastened on Antonio as he heard the case. His sternness lessened as Antonio's objective recital progressed. "It is evident that you respect the ability of General Elias," he said when Antonio finished. The Pope looked at the other members of the delegation. "I agree that the unrest in the order and dissatisfaction of the brothers can only be ended by confirming Friar Parenti as general of your order. I do not agree with those who complain of General Elias' actions in building a new church. Certainly Father Francis is deserving of a church in which his body may repose. If collecting of funds and owning a church conflicts with your Rule, it is sufficient that all rights and ownership be vested in the Holy See."

8

ANTONIO moved steadily through the Romagna, Emilia, and Venezia, to inspire the friars, to exhort and encourage the people. He saw the blessing of God on the work in a new gift—the gift of Christ to His Apostles when He gave them power to "heal the sick, raise the dead, cleanse the lepers, cast out devils."

The gift was not without pain. From the time when he placed his hand on the twisted, stiffened foot of a child and felt the flesh relax and the muscles straighten, he became conscious of a new attitude in Ruggiero. Delighted surprise appeared in the face of the big friar on that first occasion; but as wonders multiplied and Ruggiero's surprise changed rapidly to deference and adulation, Antonio understood that a new sacrifice was asked of him.

His heart recoiled from the task. He must force Ruggiero's attention from the gifts to the Giver, must turn Ruggiero's love entirely to God. Only one action could accomplish what was asked—severance of the tie that bound Ruggiero to him and him to Ruggiero—and his heart would not permit him to act. One last human affection remained between himself and the will of God, and he had not the power to destroy it.

At Padua, in December of 1230, his body rebelled again. He had preached from the balcony overlooking San Nicolo Square and turned to enter the building through the great double doors. As in a dream, he knew that Ruggiero had picked him up and was carrying him. When consciousness returned, he was resting on a great pile of straw in the small room of the brothers' house.

"You fainted," Ruggiero told him simply.

Signor Lancia returned to scold and complain and to order milk and eggs and other foods strange to a house of the brothers.

Antonio responded to the ministrations forced on him. Periods of wakefulness increased. For long periods, he lay awake, alone much of each day, listening to the quiet breathing of Ruggiero each night. A new temptation thrust at him—he had refused the sacrifice asked by God, and God had taken from him the gifts that had so affected Ruggiero. Patiently, he repulsed the temptation. God required of him only what he had power to do. If God asked what was not in his power, it was to make him admit his poverty so that he would turn to the omnipotent God and receive the power. He had not the power to sever the love that bound him to Ruggiero. He had only the power to pray that God would accomplish what was asked.

He lay in the darkness of a night, a darkness so complete that it was like the void of infinity between himself and God. Knowledge of his helplessness pressed against him—helplessness to exert his spirit against human affection. Steadily the pressure increased; just as steadily, grace held him steadfast in heart and mind to God. Quietly, so that he would not disturb Ruggiero, he moved from the straw to the window and knelt. "O Almighty, Most Merciful, neither light nor darkness measures Thee. Nothing reveals the fullness of Thy goodness nor flood of Thy kindness and burden of Thy gifts."

The weight of temptation lightened with his prayer. The veil that had drawn across his mind fell away from him. "Lord and Master, Jesus Christ, renew Thy mercy upon me. Lift me up, my Lord, that my mind may know nothing but Thee, that my will may desire no sweetness but Thee, that I may love none but . . ."

His prayer failed and ended; the darkness of night departed as had the darkness from his heart. A radiance of heaven flooded the room. Mutely he raised his arms in supplication to continue the prayer. The light swelled more brilliantly, a light that penetrated with a physical presence. A gentle pressure forced against his upraised hands, a soft body filled his arms. Close to his heart, Antonio held the body of the Infant Jesus. Rapture severed all ties with earth and time and nature. The Infant head pressed against his own, Infant eyes bestowed their blessing, an Infant hand rested against his heart, an Infant hand caressed his mouth.

"Jesus, my Lord!" he whispered.

Within him, he knew that the flame of love had consumed all other loves and that all other loves were magnified in this one love. As Francis had been granted the wounds of Christ, Antonio was granted the pure love of Christ.

The visitation was not of time but of eternity. Antonio knew neither time of appearance nor time of departure, neither end nor beginning of joy. He knew that the body of the Infant released from him gently but that Jesus had neither come nor gone—Christ abides in the heart in the manner of His eternity, unmoving, unchanging, enduring.

Darkness of the night returned as his arms lightened. He felt the presence of another kneeling beside him, another who knelt silently and adoringly in the room hallowed by the Eternal Light.

"You must not speak of this night."

Silence betrayed Ruggiero. In the radiance of heaven's light, he had been a witness, and a witness must testify what he knows, what he has heard, what he has seen.

"You must not speak of this night," Antonio repeated.

Reluctantly Ruggiero answered. "I will not speak until you permit me; but you must send word to Stephen." Ruggiero pleaded in the darkness. "Tell Stephen, Antonio, because he knew this time would come, and you told him that, when he heard, he should praise God."

Antonio hesitated so that he would not seem to reject Ruggiero's plea. "He will know at the proper time, Ruggiero. God will make known to him as much as He wishes whenever He wishes."

In the morning, the manner of the others toward him and the joy in their eyes told him that something in his expression betrayed the visitation of the night. None were curious, none questioned, none sought to discover what grace he had received. The gift of God within his heart preserved their minds from prying. Later in the day, Signor Lancia examined him but without grumbling his observations and complaints as was customary. "You may resume your work," the doctor announced.

Immediately, Paduans returned to the church of Santa Maria; their number increased and, as Christmas approached, Antonio remained longer and longer in the confessional. A message from Bishop Rainaldo summoned him to preach at San Nicolo on the Sunday before Christmas and on Christmas Day. Antonio's happiness increased with the burden of his work. He loved all men—those who came to him at Santa Maria, those who crowded before him in the square of San Nicolo, Ruggiero, and all the brothers—as

Christ had loved. God had not given him the power to end a love; God had given the fullness of love. And men loved him in return for a reason they did not know—a compelling reason that drew them and attracted them without reason.

Signor Lancia continued his visits to Santa Maria; but the doctor did not resume his manner of scolding and disapproving. When the doctor came early in February and Ruggiero was about to expose Antonio's arms and chest, Lancia dispensed with the examination. "That will no longer be necessary, Friar Ruggiero." He looked meaningly at Ruggiero and remained alone with Antonio when the big friar left the room.

Antonio raised up from the pile of straw where he had awaited examination. There was no bench in the room, nothing more than the straw to serve as his bed and the twigs that served Ruggiero. "I'm sorry I cannot ask you to sit, Signor Lancia. Perhaps it would be better if we went into the large room."

"No," Lancia said. "I prefer to speak where no one will interrupt, Father Antonio." He leaned back against the wall. "Many times, Father Antonio, I have spoken harshly to you and scolded you. I did not speak those words from my heart. I tried only to find some means to make you give care to your body."

Antonio smiled as a conspirator. "I have done the same, Signor Lancia, to men who would not care for their souls."

"Your body has swollen, Father Antonio. Even that great robe of yours can no longer hide what is happening." Lancia paused. "Is it very painful?"

Antonio nodded silently.

Lancia produced a paper and handed it to him. "My Lord Bishop commanded that I deliver this to you."

Antonio read the message quickly. "It is my wish, Father Antonio, that you recover your health. For that reason, you must discontinue the work you are now doing with the people and devote your time and attention to recording your sermons; that activity will benefit you physically and all preachers of my diocese spiritually. The noble Tiso of Camposampiero is prepared to receive you into his home so that you may work without interruption or distraction—Rainaldo."

Antonio lowered his hand and looked about the tiny room. "My Lord Bishop wishes to separate me from the people, but he is separating me from much more, Signor Lancia."

"What answer shall I give?"

Antonio raised his head quickly. "No answer is necessary, Signor Lancia. Ruggiero and I will go in the morning."

9

BEYOND the village of Camposampiero, Signor Lancia turned the carriage into a narrow drive that curved slowly up an incline to the iron gates on huge stone gateposts which marked the entrance to the estate of the noble, Tiso.

A round, elderly man with a petulant face came quickly from the house to welcome them—Antonio heard Signor Lancia murmur, "My Lord Tiso," as he bowed before the noble. Antonio noticed the precise manner of Lord Tiso's words of response and the soft clothing. Yet, as though to deny the riches and preciseness, Lord Tiso dropped to his knee before Antonio to kiss the hand of his guest. "My house is honored, Father Antonio, that you have come to dwell with me."

"Rather is it I who am grateful for your hospitality, Lord Tiso."

In the quiet seclusion of Tiso's home, Antonio worked steadily and rapidly. Lord Tiso remained carefully away from him during the day; Ruggiero disappeared from morning until the evening meal. Sermon outlines developed readily.

Signor Lancia visited Camposampiero regularly. Each Tuesday his carriage climbed the sloping driveway just before the supper hour. When the meal ended, he went with

Antonio, not to examine and probe, but to sit quietly and talk as though he had no other purpose in life.

In the first week of April, Lord Tiso came into the room where Antonio worked. "I hesitated to interrupt you, Father Antonio, but I have no other opportunity to speak to you while Friar Ruggiero is not with you."

Antonio smiled. "Sometimes work is improved by interruptions, Lord Tiso."

Tiso nodded to the papers piled before Antonio. "I wonder if you know that, in his own way, Friar Ruggiero has been working as industriously as you." He lifted a chair and placed it so that he would face Antonio. "In the last two days, three of my men have come to ask if I will release them to you and to Friar Ruggiero that they may enter your order. One is a knight and is entitled to release without hindrance. But the others, Father Antonio, are bondmen."

"Did Ruggiero send these men, Lord Tiso?"

"May I say that he inspired them, Father Antonio, without the necessity of speaking to them or sending them to me. While you have been working here, Friar Ruggiero has earned his food by working in the stables. All of the knights know him—he shows them how to use their weapons." Tiso smiled thinly. "I have not been able to accustom myself to seeing a Friar Minor show a knight how best to handle his sword."

Antonio offered no comment, though the host paused so that he would have opportunity. Antonio sensed that Lord Tiso's curiosity about him and Ruggiero had increased rather than diminished since their arrival.

"I am not averse to releasing these men, Father Antonio; but I should like some assurance that they will enter your order and are not seeking a simple way of escaping their bond to me."

"Is the amount of their bond very large?"

Petulance increased momentarily in Tiso's face. "You know that it could not be, Father Antonio. I have said I am willing to release these men; but I don't want to establish an avenue of escape for every bondman. It is the matter itself rather than the amount."

Antonio waited.

"I know your attitude," Tiso continued. "Release all who ask—it can amount to but little. Release all and turn society upon its head." His voice had begun to show traces of petulance, and he paused. "Sometimes, Father Antonio, I am persuaded to do as you preach and release all my bondmen and give all my goods to the poor." He shook his head slowly. "But that is a tremendous thing for an old man, and I have not the courage."

"You are thinking of what Our Lord told the rich young man, Lord Tiso?"

Tiso drew back in his chair as though he had already said more than he had intended.

"Lord Tiso, St. John wrote that Our Lord had no need of someone to tell Him concerning man, for He Himself knew what was in man. So Our Lord will not ask more of a man than that man can do. It is true that He told the young man of great wealth that he should sell all that he had and give it to the poor and to follow Him. You are troubled because you cannot suddenly turn away from all that you have and the life you have known; because you cannot do all, you do nothing." Antonio's voice softened until it was little more than a whisper. "There can never be an end until there is a beginning. Our Lord demanded of the young man that he turn toward perfection and sell all that he possessed. But when He came to an older man, Zaccheus, He assured him of salvation even though Zaccheus had given only half of his possessions to the poor."

Tiso searched Antonio's face silently as though still endeavoring to pierce the past. "Is it not more difficult for the old to give up half than for the young to give up all?"

Antonio looked directly into the eyes of his host and smiled with amusement. "I can assure you that it is not, Lord Tiso."

Ruggiero brought word late that day of the release of the knight and the bondmen. His eyes glowed with admiration. "Lord Tiso gave them a full bill of release."

Antonio related the incident of Lord Tiso's generosity to Signor Lancia when next the doctor sat with him.

"Why do you open and clench your hand, Father Antonio?" the doctor asked irrelevantly.

Antonio laughed. He had not been aware of his action. "I am trying to be worthy of Lord Tiso's generosity. My hand refuses to move as quickly as it should to earn its food."

Lancia examined each hand in turn. "The dampness," he decreed.

Antonio was reminded of their conversation when Lord Tiso told him at breakfast the following morning: "Signor Lancia has suggested a shelter be built for you in a tree, Father Antonio. He said you should be in the open air but raised above the dampness of the earth."

Antonio glanced at Ruggiero and back to Lord Tiso. "Will Friar Ruggiero also have a nest, my Lord Tiso?"

Tiso looked at the big friar and laughed. "A den is more befitting for bears, Father Antonio. But Friar Ruggiero will have a hut beneath your tree."

Ruggiero grinned amiably. "Father Antonio likes to live close to God, Lord Tiso. The rest of us cling too closely to the earth."

Late in May, Lord Tiso announced that the project was complete and Antonio might change his residence. Ruggiero went with them and looked curiously at the work of Lord Tiso's carpenters. Antonio smiled with amusement at the shelter in the lower branches of a walnut tree and the short ladder leading to it.

Signor Lancia's device proved more comfortable than the enclosed room and the dampness of Lord Tiso's house. Antonio rested more completely in the straw of the shelter and the pain of his body diminished. But Lancia merely nodded when Antonio reported the greater comfort to him.

One disturbance occurred soon after their transfer from the house. Antonio sat on the platform of his shelter, talking to Ruggiero on the ground below when both were attracted by sounds coming from the direction of the village. Antonio could see the road near the village, but trees obscured the village itself; his eyes wandered repeatedly toward the road as the sounds increased in volume, and he recognized the roar of many voices.

In the road below, through the clear space among the trees, he saw a great crowd walking quickly and purposefully from the village. Their voices swelled steadily as they came closer and turned into the road leading to the house of Lord Tiso. He saw the leaders stop and look toward him, then turn abruptly and lead a crowd across a field of young wheat. In the vanguard, he recognized Guardian Giuseppe of Padua.

Knights, grooms, and workmen appeared quickly from the house and stables of Lord Tiso as the crowd followed their leaders across the field. Lord Tiso himself ran from the house waving his arms angrily but was unable to prevent trampling of the wheat. The crowd ignored, then engulfed, the noble as Giuseppe strode past him.

Antonio examined the face of the Guardian as he came forward. Giuseppe's face was set in fixed lines of determination that seemed only then to be relaxing. A thick cloud of dust billowed up from the wheat field in the wake of the crowd.

They quieted as they approached as though they would be silent in the presence of Antonio; they began to smile as though relieved of some great fear. Giuseppe ran the last short distance until he stood beside Ruggiero at the foot of the tree and smiled up at Antonio. "You are safe!"

Antonio looked bewildered at the Guardian and the crowd behind him. Some were still hurrying across the wheat field.

Guardian Giuseppe explained: "Father Antonio, someone reported that Lord Tiso had erected barricades because the Veronese were coming to take you away. We came to protect you," he added, embarrassed.

Lord Tiso pushed through the crowd to stand beside Giuseppe and Ruggiero at the foot of the tree, his expression a mixture of pain and resignation. Antonio looked out at the ruined wheat field beyond the crowd. He sympathized with Lord Tiso, but he could not condemn the anxiety of his friends whose thoughtlessness had caused so much damage.

"Forgive them, Lord Tiso," Antonio pleaded softly.

The struggle within Tiso was evident in the workings of his face. He could not answer. He stood for a moment looking dumbly at Antonio, then turned and walked toward his house.

Antonio watched the back of his host, the man who had made a beginning. He turned toward the crowd, standing quietly and repentant, conscious now of their foolish impulsiveness. "Throughout life, we will do many foolish, thoughtless deeds. Some are within our power of reparation and restitution. Others are beyond our power, and we must consign those to the kindness and goodness of God, that He will repair and restore what is impossible for us.

"We have no power to repair the damage wrought here today. But almighty God, our Father in heaven, will hear our prayer. All of us will pray now, while we are together, and alone, when each has returned to his home, that God will not suffer this damage to remain between us and Lord Tiso."

When he dismissed them, the crowd held carefully to the road and avoided the field they had trodden. From the platform in the tree, Antonio watched them sorrowfully as they retraced their steps to the village.

Lord Tiso returned at dusk to stand beneath the walnut tree while Antonio looked down from the platform of his shelter. "I prayed, Father Antonio, when I left you today. I have forgiven them." He turned and walked again toward his house without waiting for Antonio to answer.

Antonio raised his hand in blessing as his host retreated. God had repaired the damage between Lord Tiso and the thoughtless crowd.

In the morning, Ruggiero's shouting of "Antonio! Antonio!" announced some joyful discovery.

Antonio raised himself painfully from the straw. Carefully and slowly his legs lifted him, and he turned to the open end of the shelter. "God be thanked! May almighty God be praised in all His works!" he breathed softly. Before him, in the field trodden by the heedless crowd, the tender shafts of wheat rippled unharmed in the gentle breeze of the morning. "Which is easier," the words flowed through his mind, "to say, 'Thy sins are forgiven thee,' or to say, 'Arise and walk'?" Which is easier for God, to heal the soul of Tiso or to heal the soil of His earth?

He could not work that day. The wonder of God's goodness enthralled him. Antonio sat most of the day on the platform of his shelter, sharing Tiso's happiness and the wonder of Ruggiero, offering thanks to the bountiful God who lavished His gifts on His children.

Signor Lancia heard the story first from Lord Tiso but would not believe until Antonio smilingly confirmed the statement of their host. The doctor examined the field carefully but saw no traces of damage or disorder. On that Tuesday afternoon, Lancia referred, for the first time, to the future. "Remember me, Father Antonio, in your prayers here and in heaven."

Until the morning of June 13, Antonio continued writing and reviewing what he had written. On that Tuesday morning, an incessant pain tormented him. He could neither sit quietly on the platform nor lie down in the straw. At noon, he called Ruggiero to help him to the ground.

Pain wracked his body, but he walked a few steps toward the table where Ruggiero had placed the food for their dinner. Without sound, he slumped suddenly to the ground as though all strength had fled from his legs.

Ruggiero was beside him immediately to lift him and carry him to the bench at the table. "Can you sit?"

Antonio nodded. He rested his arms on the table and supported his body from the violence of the pain that would have felled him again.

"Signor Lancia will come this afternoon," Ruggiero said anxiously.

Antonio heard without interest. The good doctor knew. The course was run. The day of fulfillment had come. He raised his head slightly. "We will go to Santa Maria Mater Domini, Ruggiero."

"I will get a carriage," Ruggiero said immediately.

Instead of a carriage, he brought a cart filled with straw. "I thought it would be better that you lie in this than that you sit in a carriage." A groom was with him to help, but Ruggiero lifted Antonio easily and laid him gently on the straw.

Antonio opened his eyes. "We should tell Lord Tiso."

Ruggiero nodded. "I told one of the men to search for him and tell him." He gestured to the groom, and the man went forward and took the bridle of the horse. Ruggiero jumped into the cart and huddled beside Antonio to ease the jolting.

Antonio's eyes remained closed. Painful spasms of his chest marked his breathing. They came within sight of Padua before he opened his eyes again. "Will we be in time, Ruggiero?"

Ruggiero raised his eyes and looked at the country around them. He saw the convent of the Poor Clares. "We are at Arcella, Antonio."

Antonio let his eyes close. "There is not sufficient time, Ruggiero." His chest rose and fell in violent spasms. "I hoped," he whispered. "I hoped . . ." his voice trailed away, but his eyes opened to see if Ruggiero understood his meaning. His lips curled in a slight smile at Ruggiero's nod of understanding.

"Signor Lancia is coming, Friar Ruggiero," the groom called.

Ruggiero looked forward and saw the carriage of the doctor. Lancia had already seen the cart and discerned the meaning. He had whipped his horse into a full gallop toward them.

Ruggiero pressed back against the side of the cart that the doctor might examine Antonio. "Please, Signor Lancia, Father Antonio wishes to be at Santa Maria," he begged.

Lancia gestured impatiently before he realized the strange intensity of Ruggiero's voice. He bent over Antonio, then straightened and turned to the big friar. "He will not live, Friar Ruggiero."

Antonio opened his eyes and smiled weakly, then saw the tears of disappointment flowing down Ruggiero's cheeks. "Let us turn in at Arcella, Ruggiero," he whispered. "It is the will of God." His eyes closed, but the smile remained on his lips.

Ruggiero lifted Antonio from the cart and carried him into the convent. Some Clares directed him to a cell while others ran to the cart to bring the straw. Ruggiero laid Antonio on the pile of straw, then knelt beside him. Lancia bent down briefly to examine Antonio again; then he knelt also. In the passage beyond the door, the voices of the Clares began the prayers for the dying.

Once more, Antonio opened his eyes and looked directly above him. Rapture lighted his eyes, and a smile came clearly to his face as his eyes fastened on something above him.

Ruggiero looked at him wonderingly. "What do you see, Antonio?"

Antonio's eyes did not waver from the object that held them. His smile increased. "I see my Lord," he whispered. He knew the will of God.

 TAN·BOOKS

TAN Books was founded in 1967 to preserve the spiritual, intellectual and liturgical traditions of the Catholic Church. At a critical moment in history TAN kept alive the great classics of the Faith and drew many to the Church. In 2008 TAN was acquired by Saint Benedict Press. Today TAN continues its mission to a new generation of readers.

From its earliest days TAN has published a range of booklets that teach and defend the Faith. Through partnerships with organizations, apostolates, and mission-minded individuals, well over 10 million TAN booklets have been distributed.

More recently, TAN has expanded its publishing with the launch of Catholic calendars and daily planners—as well as Bibles, fiction, and multimedia products through its sister imprints Catholic Courses (CatholicCourses.com) and Saint Benedict Press (SaintBenedictPress.com).

Today TAN publishes over 500 titles in the areas of theology, prayer, devotions, doctrine, Church history, and the lives of the saints. TAN books are published in multiple languages and found throughout the world in schools, parishes, bookstores and homes.

For a free catalog, visit us online at
TANBooks.com

Or call us toll-free at
(800) 437-5876

Spread the Faith with . . .

TAN·BOOKS
A Division of Saint Benedict Press, LLC

TAN books are powerful tools for evangelization. They lift the mind to God and change lives. Millions of readers have found in TAN books and booklets an effective way to teach and defend the Faith, soften hearts, and grow in prayer and holiness of life.

Throughout history the faithful have distributed Catholic literature and sacramentals to save souls. St. Francis de Sales passed out his own pamphlets to win back those who had abandoned the Faith. Countless others have distributed the Miraculous Medal to prompt conversions and inspire deeper devotion to God. Our customers use TAN books in that same spirit.

If you have been helped by this or another TAN title, share it with others. Become a TAN Missionary and share our life changing books and booklets with your family, friends and community. We'll help by providing special discounts for books and booklets purchased in quantity for purposes of evangelization. Write or call us for additional details.

TAN Books
Attn: TAN Missionaries Department
PO Box 410487
Charlotte, NC 28241

Toll-free (800) 437-5876
missionaries@TANBooks.com